"IF YOU WANNA STAY SANE, YOU
GOT TO PUKE UP THE PAIN.
PREFERABLY WITH BLUE INK ON
LINED PAPER."

WISE YOUNG FOOL

SEAN BEAUDOIN

Ⓛ Ⓑ
Little, Brown and Company
New York   Boston

Copyright © 2013 by Sean Beaudoin

Little, Brown and Company

Hachette Book Group
237 Park Avenue, New York, NY 10017
Visit our website at www.lb-teens.com

Little, Brown and Company is a division of Hachette Book Group, Inc.
The Little, Brown name and logo are trademarks of Hachette Book Group, Inc.

The publisher is not responsible for websites (or their content) that are not owned by the publisher.

First Edition: August 2013

Library of Congress Cataloging-in-Publication Data

Beaudoin, Sean.
    Wise Young Fool / by Sean Beaudoin.—First edition.
        pages cm
    Summary: A teenaged guitarist in a rock band deals with loss and anger as he relates the events that landed him in a juvenile detention center.
    ISBN 978-0-316-20379-1
    [1. Juvenile detention homes—Fiction.   2. Bands (Music)—Fiction.
3. Musicians—Fiction.]   I. Title.
    PZ7.B3805775Wi 2013
    [Fic]—dc23
                                                                    2012032472

10 9 8 7 6 5 4 3 2 1

RRD-C

Printed in the United States of America

For my mother, who bought me my first guitar. Every thinking person should aspire to be, at some point in their lives, the person who buys someone else their first guitar.

(L) (B) **LITTLE, BROWN AND COMPANY**
BOOKS FOR YOUNG READERS

Editor's note:

Three years ago, a very curious manuscript was turned in to our offices. It was covered with coffee stains, crude drawings, and a patina of Cheetos dust. Some sections were cut out and taped back together. Others were torn away entirely. At times, the parts seemed to be shuffled at random, like two decks of cards.

Or so we at first thought.

The manuscript arrived in a manila envelope with no return address or explanation. It sat in the mail room for nearly six months before landing on a senior editor's desk. Less than an hour after finishing it, she was attempting to locate Ritchie Sudden with the idea of offering him a contract. Using the Internet proved fruitless, as did countless phone calls and inquiries. A detective was then hired. Despite being billed for a dubious number of investigatory hours, we have still found no trace of the town, friends, or high school Ritchie refers to below—let alone the curiously named Progressive Progress.

Further, there is no Dr. Kiki Benway registered with the American Medical Association. The detective did discover that many East Coast criminal justice systems offer a ninety-day "observational detention" program for first-time juvenile offenders. As noted, Ritchie makes ninety entries and mentions "owing you ninety." Apparently, it is common practice for offenders in this program to keep a journal, which is used as a factor in determining whether a release date will be granted or further incarceration is appropriate.

Although that theory is purely speculative on our part, particularly given the gravity of his crime, as well as the fact that youth incarceration records are closed to public view, we will leave it to the reader to decide whether he or she feels this document is likely to have earned Ritchie Sudden his freedom, either from his demons or from the walls of Progressive Progress.

After two years of research, extensive discussion with legal counsel, and a protracted rights hearing, we were finally granted permission to print the ensuing pages. If Ritchie ever steps forward, any profits made from the sale of this book will be shared with him and/or the Sudden family, a legal codicil that has been enacted in perpetuity. And if, while reading this manuscript, any of these people or situations seem recognizable to you, please contact us immediately at www.suddenlyfound.com.

In the meantime, we sincerely hope you enjoy what Ritchie has chosen to share with the world. I think these are very brave pages indeed. And I hope that one day Ritchie Sudden and I, in whatever form he now takes, can sit down for a cup of coffee. Or two.

Gloria R. Quill
Executive Editor, Quality Division
Little, Brown, Inc.

1

I sit on my bunk, in a dark room that smells like a thousand stiff Kleenex and a unit filled with twenty sweaty boys. The air would taste like angst, except there is no air. The silence would sound like fear and pain, except there is no silence. In fact, there's only a constant jabber, like a hallway full of junkies waiting out their morning methadone, and a heavy fluorescent gloom that seeps and settles and makes everything green and dull and fake.

You want ninety? Fine, I'll give you ninety. And not just the ones in here. I'll give them to you coming and going.

Yeah, I'm going nowhere. Except where I'm told. Sit in this chair, eat this slop, put your toe on this line.

But it doesn't matter what they do with your body. Bodies are resilient.

It's what they do with your mind.

"Mr. Sudden, please open your notebook and re-create the sequence of events that led you to this point."

"I don't have a pen, let alone a point."

"It will be therapeutic."

"Can we skip therapy and get straight to the prescription?"

"Is that meant to be amusing?"

"My grandma always said it's the little laughs that cut the deepest."

"All right, stand against the wall and place your hands behind your back."

I let myself be cuffed and then shoved to the floor.

To the cold, wet concrete.

What's there to say?

There's the days I've earned, minus the days I have left.

Everything else is just another lame cliché.

Until you're the one standing ankle-deep in it.

And I'm not standing anymore.

So, okay, here's the beginning.

The hard truth.

The only thing you really need to know:

In the end, they want you to bend over and submit...in the end.

Actually, you don't need to know that. That's just bullshit someone carved into the wall with their fingernail.

What you really need to know is:

There's a kid in here wants to kill me.

Two of them, actually.

2

The hard truth is that no matter what you do, there's always someone better at it than you are. In my case, that's Elliot Hella. We've been friends since third grade. Or at least he's let me follow him around since then. Elliot's older brother, Nico, an original tatted badass now married and bagging groceries, was in six different thrash bands while we were still spooning up Lucky Charms. So by osmosis, Elliot has chops. I have no chops.

Especially on the folk guitar Dad Sudden left behind.

"You're getting an electric," Elliot says, wearing big black boots and stiff jeans with the cuffs rolled. "Today."

"Why?"

He shoves a poster in my face. It's for Rock Scene 2013: TWO DOZEN HOT ACTS! TWO BRUTAL WEEKS! ONE MASSIVE WINNER! Normally we're in the audience, holding our tools while lamer bands soak up all the glory. Not anymore. Not this year.

"There is only one thing standing between us and total domination," Elliot says.

"My ownership of a brand-new, bone-crushing noise machine?"

He grins and gives me a nod.

The nod.

Half the kids at school would practically carve out their spleen to have El Hella nod at them like that, the dude too cool to know it, too weird to be popular, too hardcore to give a shit. You can practically see the musk rising off of him. In fact, he'd be an absolute monster, a campus hero, a woman-slaying juggernaut, except for how he's six-four packed into five-six, built low and wide and raw, too much torso and not enough legs, compressed, tamped down, ready to explode, a heavy dose of Hella on every front, way too much for some people.

But not me.

"So can we go already?"

Elliot drives his mom's Renault like a stock car, trading paint, switching lanes, gunning off ramps, catching air.

It's terrifying.

I want to ball up under the floor mat and suck my thumb.

But I don't.

On the outskirts of the city, we park under a bridge, then take the subway straight to Jazzbox Jim's, where I'm all pretending I know my ass from an E string. *Dude, check out the action on this.* Or, *Dude, isn't this the axe Hendrix played?* The aisles are full of guys in city bands, gelled hair and wallet chains, and a fat kid in the corner playing "Master of Puppets" note for note. It's hot and sweaty. I can't stop saying *axe*. The clerk wears a Western shirt with pearl buttons, shining us off 'cause he thinks we're gonna paw through his stock all afternoon without buying a thing. He is incorrect. I clear my throat, trying to sound like a dude who gets paid for gigs.

"Let us check that purple Strat."

Western Shirt sighs and takes it off the wall. Elliot whips hair out of his eyes, slinging the guitar over his shoulder like he just rappelled into downtown Basra, ready to lay out a blanket of suppressing fire. He runs through a bunch of tasty licks, ending with this weird descending octave pattern I could only dream of pulling off, stretching the last note with creamy élan.

"Cool run," Western Shirt says, already Elliot's buddy.

"Yeah," I say. "Nice...run."

I've actually wanted an electric since I was ten. Beth was always like, *So stop talking about it and just get one.*

Beth doesn't say that anymore, even though she was right.

"How much?" I ask.

Western Shirt, starting to take me an increment of seriously, checks the price.

"Six bills."

"Six *hundo*?"

"What else do you got?" Elliot says. "Like, for the semi-employed?"

Western Shirt strokes his Strokes sideburns, pointing to the junkie trade in the corner, the dozen shit-rides he can't give away. The best of the lot is a Les Paul "The Paul." It's turd brown with ancient twin humbuckers and looks like a two-by-four with a neck stapled on it. The tag reads $299.

"Well, the price is right," Elliot says.

The Paul is cracked and worn and tired. It's covered with band stickers and band grime and the residue of a thousand out-of-tune renditions of "Sweet Home Bamaslamma." It needs tender love and care. It needs penicillin and a solder gun. It needs a blindfold and a bullet.

"Yeah, it's not gonna win any beauty contests, but at least it ain't made in Korea."

"They make axes in Korea?"

Western Shirt rolls his eyes.

I finger a chord. *Plink, plink, plink.* I play a scale and doink half the notes. I slide up the neck, go for an arpeggio, miss it by a mile.

The guitar is clearly defective.

Worthless.

A stone-cold loser.

A rope-swinging albatross.

I am totally, completely in love.

"I guess it's possible I could be talked into taking this off your hands."

"Talk away."

"You take two hundred cash?"

"You got two hundred cash?"

Elliot gets up and stands enigmatically by the window, staring at a stack of amps. Or maybe the face of Joey Ramone in a stain on the wall. I lean over and yank a roll of twenties out of my sock. Twenties I sweated hard for all summer, bussing plates of all-you-can-eat rib bones at the all-you-can-eat rib place where I never eat a single freaking rib because even the thought of them makes me ill.

Western Shirt sniffs the bills, rings it up. "So what's y'all's band called?"

"Death by Natural Causes."

"Shitty name."

"Actually, it's Death by Piranha."

"Not much better."

"Actually, it's Death by Whoreknife."

He doesn't laugh.

"Toss in a set of strings?"

This time he does laugh. At two hundred dollars, I don't even get a case, resting the guitar over my shoulder like a lumberjack.

On the subway I feel so freaking cool.

At Forty-Fourth Street, some Brooks Brother points to one of the stickers on the back, THE BLOWNUT HOLES.

"Hey, I saw them play CBGB's in college. They totally rocked!"

I turn and stare.

"You've never been to CB's in your life, suit."

The whole car laughs. A posse of cholos in the corner falls all over one another, goofing on the guy for being such a knob.

The suit frowns, goes back to his paper.

One of the cholos leans over to bump knuckles.

I reach out and we touch skin.

Elliot nods with appreciation, eyes intense, chin cleft, hair so black it's purple.

There is alchemy waiting to happen.
A band is dying to be born.
To rise from the ashes of our lameness.
Even though I do feel a little bad for the suit.
Truth is, I've never been to CB's, either.
But I do own an electric guitar.

3

You want a diary?

Diaries are for girls in pajamas.
    For teacher-crushes and prancy unicorns.
    Fancy leather bindings and tiny yellow keys.
    Best-friend betrayals and grass-stained capris.
    Fumbled bra-lifts and locker pose.
    Angsty poems and parent-loathe.
    All your random hope dreams.
    All your dirty dope dreams.

No, man, this ain't no diary.

What we have here is a forced narrative.
    What we have here is a failure to exaggerate.
    Minimum-security purity.
    What we have here is homework for a bunch of dudes who
were too slick to get caught.
    And then got caught.
    Tried and tied.

Nailed and bailed.

This notebook is for those of us who need three-punch holes, a spiral binding, and the consistency of ruled margins to provide the sort of authoritative structure otherwise missing in our single-parent homes.

Hey, this notebook isn't for you.

It's for me.

For my delinquency.

A clean rectangle upon which to get down my thoughts.

Sound my thoughts.

Drown my thoughts.

Before they rear up, bare their fangs,

Spread 'em wide.

Before they

Chomp down

Go to town

And

Eat me

The fuck

Alive.

For the love of Baal, The Paul is *loud*. I pose and strut, wind-mill Townshend, kick-leg Angus, duckwalk Chuck, crank the knobs, crank the amp, crank the stank, making Elliot admit every twelve minutes The Paul takes no prisoners.

"Say it."

"The Paul takes no prisoners."

"Again."

"The Paul takes no prisoners."

"Once more."

He gives me a look, raises his lip, a smile that's not a smile. "Don't push it."

So I pout for a while instead.

He finally slings the greasy hair out of his eyes and rubs his temples. "Fine. Your piece-of-shit guitar is less a piece of shit than anticipated. Okay, *Ritchie*?"

I shrug. "Yeah, okay."

We run through our set in his basement. Thirteen songs, not a single cover. Assuming you don't count the parts we bla-tantly stole as covers. Just a lick here, a riff there. Everyone thefts from everyone else and always has. Band to band, song to song, note to note. Blues to rock to punk. Take it and make it your own. Or at least disguise it well. But since we are on the verge of being the greatest act of all time—concerts selling out in fractions of seconds, so many records going platinum they have to discover a new alloy, Brazilian models fighting over the right to bear our children and name them things like "Amelia Beefhardt" and "Firetruck Inspektor," scientists bronzing the smell of my Nikes for the Smithsonian—we must be careful about these things.

After three encores, we're covered in sweat. My ears ring like a Weedwacker stuck between gears. Tiny threads of ceiling material waft onto my shoulders and into my lungs, settling like an asbestos lawsuit.

"We need a drummer."

Elliot frowns. "Screw that."

"Screw what?"

"We'll just sound like Fred Sabbath."

"But, dude, with the right cat on skins these songs would rock sixty-nine percent harder."

"We'll just sound like Fred Halen."

"And that's a problem because?"

"We'll just sound like the Jimi Fredrix Experience."

"Whatever," I say. "Be like that."

Elliot's face goes dark. His shoulders begin to tremble. He half turns away, voice cracking. "You *really* want to know why not?"

"Of course."

He takes a deep breath. "When I was little, there was this guy in our neighborhood."

"What guy?"

"Who dressed up like a clown."

"With big feet? And a red wig?"

"And played drums."

"No shit?"

"Yeah," Elliot whispers. "And that drummer clown...gave me a piece of candy."

"So? What's wrong with—"

"Right before he put his hand down my pants."

Water drips from a pipe in the corner. The basement, for the first time ever, is dead silent.

"Wow, man," I finally say. "That's really heavy. Do you want to talk about it, or—"

El Hella busts out laughing, then plays a massive distorted chord.

"You idiot. I just think we're better off as a duo."

Five Things Our Band Needs (to win Rock Scene 2013):
1. A name
2. A drummer
3. A singer
4. A signature song
5. A slightly less evil Elliot

I turn it loud, then louder, then loudest. We run through our set one more time, full bore, like an army of marching noise-bots. Like an amplified steel thresher. The Paul owns several major frequencies. Rude vibrations sterilize every rodent within a two-mile radius. Virgin ears beg for mercy and are turned down flat.

It's awesome.

"This is awesome!" Elliot says, looking like a punk bricklayer.

"I know!" I say, looking like the guy who invented chat rooms.

The reason we get away with making such colossal racket is because Elliot's mom is never home. And by never I mean not *ever*, all busy being this upper-crusty Greek chick out riding horses in thigh-high boots and orange mascara. Seducing stable boys in tight horse-tights. Having cocktails and sashimi and correctly pronouncing *dressage*. She's also working on her fifth husband, having killed off the first four. Heart attack. Cancer. Cancer. Heart attack. Pocketing a nice chunk of change each time. Even Elliot calls her the Black Widow.

Husband number five, name of Lawrence, has little tufts of gray hair and miles of wrinkly skull, sitting upstairs in a leather chair next to a reel-to-reel player spooling out Tchaikovsky. There's a jar of honey on the side table that he eats with a spoon. We take a break and Lawrence tells me he once worked on the Manhattan Project.

"No fooling, huh?"

"Like Oppenheimer?" Elliot explains. "The dude who assembled the first nuke? The Manhattan Project was his team. Mushroom clouds and shit. Lawrence racked the abacus and got all theoretical on Hitler's ass. He mathed up hard and ended the war."

"Well, not alone," Lawrence says.

"L-Dog, I so had no clue you were famous!"

Lawrence shrugs and nods, practically a living memory, a dream of tweed suits and chalkboards and differential equations, like Russell Crowe in that movie where he's not a gladiator.

How can you not love the guy?

Plus, he couldn't care less how terrible we are. How loud and clumsy and angry and awesome we are, amps cranked postmax, hammering through the floorboards for hours while he just sits there readjusting the quilt on his legs.

"Lawrence," I say, "you're totally getting a major shout-out in the liner notes."

"Don't get ahead of yourself," Elliot says, scratching neck stubble. "We don't even have a name yet and you're hanging the Grammy over the mantel."

"How about the Envisaged?"

"Terrible."

"How about Betty Got Eddie Pregnant?"

"Even worse. Sounds like an avant-garde theater troupe."

"How about Murder Coaster?"

"Hey, that's good," Lawrence says.

Elliot takes off his steel-toes and rubs his real toes. Dude don't wear no socks.

"Like I said, we don't even have a name."

The phone rings.

The phone never rings at the Hellas'. Literally. I have never once heard it ring before.

We all crowd around the speakerphone. "Hello?"

It's the Rock Scene people. The guy sounds too happy to be alive.

"Hey, guys, we have some great new twists this year that will be announced soon!"

"Great," Elliot goes.

"Twists," I go.

"Like live streaming. It may go viral."

"Live streaming," Elliot says.

"Viral," I say.

"Also, on the downside? We've received your application."

"What about it?"

Turns out there are two problems with our application. One is that we forgot to include the entrance fee, which is more or less a direct result of the fact that we didn't include it, since I earmarked every last available dollar for The Paul. We were sort of hoping they wouldn't notice, like, *Whoops, it must have fallen on the floor.*

No dice.

Rock Scene Guy goes, "Sorry, guys, but rules are rules. Deadlines are deadlines. Disqualified is disqualified."

We're screwed.

Until Lawrence reaches into the side table without a word, pulling out a checkbook made of, like, papyrus. He writes in the amount, one hundred shaky dollars, with this thing that looks more like an eagle feather than a pen. He actually dips it in a jar of ink.

Elliot gives Lawrence the thumbs-up, already arguing with Rock Scene Guy about the second problem.

The second problem is that we didn't fill in a name.

"Our name is Band."

"The Band? I think that's already taken."

"No. Just *Band*."

"Banned?"

"Not *Banned*. Band! We are called Band. Our fans know us as Band. The world worships us as Band. Should I drive down there and sound it out for you?"

"B-A-N-D?"

"No, genius, F-I-S-T-E-D. Yes. How many times do I have to say it? Band!"

Rock Scene Guy sniffs, like his feelings are hurt. "If you have to say it that many times, it's probably not a very good name."

There's a long pause. Elliot knows the dude is right. He clears his throat like he's about to apologize, and then doesn't. The discussion continues, the whole thing extremely interesting, but I'm not really paying attention anymore.

Why?

Mostly because I'm way off in that space I go to alone, about sixty-nine times a day.

The space where I'm thinking, hard, about Ravenna Woods.

5

It doesn't pay to think about Ravenna in here. So I don't. There're sixty dudes in one big concrete crate. Which is fifty-nine dudes too many. It doesn't pay to think about anything you do want, anything you will want, anything you ever wanted.

But let's not get too dramatic.

This is no movie.

Lockdown and solitary.

Shaw and shank.

It's mostly just a parade of dimwits, shit-lucks, knuckle-heads, fist-fuckers, finger-sniffers, ass bandits, wrong-place-wrong-timers, and dudes too weak to pull off even the most minor crimes.

Which, ironically, makes the ten guys who are actually dangerous 63 percent more dangerous.

At Progressive Progress we have classes. Like Art Therapy, and How to Do a Job Interview, and How to Not Be High All the Time. Then there's "counselors" instead of guards. Some of them are hard-asses. A couple true believers. Most of them are just bored.

But that doesn't mean it's not hairy at times.

You cram a hundred degenerates into a box, eventually one of them's gonna come up with *The Merchant of Venice*.

And another's gonna come up with Undercard.

Which two of them actually did.

What's Undercard?

Rock 'Em Sock 'Em Robots played out by juvie knucklettes.

Punch or be punched.

Do not pass Go; do not explain your bruises.

No ring, no gloves, no trainer.

It's about bouts. Kids crowding around going "Oooh!" and "Damn!" while they stand on the sidelines, safe and whole.

At least for a week.

Undercard pays in smokes. Or, as the slang-happy residents of Unit 3 call them, bones. Like, "You want to brawl, homes? No? Cost you six bones. Don't got 'em? Then you're on the list. We'll see you at fight time in the dayroom."

Saying no is not an option.

In the dayroom, there're a dozen plastic chairs. This muscle dude named Conner is barn boss. He's got eleven chairs stacked up, sitting on them like a throne, daring anyone to ask, let alone try, to take one. So people just stand. For hours. No one sits on the floor, 'cause it smells like piss. Next to Conner is his second in command, kid named Peanut.

Peanut sits on the one other chair.

A horizontal scar across his throat like a necklace.

Busy picking the bouts.

He doesn't seem to like me a whole lot.

In fact, word is he hates my guts.

If Peanut hates my guts, that means Conner hates my guts.

I'd ask them why, but that would be stupid.

"You down with Undercard, Sudden?"

"Um, well, I..."

"Sorry, son, you been chosen."

So I lost my first two fights.

Got punched and kicked until the punching and kicking stopped.

Went to lunch a little on the tender side.

"You fall down in the shower?" Conner asked, then laughed.

I paid in cigarettes to get out of the match after that.

But they didn't like me ducking.

For some reason I'm a big draw.

Apparently, people like watching me get punched.

I can't figure it out.

At all.

School starts in one week exactly. My senior year. Supposed to be awesome. King of the Hallways and all that shit. But I'm fairly sure it's just another fantasy, like winning the big game or nailing the hot cheerleader—except no one fantasizes about those things anymore, since football is a concussion factory and cheerleaders are hot pockets of chlamydia. So it's more like dreaming about getting accepted to Princeton on hardship or writing the next killer social media app.

Meanwhile, I've been playing The Paul every waking second for a month. My fingers are bleeding. Have bled. Will bleed. Wore the lame calluses I used to have clean off. Now my fingertips are like cracked leather. My chops are getting slick. I finger-pick my way down the stairs, windmill open chords through the kitchen. I play while watching TV, twang arpeggios during every commercial, beer-car-beer, buy fish sticks, buy boner pills, please tune in to Sitcom Q while some tool delivers punch lines mathematically designed for the diminution of your intellect. I diminish minor sevenths instead. I change the strings, wax the back, tweak the truss rod. I sleep with The Paul lying next to me like a skinny Russian model, all neck and no ass. Hey, you want commitment? Even on the can, squeezing out a deuce, I got The Paul on my lap, shredding through Slayer tablature and getting one out of every twenty-three notes right. Mom is yelling, but mostly it's to say, *Bye, I'm late for work. Don't forget to wipe!*

Seriously? That's not a joke.

Or is barely one.

Mom still thinks I'm six.

Possibly nine.

Assuming she's done the math at all.

Possible Band Name List #48

Death by Blender
Los Stupid Texans
Mutilhate
Your Feet, My Ottoman
Suction Solution
The Glossolalias
HoBroken
Death by Market Share
Sonata Regatta Cumquatta
Stab Habit
Death by Man, Machine, and Nature
Kiss Me Cherry
Tiniest Little Sips
We Buy Sell Hair
Kennedy Martini Left
Craw Aerosol
Hammershot Panicsmith
Death by Wipe

sMuttonChops
The Velleity
Death by My Chemical Romance
The Plenipotentiaries
Men of Mod
Death by Rat Salad
Psycooze
Incest Militia Right
The Has Binges
Pigtail and the Curls
Scrofula
Use *Suburb* in Our Name to Signify Angst.
ShockMom AweDad
Death by Arty Pretension
Ouroboros
CutYou Slim and the Four Tercels
Death by Koresh

Elliot pulls his mom's Renault up the driveway and parks next to my Saab, which hasn't moved in a while.

I don't like to drive that much.

So I don't drive that much.

Or, really, ever.

He kicks open the door and starts unloading.

There's something different about him.

I can't quite put my finger on it.

Until I do.

He's got no hair.

Not a single one.

Shaved clean.

El Hella has gone full-on skin.

I don't say so, but it actually looks pretty cool, pretty tough. He left the sideburns, which are now muttonchops, proto-Neanderthal. His eyes are black and flat. He's got a Marlboro behind his ear like he's about to reach up, dip it in ink, and sign his will.

"What?"

"Something's different. You wearing a new outfit?"

He's wearing khaki shorts and a Misfits shirt and sweating, squat and nut-brown and muscular. I'm wearing khaki shorts and a Pixies shirt and sweating, tall and pale and skinny.

"No."

"For some reason you remind me of a baby's ass. For some reason I want to powder you and swaddle you and gingerly tuck you under my arm."

"Hilarious."

"Hey, maybe when we get huge, you can endorse teen-formula Rogaine."

"Are you through yet, or do you need a few minutes to go mature in private?"

"Nope, I'm good."

He starts tugging at his amp, a Fender Bassman that's heavier than a freezer full of steaks.

"Need a hand?"

"Negative."

"You sure?"

"I am not in the habit of taking help from dicks who are all up in my fashion sense."

I grab the other end anyway, mime scissors.

"You do the honors yourself?"

"Nah, that hot waitress at Presto's clippered it off. In the back lot. Said she was going to sell the shit for fifty bucks."

"To who?"

"One of those companies makes wigs. Long Island MILFs. Cancer ladies. Ladies who need merkins."

"What's a merkin?"

"A vag wig."

"They make vag wigs?"

He shrugs. "I guess."

"Hey, you know what?"

"Do *not* say Vag Wig is a great name for a band."

"But it totally is! Besides, what hot waitress?"

"Angie."

Elliot is a pasta boy at Pasta Presto's. That means putting precooked spaghetti in these little cups of warm water just before the chef slops on the sauce.

"Angie?"

"Yup."

"Angie Proffer?"

"Yup."

"Mrs. Proffer who is Spence Proffer's mom?"

"So?"

We lever the amp into the corner of the garage, under a poster of Marc Bolan driving a tank through downtown Detroit with some ugly-ass nude chick straddling the turret. She's got a gut and a flask and this unruly brown muff that looks like half the hippies from 1974 are communing in it. But, man, she's smiling like you wouldn't believe. So open and innocent. So happy. Her eyes are like melted glass, teeth an ocean wide. People don't smile like that anymore.

I seriously love that girl.

"What do you mean, *so?*"

Elliot gets on Beth's old Huffy and pedals in circles around me.

"Mind your own business."

"You're right. Hey, what am I thinking? You should totally bareback Mrs. Proffer in the stockroom. Knock that cougar up. By the time we graduate you'll be Spence Proffer's uncle."

"That wouldn't make me his uncle."

I get on my old Razor and start doing opposite circles inside his.

"And he just might take a pass on beating the shit out of you, since your pink, beautiful, funky-tonk baby, whom you will no doubt immediately name Joe Strumma Hella, will be his half brother."

"Still doesn't make me Proffer's uncle."

"No, but when you're in the hospital with broken arms and legs, I will have to ask for a full refund for our fully nonrefundable Rock Scene 2013 deposit under a medical hardship exemption."

Elliot stops short. Beth's tire squeals. His eyes are beyond serious. He puts his cigarette out on the back of his wrist, where there are about thirty circular burns, like eraser tips, forming a lunatic's bracelet. "Under no circumstances of any kind am I missing *one fucking note* of Rock Scene 2013. You got me, Sudden?"

"Okay, okay."

I take a big stride and launch the scooter into the wall, where it chunks out a piece of Sheetrock almost exactly the size and shape of a scooter.

"What we really need is a drummer."

"Negative."

"But *why*?"

He sighs. "Drummers are dicks, okay? They're high maintenance. They're always wanting to sing and write songs instead of just keeping the beat. They're always spontaneously combusting, or choking on their own vomit, or losing an arm in a car wreck. It's just not worth the effort."

"A kept beat isn't worth a little hassle?"

"What we *really* need is a name," he says. "That Rock Scene dude keeps pestering me."

"How about Celestial Embryo?"

"Terrible. Hippie nonsense."

"How about Elliot Hella and the Smella Glove?"

"Worse. Zero funny."

"How about Mortis Trigger?"

He shakes his amazingly bald head. "Unmarketable, even to Norwegian metalheads."

"Okay, all joking aside?"

"Yes?"

"I have *the* name."

"Yes?"

"Stop Exploring. Except we insist on squeezing our legs together and saying it every time with a lisp, like *Thtop Exthploring.*"

"Hmmm…"

"No, seriously? I really have the name."

"Yes?"

"Sin Sistermouth."

"Sin Sistermouth?"

"Sin Sistermouth."

Elliot ponders it, the expanse of his skull creasing. He dumps the bike and holds up one finger.

"That, my friend, is actually not bad at all."

I pick up Beth's bike and put it back in the corner.

So, Sin Sistermouth is our new name.

And then, instead of practicing, we spend the rest of the afternoon working on cover art and a cool logo.

Five Things Our Band Needs (to win Rock Scene 2013):

1. ~~A name~~
2. A drummer
3. A singer
4. A signature song
5. An enema

Just as Elliot is splitting, Looper comes home.

Three things you should know:
1. Beth left us.
2. Dad Sudden left.
3. Looper just showed up.

Cause and effect. Euclidian geometry. The moronic triangle.

Looper blocks Elliot's Renault with her PERFECTION POOL CLEANERS van before edging to the side. Elliot sprays gravel at the end of the driveway, tires leaving a tiny French patch.

"What, you and your buddy are skinheads now?"

Looper leans against a scuffed Coleman cooler, peeling off her rubber boots. A blue feather earring dangles from one ear. She's got the tan of someone who stands next to water all day.

"I look like a skinhead to you?"

She cracks a Stroh's. "You hang out with a skinhead, I figure you're a skinhead, too."

"Well, how about you toss me a Stroh's there, Alberta Einstein, and I'll explain just how dumb that comment is."

Looper hands me one. "One."

"I know."

"And brush your teeth before your mom gets home."

"I know."

I hate beer but always ask. Mostly because I get a kick out of letting Loop play The Cool Adult Who Will Let You Drink A Beer. And she pretty much always takes the bait. In fact, for your mom's girlfriend, the person you're supposed to be colossally freaked out by and resent down to your marrow and get into these long, cinematic, tongue-tied arguments in the pouring rain with, Looper's actually a purty cool chick.

"So go ahead and explain."

"Explain what?"

"How dumb my comment was."

"Okay, Loop, here goes."

"Don't call me Loop."

"Right. So, Loop, I guess it's like, there're good skinheads and bad skinheads. They even fight at shows sometimes. The bad ones are, it's true, all with the Nazi rhetoric and such. With the tats and the pamphlets and the random kicking of steel toe. But, you know, everyone, even them, is fully aware that this mentality is unsupportable in the twenty-first century. It's a doom ride that's more about the doom than the ride. But mostly, it's the shtick of the profoundly stupid. Those guys always repent after getting canned off their last dishwash job, and then they find God and go around talking to schoolkids about how ignorant they once were. The good skinheads are really your modern-day Love Children; it's just that ever since the Internet, people are embarrassed by overt expressions of humanity and kindness."

She whistles, lighting a smoke, feet wrinkled white like baby-ass after a bath. She wiggles her toes, skin loose. I want to tear it away in strips.

"You, Ritchie, are way too smart for your own good."

"How can anyone be *too* smart?"

"You're right. I meant too smart-ass."

"Ah."

"Actually, if you had a brain, you'd be dangerous."

"Shit, homegirl, I'm dangerous either way."

She laughs. "So, anyway, I'm interested in these young skinhead girls."

"I'll bet."

She doesn't laugh.

"I mean, you're telling me they're secretly hiding good intentions behind layers of mascara? And, like, pointy bracelets?"

"Exactly. It's all a front. The good skinheads are into PETA and vegetarianism and womyn's rights."

"Would that be womyn with a *Y*?"

"It would."

Looper unbuttons her PERFECTION POOLS—HI! I'M LOOPER shirt, allowing her blue-collar jugs to breathe.

"Besides, Elliot is just trying to piss off his mom. We're totally apolitical."

"You rock gods are without a position on global warming?"

"We do not play rock."

"Do you roll?"

"We do not roll."

"What do you play? Punk?"

"Hardcore, Loop. Hardcore."

"And the difference is?"

"Hardcore is to punk as a pickax is to lipstick."

She shakes her head, rolling the filter of a Marlboro between her fingers until it's shaped like a cone.

"And when exactly can I hear some of this hardcore?"

I yawn. "After we crush skulls at Rock Scene 2013 and get signed to a megadeal, you can download the MP3s at what I'll make sure is an adjusted familial rate."

Looper blushes at the word *familial*, liking it. I kind of like it, too. It's weird. It's different. It's so much better than Dad Sudden.

"You need to burn off some serious energy, Ritchie. Crank that imagination down a notch. Or three."

"Yeah? How am I supposed to do that?"

"Handsome rocker like you? Ever heard of a girlfriend?"

Two thoughts flash behind my lids like burning neon: *Handsome Rocker + Ravenna Woods.*

"What I need," I say, "is more dating advice from Billie Loop King."

Looper smooths foam from her chin. "Just finish your beer, huh?"

I do. Or at least pretend to, but really pour it out behind my leg, toss the empty into the cooler, and head inside just as Mom pulls up the drive, since I need to see them kiss hello like I need ten grand worth of free therapy.

10

Isolation is therapeutic. It says so in all the leading penal literature. Also the leading penile literature. Today I got called on the carpet for not keeping up with my journal. A counselor, this monstrous dude everyone calls "The Basilisk" but whose real name is Joey or something, comes by every other day and checks. Screw off with the journal and they put you in administrative hold as punishment. Me and some hard-looking black-Mexican kid, who looks more black than Mexican, are in an empty room cuffed to desks in opposite corners. The dude's name is Carlos. But everyone calls him B'los. Which is short for Black Carlos. I don't call him anything.

We're in there twelve hours together.

At about hour six, I say, "You blow off your journal, too?"

He looks at me a long, long time.

Then goes, "Yup."

And that, ladies and gentlemen, is the entirety of our conversation.

At the end of the shift, The Basilisk is all like, "Tomorrow you see Dr. Benway after breakfast. Bring your journal."

"Doctor who?"

"No talking," he says, and locks me back in my box.

11

I get a letter the week before school starts. It says WELCOME BACK! It says CONGRATULATIONS ON BEING A SENIOR! It says SENIOR YEAR IS A YEAR THAT YOU WILL REMEMBER THE REST OF YOUR LIFE! It says YOUR HOMEROOM TEACHER IS DICK ISLEY, WHO YOU'LL ALSO HAVE FOR HISTORY OF THE AMERI-CAS AND BIO LAB!

> **Kingdom:** *Dick Isley*
> **Phylum:** *Dick*
> **Class:** *Dice*
> **Order:** *Dangling Human Turdlet*
> **Family:** *Dicehole*
> **Genus:** *Intestinal Fluke*
> **Species:** *Flat-Out Liar*

Truth is, I don't really dig Dick Isley.

Why?

For one thing, he wears his male-pattern baldness as if it were a matter of style or efficiency instead of being follicle-y challenged. Like he's just too damn busy educating the kids to waste time shampooing what would otherwise be a forest full of wavy locks.

Dick knows, like all the Dicks of the world know, exactly how many inches he can get away with.

For another, it's because Dick calls himself *Dice*, which he's happy to explain is a "mash-up" of *Dick* and *Mr. Isley*. He spends half of every class encouraging the girls to call him that, too.

"That sucks," Elliot says, helping himself to two fingers of whatever looks good in our fridge. "I didn't get him for a single class."

"Actually, I think it's sort of perfect."

He swigs milk straight from the carton. "I thought you hated the guy."

"Hate? Me? Dice?"

"Yeah. Hate, you, him."

I tear the letter into tiny pieces and then stuff it into a cookbook. "Okay, it's true. But there's a plus side."

"Which is?"

Which is that Dick Isley has a component stack behind his desk that he's absurdly proud of, always dusting the thing and tinkering with buttons and settings. It's got high-end equipment locked in, like a DVD player and Wi-Fi and a preamp and speakers and monitors and oscillators. He calls it the Teaching Tower, and mostly uses it to show instructional videos when he's too hungover to do the lesson plan. Or impress girls after class, playing his huge collection of Weezer bootlegs. Or for parent conferences so they rave about how down he is with the kids.

He bought it out of his own pocket, honey! Did you hear that? I swear, that's the kind of commitment teachers don't show anymore!

"Well, I'm thinking Sin Sistermouth sure could use some of that gear ol' Dice is hoarding. And now I'm gonna be real close to it every morning."

"Use like how?" Elliot says, sticking his thumb in a yogurt, licking it, and putting it back in the fridge.

"For our PA. We could hook up that preamp, no doubt. Run the mic straight through. Also, we could—"

"You mean jack the Teaching Tower?"

"Nah, Jay-Z, not *jack* it. More like borrow without asking."

Elliot shakes his head. "You wanna give the guy a hard time? I'm down. Rage Against the Di-chine? Cool. I mean, the asshole wears a trimmed goatee. But his gear's all welded in. There's about a hundred padlocks on it. Trying to steal that shit is a sure way to get busted."

"Yeah," I say. "It's a risk. Still, if a man had a plan? Like, a really smart plan, he—"

Elliot holds up one callused finger, muttonchops glistening. "The last thing we need is trouble, Ritchie. Um, Rock Scene? Um, priorities?"

El Hella, voice of reason. It's amazing.

"You don't want trouble, don't eat Looper's Chinese leftovers," I say.

Elliot scoops three fingers of kung pao and drops it into his mouth.

"I'm serious, dawg. Don't even think about it."

39

"Okay."

He eyeballs me like roadside ordnance. "I mean it."

"*Okay*," I say, in a way higher voice than anyone not named Amber should ever use.

Elliot nods, then heads down to the garage to practice.

The final reason I don't dig Dick Isley is that he was at the party.

Which party?

Beth's party.

My sister, Beth.

Have we not talked about her yet?

Beth was killed six days into freshman year.

By a drunk driver.

So for a semester I walked around school, That Drama Kid.

Suddenly everyone knew who I was.

Up and down the hallways, the whispers and looks.

The sympathy.

The weirdness.

The shying away.

Like maybe it was contagious.

Guys and their grim faces.

Girls and their teary hugs.

Standing around trying to decide whose sweater was more devastated than whose.

And then teachers.

Before class, after class, in study hall.

"Are you okay?"

"Yes."

"Are you *sure* you're okay?"

"Well, now that you mention it, no. In fact, I think I'm going to need intensive one-on-one mentoring the whole rest of the year, and especially on weekends. Do you, by any chance, have a spare guest room?"

Actually, some teachers really stepped up. So did a bunch of kids, if only because they weren't afraid to show how genuinely crushed they were. But they did it from a distance, because mostly they were all about Beth.

And she wasn't all about me.

She wasn't about anything anymore.

Her bed was empty; her clothes were donated.

There was a time for feeling really, really bad.

Until it was time to feel something else.

And then we all went home.

13

"How's that for revealing my inner pain and source of criminal inclinations?" I ask.

We're in a small office. There's a counselor right outside in case I get frisky. The psychiatrist is a tiny woman with hair pulled straight back into a bun. She's wearing a wool suit, even though it's hot as Christ. Her name is Dr. Kiki Benway. It says so on the plaque above her shoulder. Graduate of some medical school I've never heard of. Which either means it cost a fortune or it's a night-school dump that she takes a lot of working-class pride in having put herself through.

Dr. Benway only comes in a few hours a week.

But still takes the time to hang her diploma.

I think that could use a little analysis right there.

"It's a start," she says, tossing the journal back onto my lap, the corner of which spears my balls and forces me to hunch like a perv, pretending not to rub them. "But I think you need to drop the posture."

"What posture?"

"Your writing is full of attitude."

"The good kind or the bad kind?"

"There is no good attitude. There is only how far you'll go to hide your actual feelings."

I roll my eyes. I figured she'd be happy—ecstatic, even—with the stuff I'd written.

"What do you want from me, lady? That's the best I can do."

"Aside from not calling me lady? I want to know what it's really like in here."

"So do I."

"And I want to know what it was like before you came."

"So do I."

She frowns. "Give me some genuine emotion. Challenge yourself to be honest instead of merely clever."

"Is that all?"

"No. I also want to know more about Beth."

"It's always more. It's never less. You ever notice that?"

"Less is easy. More is a ticket back onto the street."

I laugh. "The *street*? I'm from Sackville. People leave their locks unlocked. Ice-cream trucks drive around all summer. Every other dude in town is a volunteer fireman."

"You know what I mean."

She's right. I do.

But it's not like I'm gonna admit it.

"Can I go now?"

"Yes."

Dr. Benway signals The Basilisk, who jumps up like he's just been Tased.

"Don't forget to give the ape a banana."

She crosses her legs. "Karl Marx once said 'Sarcasm is the opiate of the asses.'"

I shake my head. "It's 'Religion is the opiate of the *masses*.' And anyway, I heard he never really said that. It's just, like, a bumper sticker."

For the first time, Dr. Benway looks at me like I might actually have a brain.

"You could be right. But even so, I bet he never missed any journal entries."

"Damn straight," says The Basilisk, and then yanks me through the door.

I miss dinner trying to decide what to wear on the first day of school, like some flighty anorexic chick with a closet full of pink dresses. I need the perfect outfit for slouching in the hall, a shirt that says *hip yet detached*, pants that say *interesting yet bored*, footwear that says *stoic yet complicated*.

I need to impress Ravenna.

Who is not easy to impress.

It's a tough choice, but I finally go with dirty jeans, Fugazi T-shirt, black boots, no socks, and an enigmatic half grin.

Not bad.

But is it a grope-inspiring *ensemble*?

Unclear.

I stand sideways in front of the mirror. I've gotten taller. Not as skinny. Jaw a little more square, a little more stubble. Not the walking cock block I was six months ago. Ravenna could like me. It's totally within the control group of statistically possible outcomes.

I stick out my chest. Fugazi's lead singer, Ian, sticks out his mic with me.

"I am gonna run *deep* into those Woods!"

"*What?*" Mom says from down the hall.

"Nothing."

"Are you okay?"

Am I okay? Seriously?

"No, I'm about to fucking die in here."

"Sorry, what?"

"I've got a gun. I've got pills. I've got a pillowcase full of sailor cock and razor blades."

"I can't hear you through the door, Ritchie!"

"I said I'm fine!"

"Oh, okay. G'night, hon."

Hon? Seriously?

Ian doesn't bother to answer.

So I don't bother, either.

15

Hey, if Dropping Posture (great band name) is the whole point of Project Notebook here at Progressive Progress, then I will drop and give you twenty, Dr. Benway. Why fight it? I want to be better. As a person. As a friend. As an inmate. As a vessel for your insights and expertise.

So let's start with a poem.

In which Jotting for Sympathy (great band name) meets Full-Metal Honesty:

You Don't Got to Tell Ritchie Sudden Twice
A Poem
by Ritchie Sudden

It is dark and boring and hot
and sweaty.
In here.
Everything is the color of some asshole's golf shirt. The
walls and the floor and even
the light.

Fluorescing down an endless hall, through cinder
blocks and
wired glass, past a
stack of jackals
in acrid pens.
They make noise, all night.
Yells, screams,
moans, laughs.
Crying for mommy, busting
on the mommy-crier
Scratching at the bars, bleeding
in the sink
You can't sleep and you can't think.
That's the worst part;
You. Can't. Even. Think.
Actually, it's second worst. First
is how
everything smells like
piss.
Even the food.
Even the soap.
Everything smells
like everything.
Did I mention it
is dark
and hot
and sweaty

and
boring
in here?

The End

What do you think, Doc? Do I got the inside track for the next prison laureate? And, hey, does it come with a stipend? 'Cause I could really use some toothpaste.

But never mind that. Let me ask you this, from one professional to another: Do you ever actually *cure* anyone?

I mean, is it even possible to "improve," or do we all just learn strategies to hide our ugliness better? Like, did your boy Freud finally come to understand himself, standing on the precipice at the bitter end, or did he jump like everyone else?

Also, I know doctor-patient confidentiality comes into play here, but I'd be willing to bet my entire savings of three cigarettes and half a jar of peanut butter that you spend 97 percent of your time talking to the other guys about matters not entirely weighty and life-altering.

Like, for instance, an obsession with onanism.

Am I right?

Is it one big verbal tug-fest?

Do you stare at your diploma while listening to tales of the inexpressible loneliness represented by a stiff Kleenex balled up in the corner of any given cell?

Because, and here's the thing, that's all they ever talk about outside your office, too. Except, you know, hooking up with strippers and doing armed robberies and beating down rap producers who didn't pay their royalties on time.

Lies, all.

But within those lies, you can hear so clearly what every one of those guys is really saying:

"I probably could have used a few more toys, a kind word, or even a little face time with mommy back when I was seven."

No PhD required to break that action down.

But hey, either way, I sure as shit am tired of administrative hold.

I will miss no more journal entries.

For real, yo.

Now, about that whole more-about-Beth thing.

He may have been a drunk, but why call him a driver?

Beth was snuffed by a Drunk Weaver. A Drunk I-Can't-Find-the-Brake-Pedal-er. Dumbass crossed the yellow line, bam, his $65,000 luxury sedan head-on into her $1,100 beater Buick. The good thing about that, though, is he died, too. 'Cause if he'd lived, I would have had to kill his stupid ass all over again.

I know, I know.

I realize that falls squarely in the *yeah, whatever, tough guy* arena.

Nevertheless.

I would have bided my time.

I would have planned and connived.

I would have squatted in the dark.

And eventually gotten my hands around his throat.

Son, that's not what your sister would have wanted.

We already lost one young life; why sacrifice another?

Besides, this isn't going to look good to the judge.

Hey, I don't give a shit. The judge should have done some looking out when the Drunk Weaver got caught the first time. Or even the second.

Like maybe yanked his license, huh? You think?

The guy was a classics professor at a college one state over, with an ex-wife, four kids, and a salt-and-pepper beard. Went right through the windshield. Died instantly. Instant karma, doomed to reincarnate as a thousand generations of shit beetles.

Beth died fast, too. But her Buick caught on fire. There were doctor assurances, medical examiner assurances, blah blah blah, it was over before she burned. But how could they know? Really, for sure? Sometimes I close my eyes and I see her like a witch in the Salem trials. They've got her lashed to a pole while the Drunk Weaver stands there in a pointy black hat, about to apply torch to twigs.

It was her body. It was my sister. Even if she was dead. She *burned*.

Afterward all my boys were like, "That sucks, guy," and "You okay, dog?" running through the appropriately sad motions, "Let us know if you need anything." But then two seconds later they're all, "Dude, who saw *Fear Factor* last night?" and "Man, let's scrounge some change for a sixer." El Hella was the only one who knew enough to come over and not leave for a week. El Hella was the only one smart enough not to get all Hallmark, just sort of sit there in my room with the lights off while we listened to my parents downstairs. Yelling. Whose screwup was whose in the crashing sea of their otherwise parental faultlessness. Dad Sudden rode it out for exactly six months.

Job in Texas.

Blonde in Texas.

See ya.

That happened three years ago, which in Sprouting Pubes years is really a decade. So I'm not gonna sit here and be all, *Beth and I were best friends* and talk about how perfect she was. Beth was only half awesome. Actually, a lot of the time she ragged it hard.

Mostly, though, I was just jealous.

Me three years ago: skinny, sweaty, hairline zits, track shorts, serial masturbator.

Beth three years ago: older, wiser, better-looking, this verging-on-hot girl who could also smack the shit out of a softball. A girl who could do beer bongs with the woo-hooers and back-slappers from the JV squad and never puke on her shoes. She and her friends always seemed to be leaving school during the middle of the day. I'd be in algebra and see her red Buick turn onto Route 6, a bunch of laughing ponytails stuffed in back, some dude hanging out the window with his arms spread like Leo the Cap in *Titanic*.

Then one morning after a big party, Mom just home from the swing shift, uniform spattered with mustard, me with a mouthful of toast, we get a call. State cops.

"Are you related... have some bad... sorry to inform..."

That week in school there was a whole lot of crying and hugging. A whole lot of teary girls standing stonewashed in corners and doorways. They had one of those memorials in the gym with Beth's picture blown up on an easel next to the podium, and people gave weepy speeches and even read these poems, the kind of poems that are so fucking insanely rhymingly horrible that it makes you like the reader more, not less.

And then everyone's favorite teacher, everyone's best pal, Dick Isley, improv-ed a eulogy.

Dick.

Speech.

Dickspeech.

"Beth was a great girl."

(How would he know?)

"Beth really meant a lot to all of us."

(A lot? Is that less than a ton? Or more than a shitload?)

"Beth will live on in all our hearts."

(Not in yours, she won't.)

A month later, everyone was pretty much back to making jokes and grab-assing by their lockers. Except Star Petrosky, who continued to cry in biology lab all year, playing her role as Keeper of the Flame. Me and Star, we ended up dating some. If by dating you mean making out in the back of her mom's Camry. We'd be talking at a party, *How are you holding up? Are you okay? Do you want to be alone?* I wouldn't say anything and then she'd lead me somewhere dark and hug me and whisper how much she missed Beth and how everything was going to be cool, and then next thing you know my head's inside her shirt and I'm sucking on a grieving nipple while she's running her fingers through my hair and moaning my name.

Listen, I know how that sounds, *Look how hard I'm trying to prove I'm all hard and detached,* like some lame white rapper in a Kangol and six-hundred-dollar sunglasses.

I mean, I loved my sister.

No doubt.

Beth Sudden R.I.P.

Spill a forty on the ground in tribute, *splash splash splash*.

And even though we weren't best friends, like brothers and sisters in Tom Hanks movies I've never seen, we were cool for the most part, and on a good night I could almost get a glimpse of the adult friends we might have grown up to be.

Meanwhile Star Petrosky's probably in the back row of some college business class right this second, wearing tear-stained black and carving Beth's initials into her forearm with an X-Acto knife, driving proof of her ineradicable sadness one layer closer to home.

17

I'm back in administrative hold. Mostly for language, but also content. Plus, not taking my journal serious enough. B'los is there, too. He keeps his head down on the desk until about hour four, then looks up.

"What you writing?"

I'm scratching away, filling up page after page.

"Lyrics."

"For what?"

"A song."

"Rhymes?"

"Sometimes."

"No, man. Rhymes. Like, hip-hop?"

"Oh. No, hardcore."

"What in fuck's hardcore?"

I try to decide if he's screwing with me or if he's curious for real.

Mostly he just stares.

"It's like metal," I finally say. "But without the stupid hair and stupid leather and stupid lyrics. Loud and hard and fast."

"At the core of the song, not just the edges."

I look at him for a very long time.

"Exactly."

"So what's it called?"

" 'Ignore Me or Deplore Me.' "

"Stupid title."

"I guess."

An hour later, he goes, "Or maybe I just don't know what *deplore* means."

"It's, like, hating shit so hard it's almost love."

"Huh."

Another hour later, he goes, "Changed my mind. Title's cool."

"Thanks."

He nods and then puts his head back down on the desk.

Ignore me or deplore me
Floor me or bore me
Your ignorance is my bliss.
Life is nothing but tape hiss.
Background noise, expensive toys
The whole world one big
clenched fist,
One big
slit wrist
One big
tongue kiss
Me and you against the wall, trading spit
Me and you in the backseat, bleeding wit.
I got raw jaws; I got pigeon paws
I'm like Johnny Law, enforcing laws
Mirrored glasses and mustache ashes
A loaded gun and nowhere to run.

So enforce me, sir, on your knees
So enforce me, ma'am, say pretty please.

I was born to die
And
You were born to tease.
I was born to lie
And
You were born to bleed.

So enforce me, sir, on your knees
So enforce me, ma'am, say pretty please.

"That's *beyond* awesome, Sudden," Elliot says. We're in a booth at Espresso Thieves, in the middle of a room full of kids picking their noses and copying algebra homework and generally failing in any way, shape, or form to rock. Also, some old people sipping tea. Elliot air-guitars a couple flourishes and then starts jotting down chords. "That there is a grade-A number-one hit song. I knew I put up with your shit for a reason."

"All it needs is a backbeat," I say, slapping out a rhythm on the table. *Cha-kacka-cha-kacka-cha.* "Like, you know, how a drummer could give?"

"Don't worry, I'll give it all the backbeat it can handle."

"You will, huh?"

"Not will. Am."

I close my eyes.

"You praying, Ritchie?"

"Nah, I'm watching TV in my brain."

"What's on?"

"It's a future episode of VH1's *Where Are They Now?*"

"No kidding?"

"Nope. In this one, forty-year-old Elliot Hella is being interviewed behind the register of the comics shop he clerks at."

"Not funny."

"Yeah, Elliot's got a big greasy pompadour, has put on seventy pounds, and generally looks like a beer keg with legs. The voice-over mentions that for years he bounced around from band to band but, despite a small cult following and a compelling amount of raw emotion, was never able to develop widespread acceptance for his antipercussive style."

"Enough."

"Oh, and here comes the really sad part where Elliot stares into the camera and insists he was blackballed in a conspiracy between the record companies and the drummers' union. A voice-over whispers: '*Elliot Hella was briefly hospitalized for extreme exhaustion and, also, paranoid delusions.*' In the background, a classic Sin Sistermouth tune plays as he gets choked up, a single tear rolling down his brownie-fat cheek."

"I swear, Sudden..."

"Then some walking pimple asks if the new issue of *Johnny Lazer and Knuckle Boy* #66 is out yet. Elliot finds it, rings the dude up, and tells him to have a nice day. Roll credits."

When I open my eyes, El Hella is squeezing the edge of the table so hard I almost feel bad for it. His eyes are pinned. His scalp is white and tight, stretched over miles of furious skull.

As usual, I've gone too far.

Elliot leans over.

I'm about to signal for the barista to dial 911 when he opens his mouth and starts singing *"Enforce me on your knees, ma'am"* in a wavery falsetto.

It sounds kind of good. Actually, better than good.

A couple of girls turn around to watch. Elliot grabs a bear claw off their table and uses it as a mike, cackling with glee at the look on my face.

"I was born to lie and you were born to bleed...so enforce me again, pretty pretty please?"

19

"Okay, but only because you asked so nicely."

Dr. Benway's rereading the poem about Johnny Law. Her hair looks even more severe than usual. She's wearing red lipstick.

"Awesome?" I prompt, waiting for the compliments to roll in.

"Decidedly not," she says, handing it back with a sniff.

"Then what is it?"

"Guarded. Veiled. Borderline misogynistic. Full of unrevealing wordplay. The definition of style without substance."

"Huh. That sounds pretty awesome to me."

She smirks.

I put a check in the Smirk Box I keep in the upper left-hand corner of my brain.

"What it does do, through the usage of a law enforcement theme, is suggest that you saw yourself as inevitably incarcerated, even before your legal troubles began."

"Nah, dawg, that's just a coincidence."

She makes a face. "Don't call me *dawg*."

"I was just looking for something to rhyme, you know?

Paws, laws. Imprison, incision. Butter, stutter. Poetic license and shit."

"*Poetic* and *shit* rarely cohabitate successfully within the same sentence."

"All the more reason to shack them up, right?"

She starts writing. After about twenty minutes, during which she scribbles out the first three volumes of Proust, Dr. Benway puts down the pen, pops a piece of Nicorette gum, and gets all orgasm-face as whatever evil chemicals are in Nicorette ramp through her bloodstream.

"You a smoker?" I say, surprised.

"Ex-smoker."

"Still got the jones, though, huh?"

"When you wrote those lyrics, you weren't just looking for something to rhyme with. Your subconscious was guiding you, possibly to a place of self-knowledge."

"You mean like the only thing I really know is that I know nothing?"

"I mean, it's not a coincidence that you wrote 'a loaded gun and nowhere to run.'"

"Because all teenagers write dumb shit like that?"

"No, because there are no coincidences. Things happen because you allow them to. You fail because deep down part of you wants to fail."

"Does that mean you smoke because deep down part of you wants to die?"

We stare at each other for a really, really long time.

"I quit," she finally says.

"What, trying to get through to me?"

"Possibly. But no, I meant cigarettes."

I grin. "Still got the jones for us both, though, huh?"

She signals for The Basilisk, who wastes no time grabbing me by the shoulder and escorting me on out.

20

Mom half-assedly throws an arm around my shoulder before I can slip through the patio door. In some cultures they might call that a hug. "Have a great first day!"

Looper escorts me to the car, gives me the keys, gives me a pep talk.

"You can do it. Just relax. And breathe."

I start the engine.

She lights a smoke, watches me pull down the driveway and out onto the road.

Away from the safety of home.

And then I am actually driving.

All the way to school.

I keep it at a steady sixteen miles per hour. A long line of cars ride my bumper, dying to pass. They zoom around corners, cut me off, stare and yell and honk.

I keep my eyes straight ahead.

My hands shake, barely gripping the steering wheel.

My throat is forty-years-of-wandering-the-desert dry.

The thing is, I don't really like to drive.

So I don't.

Almost never.

Actually, ever.

It's just a personal choice, a matter of taste.

The way I roll, homes.

Or, you know, maybe it's because I see the Drunk Weaver bearing down every time I look up.

Or because I see Ghost Beth in the backseat every time I turn around.

Grinning at me, a sixer on her lap, wanting to crank up some Smashing Fredkins and hit the next party.

A month ago Looper got tired of tooling me around in the van and insisted I buy a car. So did Mom and so did this grief counselor I talked to a few times before blowing his beard and his slacks and his "when you fall from a horse, it's essential to get right back on" routine off cold.

"What the hell am I going to buy it with?" I asked. "Muskrat pelts?"

"You have a job, don't you?" Looper said.

"Yeah, and the huge min-wage bundle I drag home every other Friday is just enough to keep me in Slurpees and rubbers."

So Loop talked her boss into payment-planning me his old Saab. He's this crazy Dutch cat named Rude. One word, like Cher. Legally changed from Ruud van der Whatever. Aside from Perfection Pool Cleaners, he also owns Video Monster, which still stocks more VHS than DVD. He's convinced tapes are making a comeback. Or is just too cheap to upgrade. Amazingly, the place is packed on weekend nights, the nostalgia crowd snapping up all the John Cusack and Molly Ringwald movies. Either way, there's always enough leaves, dead mice, and kids squeezing out a Baby Ruth in the shallow end of the local pools to keep them busy.

My Saab cost six hundred bucks. I slip Rude forty a month, the car smelling like me even before I opened the door: worn, tired, smooth. Needing a wash, needing a buff, needing a new set of valves, whatever valves are.

"Is good? We have deal?"

I laid out two twenties and then peeled a sticker off the Video Monster gore shelf. It's this big orange circle that says HORROR. I put it in on the Saab's dashboard, where the sun immediately baked it into a shriveled, pulsing warning. It sits there like a cursed monkey paw. HORROR. The more you stare at it, the more it becomes Sanskrit.

HORROR.

I can barely drive, it's so distracting.

HORROR.

I can barely drive anyway.

HORROR.

I park in the senior lot for the first time, my final year finally begun.

HORROR.

Oh, the horror.

HORROR.

21

It's not even second period and Lacy Duplais is already pretending to fix her heel by my locker. She's wearing mascara, a pearl necklace, and a cabled sweater that has *gift from Grandma* written all over it.

"Hi, Ritchie!"

"Lacy doo-play," I say.

"Wow, you got big over the summer."

"Big as in tall? Or you mean big as in *huge* 'cause the 'roids have finally kicked in?"

"Huge," she says, deadpan.

I bust out the trembling Hulk Hogan flex. Then I wonder what the hell I'm doing a stand-up routine for.

"Maybe we'll have a class together," she says, playing with her necklace. "You can make me laugh when it gets too boring."

"You got seven periods of remedial?"

"No."

"Then we're not gonna have any classes together."

She giggles uncertainly. Actually, we're both in Dice's History of the Americas, but I don't tell her that, mostly so I don't have to say his name out loud.

"Catch you later."

"Bye, Ritchie!"

El Hella is at my side as we weave through tiny sophomore dudes in polo shirts. He's wearing leather wristbands and ten square kilometers of scalp, clearing a wide swath on attitude alone.

"That Lacy's cute."

"Yeah, I guess."

"What's to guess?"

I shrug. "She's a little...old-fashioned."

"So?"

"So for that apparently shallow and unacceptable reason, I am not all that into her."

"Into her is the whole point, chief."

"Don't freaking 'chief' me."

"Sorry, chief, but you've got a major malfunction. She's a keeper. And she's been making eyes at you since eighth grade."

"Yeah," I say. "I'm not really sure why the Lacy phero-mones don't get the Ritchie bonermones revved more, but they just don't."

He shakes his head. "You are one dumb fucker, you know that, chief?"

"I told you to ix-nay that ief-chay shit. Have some respect for indigenous peoples."

"As Sackville's only voluntarily bald man, I'm exercising my right to make fun of my fellow minorities."

"Voluntarily bald men and strident sociopolitical views are a bad mix."

"Good point. As my group's official spokesperson, I officially apologize. Also, from now on, I will be referring to you as 'champ.' Unless, of course, it offends the boxing community."

"I'll look into it."

"You do that, champ."

Elliot peels off into Applied Mathematical Concepts. I take a left toward Sociology: New Perspectives on Our World.

In front of the classroom, there's a gaggle of kids. Off to one side is Ravenna Woods. She waves.

"Hey, Ritchie!"

I practically sprint over.

"Hey, Ravenna."

She's about to say something when the sun is blotted out. It's Spence Proffer, looming behind us.

"'Sup, Sudden," he says, rocking a new perm, elaborate braces, and nostrils that flare like twin manhole covers. He looks like Babe the Blue High School Ox, a bizarre combination of hard fat and harder muscle. If he dragged a plow from class to class, no one would even blink.

"Hey, Spence," I say.

"*Hey, Spence*," he mimics.

Ravenna giggles.

I want to reach over and snap off his gold necklace, melt it down with an acetylene torch, form it into a much daintier necklace with I HEART TWINKS spelled out in cursive, and gently return it.

Instead, I do nothing.

"I got a message for your buddy," he says.

"I have no friends."

"Tell Hella he needs to step the fuck back."

"I have zero clue what you're talking about."

Spence grins, then gives me a tittie twister.

Few people understand the agony of a tittie twister pulled off correctly.

I tell myself not to rub it, not to rub it, not to rub it, then stand there in the middle of the hallway, rubbing it.

Counterclockwise.

Ravenna laughs as Spence lumbers off.

I should be mad. I should turn and walk away, leave her hanging like a counterfeit twenty.

But I can't.

Because she's playing me and every other lame at school like the deuce of hearts. Even Mercedes and muscle dudes are practically running naked into traffic and throwing themselves off clock towers to get her attention.

And the thing is, she's not really *beautiful* beautiful at all.

She's actually a little weird-looking. Asymmetrical. With a funny half smile that makes one side of her mouth turn up like the Joker's. Her eyes are too dark, just this side of cruel. More knowing than gorgeous. More weary than drop-dead. Superior. Not the princess but the princess's raven-haired stepsister. The one with the vials of poison lined up on her dresser. The one who seduces the regent while dating the dragon.

Or dating no one at all.

So why does she make every guy in school apoplectic?

Why does she walk around lobbing a toaster in the collective male bathtub?

Hey, let's not pretend.

It's her body.

There is simply no ignoring its heft and criminal perk. Its taut Austrian hydraulics. If she were flat or fat she'd still be pretty, but no linebackers would be cutting practice trying to get to know her better. Without the badonkadonk and sheik-money strut, guys would hardly be killing themselves to score her fake digits anymore.

You've got to figure that level of constant objectification and wheedling hypocrisy would make a girl bitter.

And you'd be right.

Ravenna's caught two hundred meters below the reef, unwanted sexual pressure crushing her lungs, sharks below and the bends above, nowhere to go but further inside herself.

A place where I'm already shacked up and paying my own rent.

So I don't have to walk a mile in her nine-inch pumps to totally and completely get it.

Which is why I always act like I totally and completely don't give a shit.

Ravenna's into guys who aren't into her.

A list that is exactly zero guys long.

"Um, what were we talking about again?"

She leans against me. "I was wondering if you were ever coming back to Sack."

I yawn. "Oh, yeah? Why's that?"

"'Cause the last day of junior year you said, 'I'm never eff-ing coming back to this brain-dead wax museum.'"

"Did I? That doesn't sound like me."

"Yes, it does, Ritchie Sudden. It sounds *exactly* like you."

"Well, as tempting as it was, I couldn't leave town. What with the new band I'm in and all."

"Band?"

"Sin Sistermouth."

"You did *what*?"

"That's our name. Sin Sistermouth."

"Interesting," she says in a way that makes it clear she does not find it the least bit interesting. "Who's in it?"

"Hmm. Lessee. It's a duo. Which, you know, means two people. So, there's me. And then there's—"

She makes a face. "Elliot Hella?"

"Bingo."

"Figures."

The bell rings. She closes her locker with a low-rise hip, stepping away like a runway cliché.

"Welcome to senior year, Ritchie."

"You figure it's gonna be a good one?" I ask.

She winks. "Depends on your definition of *good*."

The curves are a smokescreen, I tell myself. Inside, she's a bag of hard edges.

And I, Ritchie Sudden, am prepared to eat sheet metal.

"Take the *o* out of *good* and you've got *God*. He's pretty much all I need."

"Is that so?"

"Yes ma'am, it is."

"You'd be more convincing if you didn't have a burning pentagram on your chest."

I look down. She's right. I forgot I changed into an Iron Maiden hoodie at the last second.

"Well, I guess the devil's in the details."

Her eyes sparkle. "I guess he is."

Dick Isley struts down the hall toward us. He's every inch the Dick he was last year, except now he's got a turquoise ring on his thumb. "Get to class, people."

"Hi, Dice," Ravenna says.

"Ravenna!" he answers, drawing pretend six-shooters. "Pow! Pow! Pow!"

She turns on us both and clichés away.

Dice and I just stand there watching.

For that, at least, I can't blame him.

The fourth coil of Hades: Ravenna Woods in skinny jeans.

22

There're only five minutes left in lunch period. There're always only five minutes left. Lunch could be three hours long and the second you sat down, the bell would still be just about to ring.

It's an immutable law of nature.

Kyle Litotes clatters a tray next to me, five warmer-lamp cheeseburgers wrapped in foil. At Sackville High, you got two lunch choices, each a vegetarian's dream: a heaping ladle of that day's meat slop with tomato sauce, or wheezy little burgers with a slice of government cheddar for a buck a pop.

"Dude, you must be hungry."

He doesn't even look up. "Eff you, Sudden."

It's classic Litotes. Or, as some people call him, Clitotes. He's got a baby face, almost pudgy, prep wear and a scholarship to Amherst already locked down. Everyone knows it. Mostly because he told them. Loudly. For years Kyle made a big deal out of being one of the abstinence kids, head of Students Against Drinking and Say No Way to Drugs and Saving It for Marriage and the Anti-Masturbator's League, handing out pamphlets and padding transcript with all the many ways he was pure.

And then, at some party junior year, he had a beer.

Just one.

Bam.

Two weeks later he was pounding more tall boys than Perez Hilton, doing beer bongs and swilling gin and groping girls, filling that abstinence hole one fresh guzzle at a time. Now he walks around with a fifth in his backpack and a sixer in his duffel, saying things like, "If the party's in your mouth, I'm coming!" and doing lame hallway pranks like snapping girls' bra straps and hiding their gym shoes.

I turn and finish my conversation with Lacy Duplais and Meb Cavil, who came and sat all giggly two seconds after I parked my tray. Meb's this cute little chick seemingly unbothered by the fact that she sports a mustache every cowboy in cinema history would be jealous of. "Meb" is either short for Mary Beth or My Estrogen Brush. I'm always tempted to ask why she doesn't spare herself the stares and just spring for a can of shave cream, but my admiration for the big middle finger she's giving the world by so completely not giving a shit stops me cold.

Meanwhile, Lacy Duplais is explaining how she's halfway through some book called *A Clockwork Orange.*

"It's written in this entirely nonsense language."

"French?"

"Ha. No, like the author made it all up."

"Sounds...tedious."

Lacy smiles, reveling in the chance to explain something to someone who's actually listening. "Yeah, but it's not. It's fascinating, 'cause once you unclench your brain, you can totally understand what's going on."

"I don't get it."

"Like, okay, they say 'viddy' instead of 'see,' and you sub-consciously understand what it means because of 'video' or whatever, even though it's not really a word."

"Huh. So—"

There's a tap on my shoulder.

I brush it away.

It taps again, harder.

I turn and almost bang foreheads with Kyle Litotes.

"What's up, dude?"

What's up is he's totally freak-eyed, in a panic. I figure it's one of his usual stunts until I notice all five of his burger wrappers are flat. There's no way he porked them down that fast.

"Man, are you okay?"

He grabs my shoulder, digging fingernails in. Sweat dangles from his nose. I can sort of make out a half orb of beef in the back of his throat, especially since he keeps pointing to it. People are watching, craning their necks. My need to act is way overridden by my need not to be suckered into a prank. But he keeps making with the fish lips, no words coming out, just a deep, airless wheeze.

"Call the nurse," Lacy says.

"Yeah," Meb says.

"Right," I say, but for some reason don't move. I don't take charge. I don't leap into action. I don't leap at all.

I just sit.

Scared.

Until Young Joe Yung lumbers over in tie-dyed overalls. Young Joe has long dreads and a chin like a cruiserweight. He's big and incredibly thick in the way some Chinese are but almost all the rest aren't. He grabs Litotes from behind, just below the ribs. They do this funky little dance, finding just the right balance and leverage, and then Joe Yung's massive forearms constrict. There's a sound I've never heard before and don't ever want to hear again.

It's intestinal, slithering.

Kyle's mouth distends into a gaping oval. His body recoils, and then a perfectly formed cylinder emerges from between his lips. It hangs there for a second, and then plops to the floor with a wet *smack*. It's like he just gave birth to a can of Pringles. A quivering yellow foot of chewed and compacted burger.

"Oh hell no," someone says quietly.

Litotes gulps air, already in tears, turning and giving Young Joe the *thank you oh thank you oh thank you* routine. The burger tube, meanwhile, has a rapt audience. A hundred people stare at it with a mixture of fascination and disgust.

No one dares to move.

No one dares to breathe.

Then the thing sort of shivers.

Maybe it's just a trick of the light, a flicker of the fluorescents, but for a second it seems like it might rear up and attack.

Some girl lets loose a curdler of a scream.

And then it's madness, people streaming toward the exits, trampling freshmen underfoot. The bell rings. Lacy wipes away a few tears, looking over Meb's shoulder, wondering why I'm not the one rubbing her back instead.

Joe Yung and I walk to our next class.

"Nice work, dude."

He swings dreads out of his face and smiles. "Just taking it as it comes."

Even though it was only two years ago, I still sometimes forget that Joe used to be a Sackville legend, a sports god, on every team, good at everything. And then suddenly hung up his cleats to became a man of peace. A grinning mountain. The rare hippie half the football team wants to fight for being a traitor, while the other half still looks at in awe.

"No, for serious, man. That was first-responder shit. I am majorly impressed."

He considers for a second, then holds up one finger. "Well, my mom always said chew before you swallow."

"I thought she said spit don't swallow."

Young Joe busts out laughing, holding his big overalled stomach as Ravenna Woods comes out of the girls' room and walks toward us.

"Way to go, Joe Hung," she says in a voice so suggestive it stings.

Young Joe stops laughing. His jaw drops, an elevator with the cable snapped, penthouse to basement in a second flat. He looks like he's going to melt, right there, into a huge puddle of earnestness in the middle of the floor.

Ravenna turns to me. "Way to get involved, Sudden."

"Um."

"Remind me not to call you if I ever have a problem."

"Um."

"Unless, you know, it's one of those special emergencies that requires someone to just sit on his ass and watch."

"Um."

Ravenna makes a face, spins on one very high heel, and then metronomes back on down the hall.

Tick, tock, tick.

The ninth coil of Hades: Ravenna Woods in a skintight turtleneck.

It takes us a few long minutes to get back even a semblance of cool, and by the time we make it to class we're way late. Miss Menepausse, in her ironic fifties skirt and vintage pink sweater, signs a pair of detention slips without even looking up.

"That's not fair," I say.

One of her two dozen unnecessary barrettes comes unsprung. "Oh, really? Why in the world not?"

"Well, for one thing, we're only late 'cause Young Joe Yung just Heimliched the fuck out of Clitotes."

"Language, Sudden! Besides, Kyle Litotes? Wouldn't we all be better off if you'd simply let him cross to the other side?"

My face goes blank.

Miss Menepausse looks up and gasps, realizing she's just made a death joke to The Tragic Kid.

We eyeball each other.

Her pores are enormous behind tortoiseshell glasses.

Her lipstick is rude, red, messy.

She wants to apologize, but that would mean bringing up Beth.

I don't want her to apologize, because that would mean someone I care so little about bringing up Beth.

Besides, in that long second I have an epiphany: Maybe she's not the bitter post-hipster stuck in a dead-end job I always assumed, but is actually a melancholy cat-loving midnight-merlot-guzzler who would otherwise be cool if she could only come to terms with the fact that she will never make a living off the prize money from Tuesday night swing-dance competitions at Jack Rabbit Slim's.

"No, seriously," I say, letting her off the hook. "Joe just saved the kid's life."

Miss Menepausse sighs, trying to decide if she's being taken for a ride, concludes that you cannot bullshit a classically trained bullshitress, and tears the detention slips in half.

"Please be seated, gentlemen."

Gentlemen?

Young Joe Yung, maybe.

But I'm just another worthless tool, sliding into an empty desk, all the way in the back row.

23

There're five minutes left in lunch period. I'm in the chow hall, which is actually a rectangular room with a raised walkway for counselors to stare down from. Not really a cafeteria at all. More like a Vegas club designed to look like a movie set designed to look like a cattle pen. B'los is at the far end, sitting with other Hispanic dudes. Conner and Peanut, everyone's favorite interracial couple, have their own table. Tough white dudes sit together on the near side. Pussy white dudes sit in the middle, the worst spot. A mix of kids everyone calls United Nations take up the only round table—a couple Asians, an Indian, a black kid with glasses, a dude who claims to be from Madagascar (which immediately cemented his new name: WhereverTheFuckThatIs), some white kids who have somehow avoided picking sides, an Arab who prays on a towel five times a day, and a kid who gets special meals (peanut butter and jelly for breakfast, lunch, and dinner) because his father's lawyer convinced an appellate court that chronic gag reflex was a federally protected disability.

If I sit down, I'll end up talking to someone. Then Peanut will see, and I'll get matched up with that person for the next Undercard.

It pays to have no friends.

Besides, I'm out of cigarettes.

I can't afford to not fight again.

So I stand with my tray against the wall and choke down everything I can in less than a minute before telling this tall redheaded doofus everyone calls Meatstick that I'm ready to go back to my box.

"So soon?"

He's got a new bristly half mustache growing in, the belly under his uniform tight and round like he's trying to shoplift a George Foreman grill. He stands there, beating out a funky rhythm on it, *smack-a-smackity-smack.*

"Went on a little date last night."

"Oh, yeah?" I say. "With who?"

He doesn't answer, just winks.

"The Meatman gets around, huh?"

"You better believe he does."

Peanut eyeballs me across the room, like, *What you talkin' to the po po for?* Conner doesn't bother. Which is even worse. I keep expecting someone to elbow me in the ribs and whisper, "Yo, Sudden, you down with Undercard?"

I mentally count how many days I have left.

I divide them by three, then by five, then by nine.

I add an extra month for bad behavior.

Subtract a week for quality journaling.

84

And then stand there, thinking about absolutely nothing.
Which is harder to do than it sounds.

Finally, Meatstick leads me down the hall to C unit, clanging open the door to room number six.

"Sweet dreams," he says, clanging it shut again.

My room is tiny and dark and smells like sweaty sheets. The window is wide open, but there's still no air. A heavy pre-lightning gloom overwhelms my clankity-clank fan.

I can't play any more scales.

I can't practice another chord.

So I crank up "Sway," my favorite Stones tune. Shit's more than forty years old but still makes every new band, all the loops and samples and alterna-hype, sound like just another thin approximation. It's off *Sticky Fingers*, the album with the Andy Warhol cover, the one that 99 percent of hypermacho dudes who have ever owned it had no clue was a celebration of illicit men's room blowjobs.

Which is a beyond-hilarious FU to the mindlessness of fame, fans, and the myth of "Rock 'n' Roll."

How can Sin Sistermouth possibly compete with that level of genius? Mick and the boys have us beat solid. Keef runs circles around us before the sustain from the first note even begins to fade.

Everything I have ever written sucks.

Everything I have ever played sucks.

So I either need to develop a sudden interest in clothing retail or stick out my thumb and get the hell out of Sackville.

Go experience something worth writing about.

Write about something worth experiencing.

Live in a place where people are revered for being clever, funny, and creative, instead of rich, annoying, and on television. Where they inspire. Where they aspire. Where they dream of the perfect sentence, or the perfect drawing, or the perfect chord. Where singing a line that sums up your generation with a run of simple, cutting words is more valuable than a million Likes or Follows or dumbass Retweets.

It's just that evil life that's got you in its sway....

Mainly, though, I think it's all Andy Warhol's fault.

Everything changed, forever, when he decided to play the greatest joke of all and corner the market on dumb. No one will ever sing or play or write anything dumber than a painting of a can of tomato soup.

Even murder is less dumb than tomato soup.

Even a car crash is higher art.

And there's just nowhere left to go from there.

I'm half asleep when my cell phone explodes, the ringtone Brian Eno crooning *"When I got back home I found a message on the door, sweet Regina's gone to China cross-legged on the floor."*

It's El Hella.

"Who is this?"

"Fuck off. Wanna jam?"

"Thank the lord," I say, already dressed. "I thought you'd never ask."

"There's only one thing."

"There's always one thing."

"You gotta drive. Something's wrong with the Renault."

I never drive in the dark. "But it's nighttime. It's dark out."

"Time to cowboy the fuck up, Sudden. Time to man up like a man."

He's right. I totally know he's right.

"Be there in twenty."

"Make it ten."

I'm palming an apple from the fridge when I hear Mom's voice go, "It's way too late to head out on a school night, honey."

I take a second to wonder who she could possibly be talking to.

Right before I slam the porch door.

We're on the lip of the sixth tee. I have Dad Sudden's old nylon string ride and Elliot has a beat-up Gibson acoustic, since even the Black Widow doesn't dig us practicing in her basement late night.

Sackville Knolls is a backwater nine-holer, trash and dog shit littered across the fairways, the kind of place no one with a shred of talent would be caught dead hacking at.

So of course Dad Sudden used to drag me and Beth here as kids, make us watch him flub and swear and snap clubs over his knee, through the sand traps, through the water hazards, lost in the tall grass muttering how his string of triple bogeys were mainly due to our silent judgment.

I hate golf.

It's for loudmouths and tam-wearers.

It's for martini guzzlers and rich dicks.

But it's a great place to jam out.

The sixth tee is on a sort of promontory that overlooks an entire hillside. You can park on Tilden Road, which is unpaved and no one uses except groundskeepers. There's a sweet view looking down over the vista of Sackville proper, not to mention the approval of a thousand crushed malt beer cans and used rubbers winking in the moonlight.

Five Things Our Band Needs (to win Rock Scene 2013):
1. ~~A name~~
2. A drummer
3. A singer
4. A signature song
5. Less proximity to used rubbers

We run through our set, Sin Sistermouth unplugged. It's a good change of pace, doing songs slower and more poppy just to see if they got any hidden pop in 'em.

We're halfway through a ballad-y rendition of "The Bloviator" when a car pulls up, high beams on.

A car never pulls up.

A car never has its high beams on.

"Should we run?"

"With our *axes*?" Elliot says. "Besides, run where?"

I nod. "Yeah, screw it, let's get arrested. It'll be killer publicity. We'll do a hunger strike. You be Che and I'll be Nelson Mandela."

"Who and who?"

"Charlie Sheen and Michael Vick."

"That's better."

"Maybe we can even do a live album from inside Sackville County Prison."

Doors slam and two guys walk over. They're wearing leather jackets and holding guitar cases. They're wearing girls' skinny jeans and ironic tour shirts, and have hair down to their asses. It's like *21 Jump Street: Biker Edition*. They're the least convincing undercover cops I've ever seen.

"You lames are in our jam spot."

Elliot leans back and lights the smoke from behind his ear. "*Your* jam spot? We been coming here since the summer of seventy-two."

"So you're the ones always leaving cigarette butts in the cup, huh?"

"Why, is it ruining your handicap?"

The bigger one fakes a yawn. "We're—"

Elliot fake-yawns back. "We know who you are."

They're Bob "Flog" Toggle and Angelo Coxone. Flog and Angelo are in Püre Venum, the biggest band around. They graduated from Sackville, like, eight years back and have won Rock Scene twice, in '04 and '06. They even had a minor hit called "Fade You to Blue" that made it up to #687 on the hair metal charts. Now they play the local dives, like Toad's Place and the Question Mark, in front of big crowds, sticking mostly to Clapton covers, Tom Petty covers. Girls dig them, dancing around. Guys dig them, holding up lighters and singing along to the chorus of "Layla" or "Runnin' Down a Dream."

"What we seem to have here is an impasse," Angelo says.

"Well, at least you brought your thesaurus," Elliot says.

"Yeah," I say.

"Tell you what, ladies. You go ahead and play us something. You're any good, we'll take off. The spot is yours. You suck, you have to split so the real musicians can jam."

"Sounds fair to me," says Flog.

I raise my hand like we're in class. "Who's to say what's good? Who's to say what's fair?"

"We are."

Elliot blows a plume of smoke. "How about you split now, since we were here first, and fuck your dumb idea?"

Angelo takes off his leather jacket. He's got a beer broiler, but he's thick through the shoulders and chest. His hands are lined with heavy silver rings, the typical bats and cherubs and emerald-eyed tigers. Even in skinny jeans, he towers over both of us. "How about I stop having a sense of humor and just kick your ass instead?"

Elliot looks at me and shrugs. "Should we do 'Beast Cream'?"

"I ain't playing that," I say, for some reason saying *ain't*.

"Well, how about 'Lungfish Wish'?"

"I ain't playing that, either."

"Time's running out, boys," Flog says, pointing to a spot on his wrist where a watch would be, if he were wearing one.

Elliot gives me a disappointed look and goes, "This is a new song I wrote."

Flog smiles. "Bust out the new tune."

"Yeah, guy," Angelo says. "Kill it for us."

Like a total wuss, I stand up and watch.

Elliot starts out fast; it's a good rhythm. *Chunka-chunka-chunk.* Quick chord changes, almost like a chord solo to open, and then he sits in the pocket of A-minor for a while. He's singing. It's not bad. Verse, chorus, pretty hooky. I like it. I like it a lot. No way it's hardcore. No way it fits within the tight constraints of Sin Sistermouth, but it's solid. I look over at Flog and Angelo. They seem impressed. Or at least listening. I realize, for once, we're going to win this round. I realize I should sit my ass back down and try to play a lead. I almost grab my axe, when something about the song starts to bother me, like an itch at the back of my neck, creeping all the way up to my temple.

I know this tune. I've heard it before.

And it wasn't Elliot playing it.

It's "Carrie Anne," by this corny old fifties band The Hollies.

One of Dad Sudden's favorites. We listened to the *Best-of* CD on the way to school for years.

Except El Hella has altered it just slightly. He's changed the girl's name. He's changed the chorus. But it's still pretty note for note.

He wraps up with a nice little crescendo thing and then a big sweeping open G.

"Buddy Holly, everybody," Flog says.

Angelo pretends to clap. "You wrote that, huh?"

Elliot just sort of stares at them. I put my guitar in its case and start packing up.

"Not Buddy Holly," Angelo says, pushing by and taking my spot, making sure to shoulder me in the chest. "The Hollies."

"Right." Flog laughs. "Nice cover, James Frey."

"What a coupla faggalahs," Angelo says, pulling beers from his backpack.

Elliot smiles, raises his lip, the smile that's not a smile.

I know what's going to happen before it happens.

"Okay, okay, we're going," I say. "So how about a couple brews for the road, no hard feelings?"

"How about no?" Angelo says. "How about fuck yeah, hard feelings?"

Elliot swings, but Flog's ready for it. He twists, and the punch catches him harmlessly on the shoulder. Angelo grabs me and puts me in a headlock. Flog swings back, slamming Elliot in the stomach, all his weight behind it. Elliot collapses, curled up, holding himself. Flog kicks him a couple of times in the side and then grabs Elliot's Gibson. He winds up and smashes it against a tree. The guitar explodes, body separating into tiny pieces, chunks of wood flying everywhere. Flog walks back over and jabs Elliot with a pointy shard.

"Now get out of here, princess, before I do the same to your pygmy-ass legs."

Back in the car, neither of us says anything for a while. I wonder if it's a good time to mention that we need a drummer.

"Stuck-up pricks," Elliot finally groans.

"I know. I hate those guys."

He gingerly raises his shirt. A line of fat bruises is already purpling. It looks like mainland Japan, along with a bunch of the lesser islands.

"Let's find something heavy. Some lead pipe. And go back."

"Are you serious?"

El Hella is grinding his jaw, actually considering it.

I grind the starter instead. The Saab coughs weakly, fires a piston, agrees to reanimate, *chugga chugga*. I gun it away before he can change his mind.

"Their band blows," he says, wincing as he probes rib.

"Yeah."

"Tom Petty practically does covers of himself to begin with. Like he needs Flog and Angelo to do even lamer versions?"

"Yeah."

We're halfway across town and Elliot is staring at the HORROR sticker.

"Way to have my back, Sudden."

"Man, okay. I froze."

"Bet your ass you did."

I roll up my sleeve. "You want to punch me? Go ahead. I don't even—"

He goes ahead and punches me. It really hurts. I don't rub it. He pokes the play button on the boom box with his toe. This band Fear immediately blares out, Lee Ving screaming, "*New York's all right if you like saxophones! New York's all right if you like tuberculosis!*"

"Feel better now? I hope that—"

He leans over and punches me again. In almost exactly the same spot. It hurts so bad it almost doesn't hurt. This time I do rub it.

"I will have revenge," he says.

"What, on me?"

"Yeah, on you."

I try not to drive off the road. My hands are trembling.

"No, dipshit, on them. Flog and Angelo. Am I supposed to swallow being dissed like that?"

"Did you just say *dissed*?"

"Yeah. So?"

"Just checking, Hammertime."

El Hella actually laughs, and now I can breathe. He starts throwing pieces of busted guitar out the window like a trail of bread crumbs.

"This was my dad's, you know."

"Which dad?"

"First one."

"No shit?"

"Nope."

I've never heard him mention his first dad. The second one owned a frozen-yogurt chain that went bankrupt once people wised up that frozen yogurt tastes like frozen shit, and the third one was a concert pianist. We wasted an entire summer constantly referring to him as a "concert penis-ist," and then being all wide-eyed and innocent, like, "What? *What?*" while he stormed around the house in a fury. Except for Lawrence, none of them ever seemed worth keeping straight.

"Wow. Heavy."

"I will have revenge," Elliot says again. "Greek style."

"You're going to stuff their navels with feta? Plato them to the wall?"

His face gets grim.

"Go ahead. Talk shit. That's all you do, right? Talk?"

I slow down. And then go even slower.

Ghost Beth is in the backseat, telling me I should have played a song with him.

Why didn't I play a song with him?

"Sooner or later," Elliot says, almost whispering, "I will bring the pain."

"You sure you don't have enough enemies already?"

"What are you talking about? Everyone loves me."

"Um, how many times I got to say it? Spence Proffer told me he's gonna—"

"Ah, screw that guy."

"Says the guy with three broken ribs."

"They're not broken."

"Dude, have you ever really looked into his eyes?"

"Whose?"

"Proffer's!"

"No, have you?"

"Not 'cause I wanted. But there's nothing there. Dude's a complete blank. Talking to him is like trying to explain calculus to a pig. That guy scares me."

"Everything scares you."

Could it possibly be that obvious?

"The thing is, Proffer's three times the size of Flog and Angelo put together."

Elliot says nothing.

Fear segues into The Replacements, a very weird but perfect transition, Paul Westerberg singing, "*We are the sons of no one, bastards of young!*" in his beautifully ratty voice.

"So you wanna go home?" I ask, just out of habit. "Or should we hit Scumbies?"

Scumbies is Cumberland Deli. They're open until midnight, the only place around with smokes and coffee and a curb to sit on where any random bastard of young can wolf frosted snack cake in peace.

We always go to Scumbies after a jam.

Always.

It's a tradition.

"Nah, take me home," Elliot says.

"You serious?"

He looks out the window, not even bothering to answer.

26

Meatstick comes up behind me in the hall. I about leap out of my pants and he laughs. The other counselors, like Jimbo or Yunior or Lamont, you call them a name, they'll smile and then later get you alone for a little talk about respect. But Meatstick doesn't seem to mind.

I couldn't figure out why, until finally someone explained the name wasn't an insult. Apparently the dude is known throughout the rehab/incarceration community for toting around thirteen inches of redheaded schlong.

Now I know why he's always smiling.

"Sudden, you got a visitor."

"I signed the paperwork. I don't want any visitors."

"Well, you got one. She's waiting."

She?

Ravenna?

Meatstick walks me to the visiting area, which is this carpeted room with a couple tables and couches. There's a place in back with a booth for a counselor to watch what's going on, but it's not like the movies, no phones or Plexiglas. I open the door, and there's B'los with his family, a bunch of little kids running around, sisters and brothers playing with grimy plastic toys abandoned by the grimier kids who came before them. B'los is hugging his mom, head on her shoulder. His dad is holding his arm by the bicep, like he doesn't ever want to let go. They hear the door and start to turn, but not fast enough. B'los moves away from his mom, looking down, wiping his eyes.

Looper's at the other table. I walk over and sit with her.

"Loop. What's shakin'?"

She grins. "Don't call me Loop."

"Right. Anyway, what are you doing here, Loop?"

"Your mom really wanted to come."

"Yeah, huh?"

"But it's crazy right now, the shifts she's working."

"Sure, sure."

"Plus, you know, this place. It makes her nervous."

"I understand. Ma's real sensitive."

"No, it's just that she's—"

"How did you get in, anyway? I signed a paper said I didn't want to see anyone."

Looper blushes and then points her chin at Meatstick. "That redheaded guy seems to like me. I let him think he could give me his phone number."

"That's smooth, Loop. You and Meatstick should go grab a pizza. Maybe bowl a few frames when he gets off."

"His name's Meatstick?"

"In here it is."

She makes a face.

"Everything okay, Ritchie? I mean, are you, you know...?"

"No, I don't know. Am I what? Surviving? Yup."

Looper bites her fingernail. "Anything I can do?"

"Yeah, actually, there is."

"Shoot."

"I need you to put some money in my commissary."

"Your what?"

"The account we're allowed to have. To buy stuff. Tooth-paste, soap, cookies."

"You want to buy cookies?"

"No, cigarettes."

"You're smoking now?"

"No, I'm not."

"Then what do you want cigarettes for?"

Undercard flashes above her head like a neon sign.

"Listen, Loop, can you just trust me on this one?"

She stares at her hands, sighs.

"I'm sorry, Ritchie, but I'm flat broke."

"You're shitting me."

"Rude has been cutting my shifts. Things are slow."

"Right, who can afford a clean pool these days?"

"I'm serious. I might not make rent this month. And I'm not going to ask your mom to cover. Again. Since, you know, we're saving and everything."

"For what, the United Lesbo College Fund?"

Her eyes narrow. She's about to lay into me, and I half want her to. I totally deserve it. But then she just sighs instead.

"I'll see what I can do."

I stand up. B'los and his family are gone.

"Thanks for coming, Loop. Really. But do me a favor and don't do it again."

"Ritchie..."

"Meatstick?" I say. "This chick is totally hot for some guard-on-citizen action. Just don't count on going Dutch."

"I'm not a guard," he says. "I'm a counselor."

"And I'm a ballerina," I say, walking on through the door.

Ravenna Woods comes up behind me in the hall and puts her arm around my waist. I about leap out of my pants, and she laughs. Her posse of friends laugh, too, standing in a line behind her, left to right, in descending order of attractiveness. Ravenna sweeps her hair around her shoulders in this slow-motion wave, like an ad for shampoo. Or bottled orgasms. She smells unbelievable. Like the slow, gentle union of a field of stamens and a meadow of pistils. I want to swallow her whole.

"Ritchie Sudden?"

"Yes, ma'am?"

Her eyes are half closed. I am infinitely aware that every single dude in school is infinitely aware that Ravenna Woods is touching me. They're probably already talking about it in the caf, arguing about it in the gym. Which means I have just acquired two hundred hardened, bitter enemies (comprised, essentially, of everyone at Sackville not currently being touched by Ravenna Woods).

She hands me something, smirks, and then walks away.

Her posse follows. The last girl in line turns, winks, waves.

There is a tiny square of paper in my hand.

I unfold it carefully.

In the middle is written one word:

SOON.

28

Elliot comes up behind me in the hall but does not put his arm around my waist. He's holding a poster he obviously just tore off some notice board, sticking it in my face instead. It says ROCK SCENE 2013, in a font made out of medieval-style daggers engulfed in flames.

"No shit."

"Keep reading," he says in Rock Scene Guy voice. "New twist this year."

"Yeah," I say with a laugh. "Can you believe anyone still uses the word *viral*?"

"Just read."

It says, WINNER GETS $1,000 CASH! It says, WINNER TO OPEN THREE GIGS FOR LOCAL ACT PÜRE VENUM! It says, WINNING BAND TO ALSO RECEIVE DELUXE FENDER STRATOCASTER PACKAGE INCLUDING STRAP, PICKS, AND CASE COURTESY OF JAZZBOX JIM'S!

"No way."

"Way."

I really, really want that guitar. I imagine holding it. Playing it. Plugging it into a huge stack of amps. Being onstage. The incredible loudness. The thousand volts of savage distortion at my fingertips. I imagine Ravenna standing below me, rapt, swaying to the beat as I knock out yet another effortless Hendrixian solo. In my mind I am making sweet, sweet love to a brand-new Fender Stratocaster and I am being very, very gentle.

"I really, really want that guitar."

"Fuck the guitar," Elliot says, giving me a backhand to the chest. It hurts. There's zero humor in his eyes.

"Um..."

"Read the bottom."

At the bottom, in a tiny Surgeon General font, it says: WINNING BAND ELIGIBLE FOR SLOT IN REGIONAL BAND SHOWCASE, FROM WHICH BANDS WILL BE SELECTED ON NATIONAL LEVEL FOR POSSIBLE SCREEN-TEST TRYOUTS IN CONJUNCTION WITH UPCOMING REALITY TELEVISION SHOW *REAL GODZ OF HOLLYROCK*. ELIGIBILITY SUBJECT TO CHANGE WITHOUT NOTICE.

"We are so winning this, Sudden. You hear me?"

El Hella's teeth are frighteningly close to my teeth. I can practically smell his enamel.

"Dude. Of course. That's the plan."

"No, man, that *was* the plan. Glory and girls? Pocket some cash? Well, screw that noise."

"Can you actually screw noise? Because, if so, man have I wasted a lot of time alone in the bathroom."

He bunches my shirt and shoves me against a locker, up on the tiptoes of his steel-toes, whispering in my ear. "We are going to *win* this, and then we are going to *blow* Flog and Angelo off the stage, and then I am going to *laugh* in their fucking faces."

"We are?"

"Greek style, homie. Right before I kick their faces in."

"You are?"

"I am."

His scalp is slick with sweat. His eyes are pinned.

"Oh."

"They broke my guitar."

"I know. I saw."

"My first dad's guitar."

"I know. I heard."

"We are going to win our regional slot. We are going to advance to nationals. We are going to be on television. I will accept nothing less."

"That is becoming clear."

"You and me, baby, we are the Real Godz."

"The Real Godz of Sackville?"

"Vengeful gods," he says, flashing the smile that's not a smile. Then he pulls a pen out of his back pocket, spears the poster like a wiggling devilfish, and jams it into the wall. Hard. The pen snaps in half, entering his palm. Blood droplets fall to the tile in pairs. Elliot holds his hand up and licks it. There's blood in his gums, blood in his smile.

"You're either on the bus or off the bus, Sudden."

I wonder, for the very first time, if maybe Elliot Hella isn't just a tiny bit insane.

"I'm so on the bus."

He pats my cheek, and then walks away.

29

B'los comes up behind me in the hall. He does not put his arm around my waist.

"You ready, Sudden?"

B'los and I have been assigned to the library. It's a cake job. Mostly because "the library" is really four shelves and a folding table. Almost no one ever comes in. We pretty much just alphabetize the books and talk while The Basilisk makes his rounds. Turns out B'los is pretty cool. He digs sci-fi. I told him about *Stranger in a Strange Land*. He knows I dig hard-boiled and told me about *A Rage in Harlem*. There's not a ton to choose from otherwise, a bunch of religious stuff and moldy Westerns and self-help. And then pretty much every Lexington Cole mystery ever written. If you can call it writing. There must be a hundred of them, all exactly the same, but everyone wants to check out *The Hypotenuse Crux* because a rumor went around it was slang for pussy.

It is so not.

We're sitting at the table sorting a box of donations. B'los has been quiet since the day in the visiting room. He doesn't look up, pretending to be all busy with a half-destroyed copy of

Still Life with Woodpecker that some genius figured he'd donate instead of throw away. A few pages missing? Hey, no sweat. You kids aren't going anywhere soon, right? Just make the missing part up!

B'los clears his throat.

"That your moms? At visiting? She don't look nothing like you."

I eyeball him, scanning for shit talk, but he's just staring at his book.

"Who, Looper? No, she's not my mom."

Now he does look over. "Yo, man, is that your *girl*friend? She's the bomb!"

I laugh. I'm tempted to say, "Yeah, she's one of them, anyway." It would raise my profile about a mile and a half in here.

"Nope, not mine."

"Then whose?"

It's my turn to clear my throat. "My mom's."

He squints, trying to work it out.

"So, she's, like, your mom's..."

"Girlfriend."

"Like, they besties? Go shopping together and whatnot?"

"Yeah. Also, she lives with us."

He drops the book, covering his mouth.

"Wait, your moms is a *dyke*?"

I look at him hard, but his expression is so comically astonished I know he's not being a tool. At least not on purpose.

"Yeah, I guess. I mean, I don't guess. She is."

"Wow."

"Yeah."

"And you don't...mind?"

I tear *Still Life with Woodpecker* in half and toss it in the garbage.

"Well, my old man split. And, also, they didn't ask my permission."

He crosses himself, sizing me up all over again.

"That is seriously heavy, dude."

"Big time."

B'los is quiet for a minute.

"Listen, about you seeing me with my parents the other day? I wasn't...I was just—"

"I didn't see nothing."

"No, I mean—"

"I'm telling you. I had a visit, room was empty."

B'los enters in two new paperbacks, stamping PROGRESSIVE PROGRESS on the inside cover. Then he glues an envelope and slides in a date card.

"Thanks."

"For what?"

"Right."

When I was little and Grandma on Dad Sudden's side was still alive, she used to live in an old motel by the airport with a shared kitchen and TV room. Gramps died there on vacation nine years before and she refused to leave. Just never came back, not even to get her stuff. Dad Sudden sold off their house and all their junk and put the money in an account that she drew off of. She also called me a lot. To be honest I have no idea why—she never called Beth—but I liked listening to her stories. She would say how Dad Sudden loved me but had a hard time showing it. She said Dad Sudden didn't know how to access his emotions on account of being spoiled, plus once dropped on his head. She admitted, even though Dad Sudden was her only son, he'd always been sort of a selfish cock. She also told me stories about the motel residents, walking to the deli for lunch, playing pinochle in the day room, and listening to the planes land.

I loved Grandma.

She was tiny and angry and wore a silver wig, but at least she was mine.

Phone Call from Grandma

A Poem
by Ritchie Sudden

I hear something; do you hear something?
Has anything good ever come from that woman down
  the hall?
There's a light under her door.
There's scratching, and everyone knows she bites her
  nails.
It can't be her nails making that noise, can it?
Sounds like a fan. It's not hot. Not hot enough for fans.
  It's a waste.
She doesn't mind wasting, not the food she leaves on
  the kitchen counter, or the dishes caked with rice in
  the sink. It's take-out men coming up and down the
  stairs night and day, delivery this, delivery that.
Is that a cry? A child's cry?
She could have been pregnant, who knows, she hardly
  ever leaves.
Or maybe it's a cat.
We're not supposed to have cats.
It's against the rules.
I should call the manager, but he drinks.
Also, something needs fixing, suddenly he no speekee
  English.

Wait, is that a crash? Did you hear a crash?
Whatever it was, it sounded expensive.
I hear music. Singing. Is that music? It's a pounding.
A pounding and a laughing.
There must be whiskey. There must be a man.
I can practically smell him from here.
Blond hairs come through my heating vent, Ritchie.
Blond hairs come like messages and settle in the corners.
They're telling me to lock the door.
They're telling me to leave the light on at night.
One time I knocked, said please keep it down.
She asked did I want a cup of tea.
I did not want a cup of tea.

I did not want a cup of tea at all.

Elliot's late for practice.

Elliot's never late for practice.

I pace around cursing, until the bell finally rings.

"About hella time," I yell, yanking open the door.

But it's not Elliot.

It's Looper's boss, Rude. He's tall and blond and bent and slack, eyes enormous, pale and loose like he needs a couple turns with a wrench.

"Loop isn't home," I say, The Paul slung around my bare chest.

"Not looking for Looper."

"Then who you looking for?"

"No one."

I take a second to consider this.

"I made my last payment. Even though that Saab barely runs."

"Not here for payment. You wish to bring back, bring back."

"I'll keep it."

Rude wipes his nose. Fidgets with his keys. He's wearing the same Irish cabdriver's hat the guy from AC/DC wears to hide his bald spot.

"Then what do you want?"

He frowns. "I need date."

"Try the Internet."

"I go to DVD release party, but do not wish to go alone."

"Video Monster carries DVDs?"

"Ha-ha. VHS is making comeback. You wish to join or no?"

"Why me?"

"Why not?"

"What's a release party?"

He shrugs. "Studios hawk latest masterpiece, hold screenings for store buyers. They hope you to fall in love and order max copies."

"What's the movie?"

"*Scream Me Up to Hell.* Has Dolph Lundgren, Brian Bosworth, and blond lady is built like state of Kentucky."

"I'll pass."

"And free preshow buffet."

"I'll pass."

"And many attractive city women."

"Let me just go grab a shirt."

Upstairs, I call Elliot's cell. No answer. I call the Hellas' house. Lawrence answers. Mozart booms in the background.

"Lawrence, this is Ritchie. Elliot's friend?"

"Yes?"

"Sorry to bother you, dude, but Elliot was supposed to come to my place and he's late. I was wondering if maybe he's still there."

"No, I'm sorry, but he left."

"Already? Great, I—"

"With a woman. Somewhat older than expected. His teacher, perhaps?"

Angie Proffer.

"She's teaching him something, all right."

"Excuse me?"

"Nothing. Okay, thanks, dude, gotta go."

"Yes, we all do. Eventually."

I hang up. *Shit shit shit.* It's official. El Hella is doomed. Spence Proffer is going to kill my one and only bandmate. Gut him like a twelve-point buck, lash him to the hood of a jacked-up Mustang, jam an apple in his mouth, and rumble around town showing off the carcass.

Which, if nothing else, will seriously put a damper on our chances for Rock Scene 2013.

Rude is waiting by the van, tapping his foot. I don't even have the door closed before he's spraying gravel. At the end of the driveway, Mom pulls up. She idles at Rude's window, all sad eyes and blond bob and Burger Barn wrappers crumpled on the passenger seat.

"Where are you two going?"

"I am taking Ritchie for the golf. We will chase small white ball around course. Be back in one hour."

Mom looks dubious. She doesn't like Rude. Why would she? He and Dad Sudden went to high school together. They used to be friends.

"Where's Looper?"

"Right this second? Hard to say."

"Try harder."

Rude considers. "Unplugging someone's drain? That is one guess. Adjusting someone's pH balance? There is another."

Mom nods. "And you'll only be gone an hour?"

"Is possible less."

She raises her window and inches up the driveway. Rude holds out a hand for a high five, which I decline. He laughs and punches my arm instead. On the highway, there's a ton of traffic. I kill time thinking of the worst song title ever, finally deciding "Cuts Like a Knife" is the winner. What the hell *else* would it cut like? A banana? A softball?

"You are having the female problems?" Rude asks.

"Ex-*cuse* me?"

"By the way you sit, I can tell."

"Trust me, I'm fine."

"You are not fine. Is clear. I wish to give you a truth."

I sigh. "Lay it on me."

"Women? They want romance. But also manners. The door open, the seat held out, the flowers on day of Valentine's. Men? They want to empty paste on bare thigh. Is law of nature."

"Paste? Did you say *paste*?"

He shrugs. "Is simply facts. Do not shoot messenger."

"Oh my god. Can the messenger just keep his eyes on the road?"

"This is possible," Rude says, turning up the radio.

When we finally get into the city, he pulls into some sort of zone. The sign has been heavily graffitied, but it's clear you can't park there. He's got two wheels up on the curb before I can even say anything, so I don't bother.

The guy at the door doesn't want to let us in. It's a fancy old theater, ornate, like they once had vaudeville, guys juggling pies and wrestling bears and singing in barbershop quartets. Rude flashes his VIDEO MONSTER OWNER'S PASS, and the door guy, with his shaved head and ham-size biceps, says in an unexpectedly high voice, "Fine, whatever, you're holding up the line."

The lobby is inlaid with beautiful pink tile. Beautiful pink women hold champagne flutes and finger their pearls and laugh at jokes about hedge funds and Ponzi schemes. Rude elbows his way to the buffet. There's quiche and fruit and scallops and ham. His translucent bangs dangle inches above the food. He takes a popcorn bucket, empties it into the trash, and then leans over the shrimp platter, netting about four pounds.

"C'mon, Ritchie."

We find our seats. Rude tosses shrimps in the air, catching them in his mouth. The movie is fairly predictable. The devil desires the blonde, as all devils do. She has her shirt ripped off a few times, then air-screws an invisible demon. Dolph is an ex-Marine with a chin like an anvil. Bosworth is an ex-boozer priest with a heart of gold. They challenge the devil to a game of chess, with the world and the girl in the balance. Dolph wins. The devil takes some screaming stockbroker guys back to hell with him. Bosworth artfully expires. The blonde and Dolph rent a U-Haul and move to Connecticut. She's about to give birth in the final scene. Angel baby? Satan spawn? Poor excuse for a sequel? Roll credits.

"Is such ridiculous piece of shit!" Rude says, drunk on shrimp.

No one laughs.

"I place only single order. In fact, I put sign next to register saying every rental donates to Al-Qaeda!"

No one laughs.

"But, yes, if I am honest I suppose I, too, would air-fuck devil for nice house in Connecticut."

No one laughs.

I drag him through the lobby. Security mumbles into their walkie-talkies as we pass. When we get back to where the van was, it's not there anymore.

"Is strange."

"Yeah, you think so?"

"I am sorry, Ritchie, but you must find other way home."

"Story of my life."

He pokes through his wallet and then hands me some cash.

"Happy birthday."

A five and five ones.

"How'd you know it's my birthday?"

He punches my shoulder and walks away.

"Hey, Rude!"

At the corner, he turns and cups his ear. "Yes, huh, what?"

"Did Dad Sudden put you up to this?"

"Naw, man. Is no chance."

"Cut the shit. He called you, didn't he? Said take a roadie, see if I'm all right?"

Rude strokes his chin, shrugs. "Yeah."

"Well?"

"Well, what?"

"Am I all right?"

Rude gets a green light, bends forward like a crab, and hustles across six lanes of traffic.

32

My cell goes off six times. The ringtone is the first eight bars of Sweet's "Teenage Rampage," Brian Connolly going, *"All over the land the kids have found it's time to get the upper hand. They're out on the streets, they turn up the heat, and soon they could be completely in command!"*

I'm still half asleep. I paw around for the phone, knock it on the floor, curse, half grab it, push it farther under, slide off the mattress, land on my back, and finally flip it open just as Elliot's voice wavers through. It's like one of those Kevin Costner movies where Kev talks to his dead father through a toaster.

"Dude, I've been thinking."

That's funny, I've been thinking, too. Like, about how out of nowhere Dad Sudden decides to stick his beak back into my life but is too lame to do it in person, sending Rude as the world's smartest emissary instead. I had to walk forty blocks back through uptown and down skid row. Past guys in nice suits and guys in tracksuits. Past girls in cut Spandex and girls in Kate Spade. I finally reached the station, waiting on a hard orange bench for the last bus. Got back to Sackville at four in the morning. Made a call. Two rings. Looper came. Didn't ask why. Didn't bitch. Just came.

"I talked to your boss," I told her, shivering. She had the heat cranked. Inside, the van was nice and warm.

"Oh, yeah? About what?"

"Dad Sudden."

There was a pause.

"What about him?"

"He's been making inquiries."

Looper lit a smoke with one hand, all Jenny Depp, cool as fuck. "Lemme guess. He wants to know how strapping you've become but is too lame to ask himself?"

I laugh.

She laughs.

Which totally fails to hide the fact that both of us are scared to death Dad Sudden might actually come back.

Meanwhile, I can hear El Hella breathing into his phone.

"Dude," I finally say, "you blew off practice."

"What're you talking about? I came by and you weren't there."

"I called Lawrence. He said you took off in a car with someone."

"I was downstairs running scales! I was packing up gear!"

I picture him getting into Angie Proffer's car.

"Lawrence said—"

"Who gives a screw what Lawrence said? Jesus. Lawrence thinks it's 1941. Lawrence thinks Mussolini is president. Lawrence thinks any day now someone's going to invent shortwave radio. Is there a reason we're still talking about this?"

Let alone a percentage in it?

"Sorry. No. You were saying something?"

Five Things Our Band Needs (to win Rock Scene 2013):

1. ~~A name~~
2. A drummer
3. A drummer
4. A drummer
5. A drummer

"I was saying if we're going to win Rock Scene 2013, we probably need a drummer."

I almost squeal, but manage to go pure deadpan instead. "I dunno. Are you sure?"

Elliot coughs. "It now occurs to me, despite my earlier... position on the matter, that to truly crush Flog and Angelo, to grind them down to fecal dust, to pack them like cold lunch meat into an old Ziploc bag, a duo's not enough."

"Hmm. Good point. I hadn't really thought of that."

"Besides, once we're on *Real Godz of Hollyrock*, they're gonna make us have a drummer anyway."

"Oh, yeah. First thing the producer says."

"And so it would be unwise for us to continue in this percussionless fashion. Do you agree?"

"Entirely."

"So go get us a snare-banger."

"Fantastic. But why do I have to do the legwork?"

He clears his throat. There's a woman's voice in the background. It doesn't sound all that much like the Black Widow.

"I'm sorta busy."

"Cougar hunting?"

"Not funny."

"Out trolling for desperate housewives?"

"Just shut up and do it."

"Fine. I'll put up a flyer at the café. Any other solemn dictates or personal wishes you need fulfilled?"

"Well, there is one other thing."

"There's always one other thing."

"No dicks."

"Come again?"

"If this theoretical drummer is a dick, it will not fly. Sin Sistermouth will implode. I don't care if the guy is all Neil Peart with the time signatures or hung like hair-bag Tommy Lee. No dicks."

"No sweat. I'll make that the first line, black marker, all caps. *This band is a dick-free zone.*"

"Actually, don't. People will think we're eunuchs."

"Even better. Everyone wants to be in a eunuch band these days. Don't you watch the Internet? Going sans-ball is total fashion. It's the new tight pants and trucker cap."

"The ladies are said to dig it?"

"I imagine there's a newfound sense of lightness."

"A diminishment of distractions?"

"Testosterone is so yesterday. So Super Bowl. So bar fight."

"Whatever. Just get us a drummer, stat."

"Consider one found."

"Good. I gotta go."

"Say hi to Lawrence."

"Hi to Lawrence."

"Say good night, Gracie."

"Good night, Gracie."

"Say it with flowers."

There's a murmur in the background, then a giggle, then a dial tone.

Night Flight
a new song
by Ritchie Sudden

A grim organic motor pulses in my head.
A grim organic motor pulses, pulses.
A grim organic motor pulses in my head.
A grim organic dread.

A dead muscle slows my heart.
A dead muscle slows, slows.
A dead muscle slows my heart.
A dead muscle grows.

A crunching static fills my ears.
A crunching static fills, fills.
A crunching static fills my ears.
A crunching static still.

An angry need jangles my bones.
An angry need rises, rises.
An angry need tangles my jones.
An angry need surprises.

A roof to leap from lightens my feet.
A roof to leap lightens, lightens.
A roof to leap from lightens my feet.
A place to land in the middle of the street.

"It's beautiful," Lacy Duplais says, like she's about to cry. At first I think she's kidding, but she's not. We're in History of the Americas (what the totality of *Americas* actually means being explained by Caucasian, omelet-eating, never-been-south-of-Cleveland Dice). Lacy's sitting close enough to wear my cologne. She ditched the grandma sweater for big hoop earrings, leather boots, and a tight skirt. Either it's my imagination, or Lacy Duplais has gotten some serious style together.

"Can I have it?" she asks.

"The song?"

"Um, yeah."

I was going to give it to Elliot, see if he could come up with a chorus or two. Instead, I tear the page out of the textbook, where I've written the lines in between two Venn diagrams, and hand it over.

"I sincerely hope that was not your textbook, Sudden," Dice says without even turning from the board. He's writing

ANDREW JACKSON in chalk with one hand, spinning the knobs of his Teaching Tower with the other. We're going over the basics of how Old Hickory ended up on a twenty-dollar bill, despite being a genocidal maniac, with Graceland as background music.

I take a deep breath, close my eyes, and attempt to destroy Dice with the deadly power of thought. With wave after wave of pure brain-hate. I mentally will him to melt. To burst into flames. I clamp down and demand that he deconstruct and then re-atomize as a roof shingle. As a loaded diaper. As a hermaphroditic squid.

When I open my eyes, Dice is still there. Whole and composed and, if anything, even shinier than usual.

"No, sir," I say.

Lacy winks, letting her hand dangle between our seats.

Lonely.

Unheld.

I do not lean over and take it in mine.

Her bottom lip trembles, almost imperceptibly. A recent poll shows I feel 44 percent more like an asshole.

Dice drones on about the Dreyfus Affair. Some people giggle at the word *affair*.

Dice drones on about the Trail of Tears, which he makes sound like an unfortunate but necessary corrective.

Dice drones on about the role of mindless droning in our nation's educational system.

"Lacy," I whisper.

She won't look over.

"Paging Miss Duplais."

She won't look over.

"Yo, homegirl."

She won't look over.

"Lacy!"

"*What?*" she says, way too loud.

Dice looks up. Graceland's diluted ethnicity goes soft.

Even softer.

He sighs and strokes his goatee.

"Is there anything you'd like to share with the rest of the class, Mr. Sudden?"

I nod. "How about some cigars and a bottle of whiskey?"

Young Joe Yung holds his big overalled belly and guffaws. Pretty much everyone else just stares in disbelief.

Dice smiles, as if he doesn't really mind a little midlesson repartee. Having a sense of humor, after all, helps him relate to the kids. But his eyes don't fool me, hard and black and flat.

His forehead is tight.

The chalk in his hand begins to crumble.

Do I care?

I do not.

After all, I have a new song called "Night Flight."

Dice does not have a new song called "Night Flight."

In fact, I'd be willing to bet Dice will never have a song of any kind at all.

34

"You're a poet," Dr. Benway says, finishing "Night Flight."

"No, I'm not."

"Then what are you?"

"A lyricist."

"And the difference is?"

"One gets you zero cash, no respect, and frequently beat up. The other gets chicks and drugs and royalties."

Dr. Benway looks at me for a very long time.

"Have you ever read Keats?"

"No."

"Or Yeats?"

"No."

"Or Frank O'Hara?"

"No."

"Or Bukowski?"

"No."

"Well, even hotshot lyricists would probably be wise to spend a little time with the classical poets."

"That would be your professional recommendation?"

"It would."

"I have a theory," I say.

"Which is?"

"Every dude in here is in here for taking bad advice."

Dr. Benway opens her tiny bird mouth and laughs and laughs and laughs.

Beenie Sloat and Young Joe Yung are in the caf, at the vegan table, slouched hard in their hemp pants and hemp sandals and dirty T-shirts that say RAW HEMP ROCKS! Beenie's not big on soap and combs. In fact, he's thin and pale and looks like he just stepped out of a long, hot cigarette shower. It makes you want to stuff raw hamburger in his gill slits just to get some niacin into his bloodstream.

Joe is leaning over, whispering. They're in intense negotiations. I spin a chair around and lean over the back, like a homicide detective.

"And what might you dudes be rapping about?"

"Liquid A," Beenie says.

"Assets?"

"No, acid."

"No shit?"

"No, sir."

"What about it?" I ask.

Joe Yung's grin is pure serenity. You could snip off his toes with a bolt cutter one by one and he'd keep smiling all the way down to the pinkie.

"I read where you can put it directly on your eyeball with one of those...uh..."

"Eyedroppers," Beenie says.

"Yeah, eyedropper. Supposed to make the hallucinations way more intense. Supposed to, dude, be, like, exponential cartoons."

"Read where?"

Young Joe shrugs. "I dunno. Maybe I dreamed it."

"Awesome, right?" Beenie says.

No, not awesome. It sounds beyond terrifying. But I don't tell them that, because that would make me sound uncool.

"Anyhow, I'm doing two drops," Beenie says with a yawn. "One in each eye."

"I'm doing three," Young Joe counters. "Left, right, left."

Beenie raises an eyebrow, like, *Can you believe this crazy but ultimately lovable guy?*

"Okay, four."

"Five."

"Six."

Joe Yung considers long and hard. His twenty chin whiskers are set. His eyes are fierce.

"I can name that trip in seven drops."

Beenie doesn't want to give in, but he knows he's beat. He fishes a peanut butter Tiger Bar from his fanny pack, sharing it with Joe, and then opens his palm. There's a tiny vial with clear liquid in the center of it. "Wanna come for the ride, Sudden?"

"Yeah, I wanna come," I say, watching through the window as a gym class troops by. Ravenna Woods is wearing the world's tiniest pair of shorts, showing off the compact absurdity of her ass. Lesser ponytails bob all around her. The girls are laughing and nattering and cooing and goading. They're pulling and poking and stretching and flouncing. Each and every sound makes each and every inch of my body ache.

"Great. Plenty for everyone."

I shake my head sadly, like it was a tough choice. "But I can't. I got homework. You dudes'll have to hit the launchpad alone. Just make sure to say hi to Space Elvis for me."

Joe Yung laughs his granite laugh. "We'll say hi to God, for sure. We'll even tell him he should let you in the gates when the time comes."

"Wait, I'm on the golden list?"

"Dude," Beenie Sloat says. "Compared to all the dickholes at Sackville? You're totally in, like, the top five."

"Right on," I say, then get up and walk across the caf, almost positive Ravenna Woods is looking through the window, her face pressed against the glass, watching my back get smaller and smaller.

I split a pizza with Looper, Canadian bacon and pineapple, then lie on the carpet until Elliot swings by in the Renault.

"How's it going with the drummer?" he asks, the door not even closed yet.

"It's going."

"What does that mean, man? Are you doing it or not?"

"Hey, you want to start screening calls yourself?"

Elliot stares like he's about to lean over and bite a steak out of my neck. Then he exhales and rubs his face with his palms. "Sorry, I'm losing it a little."

More than a little. He looks haggard. In desperate need of a shower, a shave, and about ninety straight hours of MILF-less sleep.

"Seriously?" I say. "You should hear some of the freaks who have responded so far. This chick with a Mohawk who never played before but 'wants to learn.' This guy says he's into doing Limp Bizkit covers but 'way, way faster.' A jazz-band kid who thinks we should also add his buddy on flute. And then some other dude who sounded cool until he finally goes and admits he's in his *thirties*."

Elliot laughs. "And now, on drums, give a big hand to... somebody's ancient dad."

"Exactly."

"Still, we're running out of time."

We take a corner hard (Beth). I have to hold on (Beth) with two hands (Beth) to keep from slamming my face (Beth) into the dash.

"Whoa there, hoss," I say.

Elliot laughs. "Jus' followin' the yella line."

Way back in olden times, Sackville was all farmland. But when those people died, their kids sold off the yokes and looms and butter churners and built nine million identical houses on tiny lots facing one another. So now there're these courts like High Ridge View Estates and cul-de-sacs like Louis the XIV's Nut Sac Terrace, but it's still mostly woods where they haven't clear-cut, and the streets are just old cow paths that have been

136

paved over. Consequently, Sackville is one of the most dangerous towns in the state, every single road narrow and windy and
mostly based on where Bessie thought the next mouthful of
sweet clover might be.

Elliot takes another corner like he's at Daytona, trying to
get the back end to spin out, and then rams a CD into the slot,
cranking something that's hard and fast and harsh and fast and
awesome and fast and loud and fast and fast and fast.

"Who's this?"

"My friend, this is the Germs."

"Which album?"

"Actually, it's their only album."

"Slackers."

El Iella nods thoughtfully, holding up a finger for a round
of Ask the Punk Professor.

"You see, the Germs' lead singer, Darby Crash, fell out in
the eighties. You know, way after rockers of the Morrison-
Joplin-Hendrix stripe had already made an art form of ODing."

"Why have I never heard of this Darby Crash?" I ask.

"You've never heard of that Darby Crash mostly because
the dude snuffed himself the very same day John Lennon got
shot."

"What a moron."

He cackles. "I know, right?"

"Total punk timing. Of all the days to pick."

"The building of a legend begins with but a single misstep.
Now please turn to page sixty-three in your text for a pop
quiz."

It's actually just a dumb game we play. I know all about Darby Crash. In fact, I turned Elliot on to the Germs to begin with. But, you know, Punk Professor passes a few minutes, which comes in handy most nights in a numb-dick town like Sackville.

Elliot cranks the volume post-max, sheer distortion, as Darby wails.

" '*What we do is secret! Secret!*' "

We're pounding the dash in time, metal fingers, head banging.

" '*Secret! Secret!*' "

The car zooming around another corner.

" '*Secret! Secret!*' "

When out of the woods clomps Beenie Sloat, right into the headlights. El Hella mashes the brake with both feet.

The Renault whines, bucks, and *scree*s, losing rubber off the edges of all four tires. We skid toward Beenie sideways, a sickening lunge of metal and velocity and inertia, stopping about a foot and a half away from his kneecap. Beenie Sloat doesn't even flinch.

"You okay?" Elliot asks.

"No."

My body drips with nausea and fear-sweat.

Young Joe Yung creeps from the scrub like a wolf. The Renault ticks and steams. We sit there for a while, quiet, dark, crickety. I finally get out, headlights blazing, the dead voice of Darby Crash going, " '*Yeah, yeah, yeah, YEAH!*' "

"Hey, dude. Everything cool?"

"Cool?" Beenie says in an alien voice, eyes like garbage lids.

"I mean, do you need a ride or whatever?"

He just stares at the car, like it's about to dematerialize.

"You good, Joe?" I call.

Young Joe doesn't answer. His pupils are rotating backward. His grin is widening a tear in the time continuum.

"What the fuck are they on?" Elliot asks.

"Acid."

"Dirty hippies."

"Ah, they're all right."

"Dude, they are so massively far from all right."

"True, but still."

I'm about to ask Beenie how many drops they actually droppered when he turns and gallops back into the woods, leaping over trees and branches and rocks, long hair flashing in the moonlight.

"How, Kemo Sabe," Joe Yung says, raising his hand. I give him the peace sign. He scampers among the trees like a wraith.

The engine whines, headlights boring into the dark. We listen to them stomp around the underbrush, giggling, as Darby Crash giggles a half beat behind.

"Man," I finally say. "I know I talk a good game. How we're alternative and radical and punk and all. How our ironic T-shirts are threatening the very foundations of straight society. But you know what? It's a total pose."

"I hear you."

"Those dudes? *That's* alternative."

"No safety net there."

"Sheer breaking on through to the other side."

"Human performance art. Chemically returned to infancy."

"Even so, though?"

"Yeah?"

"Give me a wife and kids and a boring job any day if it means I never have to be that far out on the coil."

The Renault sputters and coughs. The headlights begin to fade. The giggles of Young Joe and Beenie Sloat have already faded away.

Elliot nods. "How about we go back to the Black Widow's, make a grilled cheese, and watch some cartoons?"

I don't even answer, just get in and buckle up.

Stepdad, Step Lad
a new song
by Ritchie Sudden

It would be good if you got killed
Killed in Iraq
It would be good if you got killed
'Cause I hate it when you fuck with my Marshall Stack
I hope you're drafted
I hope your head's whitewalled and you die
I hope you're blasted by a scud
Like a tear from Allah's eye

It would be good if you stayed gone
If you re-upped and lied
If you never came back from Basic
If you grew a beard and became a Kuwaiti spy.
I hated you
Ever since my mama dated you

Since you stained the sofa with your Quarter Pounder
  and fries.
It would be good, yes good
Oh so good if you took the IED ride
Died in Iraq, died in an attack, died like a one-eyed jack
While absolutely no one cried.

Stepdad, dad of step
Stepdad, you had a rep.
Sign him up; line him up
A marine machine
A lean McQueen
Grind him up
Wind him up
Flee the scene
Clock his clean

Stepdad, dad of step
Stepdad, you had a rep
You're not the first; you're not the last
You're just the latest
Dad I hated

Just the latest
Dad I hated.

Elliot puts the paper down. "That's fucking awesome, Sudden."

"Thanks."

"It's, you know, a little intense. But awesome."

"You sure? 'Cause I could change a few—"

"No way, man, don't change a thing."

Elliot straps on his guitar and starts playing around with riffs. In an hour we got the verses and chorus down. An hour after that, the break. I even bust out a solo that almost sounds good.

"So, like, is it about Looper?"

"What do you mean?"

"Well, you know, if you want to get all technical and shit, she's pretty much your stepdad."

I hadn't really thought about it that way. "She wasn't in the army, though. At least I don't think."

"True."

"Also, I don't hate her."

"Amazing, but also true."

"No, it's sort of more about the universal experience of living under the yoke of step-daddery."

"You know what would be radical?"

"People actually staying married?"

"No. A song about a cool, friendly stepdad. Who, like, hated beer and had a good job and treated your mom well."

I laugh and start changing the lyrics, making it friendly and sad and wholesome, begging for the dude to come home and have French toast with the whole loving family. When I'm done, it's eight million times more subversive.

Elliot cranks the volume and strums a massive bar chord.

His amp makes a tortured squall, one long agonizèd note, then dies. A tiny puff of smoke comes out the top.

"Damn."

I find a screwdriver and take off the plate in back. We look in, where a bunch of wires are all fused together, smoking.

"I do believe this amp has shit the bed."

"We need some real equipment," I say.

"So does Looper," he says.

We both laugh, but Elliot laughs harder.

"So does Lawrence," I say.

We both laugh, but I laugh harder.

"No, I mean high-quality equipment. Pro gear. Like you might find bolted into a Teaching Tower."

"I thought I told you to forget that."

"Yeah, you told me."

He gives me the El Hella stare, a stare that has been intimidating weenies, wetting waitress panties, and clearing the backseat of the bus for years.

"I'm not kidding."

"I know you're not," I agree, without agreeing at all.

"Good. So should we do a funeral at sea?"

"Osama-style!"

We both grab an end and then carry the amp up to the roof. The thing is the size of a small refrigerator. We have to balance it against the weather vane and steady our feet.

"Want to say a few words?"

I nod. "You've served us well, rectangular noise funnel.

May you die with the same style and élan with which you rudely amplified our many funky chops."

"*In magna exspirare nobis otium,*" Elliot says.

"One, two..."

The amp lands in the middle of the driveway and smashes into two large pieces.

We climb down and get them and toss them off again.

Four pieces.

We do it again.

Eight pieces.

Then sixteen.

Thirty-two.

Sixty-four.

Eventually the thing has spread all across the driveway and the shrubbery and the lawn, a deconstruction so thorough it's impossible to imagine that the chunky strains of Sin Sister-mouth ever came out of its colorful component parts.

"Mission accomplished," Elliot says, lighting the smoke he'd had wedged behind his ear.

37

Kids come into the library all day long, giddy, amped. "Gonna be a fight in the dayroom, yo!"

"Oh, yeah?" I go.

"Fight today. After lunch."

"Oh, yeah?" B'los goes.

"Fight's on."

"Right."

"Fight later."

"Gotcha."

"Fight happening."

"Good to know."

"Don't anyone want to take out a book anymore?" B'los asks.

I'm checking in a new one. It's a Lexington Cole mystery called *The Pugilist, the Pulchritude, and Scenes from the Velvet Past.*

"Or at least a book about fighting?"

"Party in the dayroom!" says Jeremiah, poking his head in the door. He's a short kid who gets picked on a lot. There's a huge smile on his face. He does a shadowbox, throws rights and lefts. "Gonna be some major Undercard! You all coming?"

"Thanks for the invite," B'los says.

We listen to Jeremiah's voice all the way down the hall.

"Little dude's just glad it's not him."

"It'll be him soon enough," I say. "Then he'll be in here trying to hide under your skirt."

B'los frowns. "When was your last bout?"

I pretend to think, even though I know exactly, down to the minute.

"Nine days."

"Peanut don't like you much."

"I can't figure it. I keep my mouth shut. I mind my own business."

"Minding your own business is bad business."

I look up. "Is that really all it is?"

"You want to know the truth, dog?"

"Yeah."

"There's just something about your ass."

"Whatta you mean?" I say, a tiny bit scared he's going to talk about its firmness or curvature.

"You just so goddamned...certain."

"Of what?"

"That you don't belong up in here."

"What's wrong with that?"

B'los laughs. "Nothing. Except it being a walking reminder on how everyone else does."

On Friday night in Sackville, everyone pretty much goes where they're told. There're six or eight major party spots, and they each have a name, like nightclubs you have to have a special password to get into even though they're mostly just clearings or empty lots cops tend not to check on much. There's Ox Hill, which is not a hill and certainly 100 percent ox-free. It's really just a turnaround at the end of an unpaved road with a make-shift fire pit. Every possible brand of cheap booze has been emptied and tossed, smashed against the rocks and ground underfoot, so many beer cans flattened in rows they look like arty bathroom tiles. Someone lights a fire, someone backs a car up and opens the trunk so Fred Zeppelin blares out; add two cups of water and a dash of soy sauce and it's instant party.

There's also the Pines, which is full of pines. It's a slant on the side of a hill that you have to park below and hike up to, perfect visual cover, no pastry-ass cop about to climb the grade even if half the Taliban were sucking down Four Lokos and eating rat meat in the scrub, biding their time for a frontal assault on the mall. Then there's the Bridge, which, yeah, is a bridge, but with no water underneath, troubled or otherwise.

There's Currytuck, which is really just a pile of abandoned tires. And Sack Rock City, which is the foundation of an abandoned house. And Stevenson Dam, which is a dam. There's the Grove, the Bear, Bear II, and the Pump. Occasionally one of them will get tossed from the rotation once the cops get hip to it and fifteen minutes after everyone parks they're hitting the flashers and checking IDs. Someone will be like, *Bear II is so over*, and then someone else will discover a big rock in a field and start calling it "the Pigeon Beak" or some shit and then it'll be, *Y'all gonna be at Beak's on Friday?* like it's been called that for years, and everyone will show up and stand around a trash fire and drink their asses off until the movable feast moves again.

So we're at the Pigeon Beak.

"Wanna beer?" people keep asking me.

"No."

"Wanna brew?"

"No."

"Cold one?"

"Nope."

"Dude, brewski?"

"Uh-uh."

Elliot and I play a couple of tunes by the fire. There're maybe thirty cars, people standing around in twos and threes talking. Girls listen and sway a little when we hit a nice harmony. Guys suggest lame covers and then say dickish things under their breath when we tell them we don't know (or want to know) how to play any Radiofred. Or Fredtallica. Or Fred

Against the Machine. We play "Nipple Ring Hero" instead, a killer early Sin Sistermouth tune, real punk style, which totally and immediately clears the place out.

Just as a Volvo pulls up.

It's Dick Isley.

"Oh, for Christ's sake," someone says.

"Him again? Seriously?"

People hide their drugs.

People make a halfhearted attempt to hide their booze.

But no one freaks out too much, because Dick Isley parties. Dick Isley goes to a lot of parties. Dick Isley is the life of the party.

"Look! It's Dice!" say a couple of girls, running toward him. A couple other girls run in the opposite direction. Pretty soon Dice is reluctantly agreeing to have a beer, "Just one for me!" and high-fiving with the football guys. He's got his arm around Katie Corcoran. He's got his arm around Zeke Rye. He's laughing and every time someone tells a stupid joke his goatee splits wide, showing all his perfect teachers' union dental plan teeth, everything so witty and open and hilariously cross-generational.

"What a douche," someone says.

"Really? I think he's sorta cool."

"He makes me taste my omelet twice."

"No way, Mr. Isley is the best."

"I hear he got Jen Slater preg."

"I hear Jen Slater is a massive liar."

"True, but still."

I'm only half listening, head on a swivel hoping to spot Ravenna Woods, but she hasn't showed.

"That's so unc," says a freshman in an Izod the exact same color as his skin.

"What's that?" someone else snaps. "Unc? Is that short for *uncle*?"

"Um, no, you know. Uncool."

"Never say that, okay? I mean, just do not ever use that phrase in my presence again."

"Oh. Sorry."

"Follow-up question: Is it still cool to say *wack*?"

"Not unless you just took a time machine back to 1987."

"How about *chill*?"

"Nope."

"*Five-O*?"

"Nope."

"*Fo' shizzle*?"

"That's safe. That's totally a classic."

"You guys are morons."

Another car pulls up. A bunch of girls, none of them Ravenna, jump out squealing, "Look! It's Dice!" They all run over.

"Let's play a fucking song already," El Hella says, all serious all the time now. Rock Scene 2013 is less than a month away. There are no songs that are just about screwing around anymore. Each note is vital practice. Every chord is a knife, a personal message to Flog and Angelo.

It's like hanging out with Matt Drudge but even less fun.

I put my hand on my chin. "Hey, I know, why don't we play

that little number...what's it called? Oh, yeah: 'Dick Isley Should Be Immediately Stuffed into a Mulcher and Spread Over the Arid Soil of Western Africa to be Used as Nitrogen-Rich Fertilizer.' "

"Grow up, already," some girl says, walking by.

"Is that really a song of yours?" the unc kid asks.

"You bet your ass," Elliot goes, busting into "Tattooed Bank Robber Forgot His Gun." "And it goes a little bit like this...a-one, a-two, a-one-two-three..."

He plays it way faster than normal. I mess up the intro. I come in too late on the bridge. Two times I play the wrong chord entirely. My solo blows soup chunks. It's so off-key it travels around the circle of fifths and lands in the right key but is still objectively terrible.

When it mercifully ends, a couple of people clap. Someone croaks a "woo-hoo" out of pure sympathy. Elliot refuses to even look at me, furiously packing up his gear.

I'm putting my guitar in the Renault when I feel a hand slip into my back pocket.

Ravenna.

The hand gives my ass a squeeze.

No way.

Ravenna Woods is squeezing my ass. Her arms go around my waist. She feels good against me. I smell beer on her breath, on the back of my neck. It's cute and ladylike, mixed with jasmine and gum.

I close my eyes, count to three, turn around.

No way.

Her lips are on my lips.

Our tongues touch.

I am seriously about to freak out.

But mostly because when I open my eyes, it's not Ravenna Woods I'm kissing.

It's Lacy Duplais.

Prison Fun Fact #17

Everyone abides by the courtesy flush. Sitting on the pot? You keep that water moving for your cellie's sake. There can be no stink that lingers. Had a bad mac and cheese? Flush a dozen times before you get up. The toilet water is the only thing an inmate truly controls in prison, so you got to control it right.

Prison Fun Fact #29

Pruno is cell-booze. It's made from apples, oranges, raw sugar, fruit cocktail, or ketchup. Bread usually provides the yeast for the Pruno to ferment. It can be made using a plastic bag, hot running water, and a towel or sock to isolate the pulp during fermentation. A batch that has been heavily steeped in a warm, dark place can deliver a deceptively high proof. Which means it's usually hidden in a Ziploc in the toilet bowl. Not for connoisseurs.

Prison Fun Fact #37

A shiv (from the Romani word *chivomengro*, or "knife") is a slang term for any sharp or pointed implement used as a weapon.

Inmates in prisons around the world make shivs. Inmates in prisons around the world frequently puncture each other with them. A shiv can be anything from a glass shard with a rag wrapped around one end to form a handle, to a straightened mattress wire. Toothbrushes can be softened with a lighter and then sharpened against a wall. A "Christmas Tree" is a piece of metal with angular cuts that ensures maximum damage when pulled from a wound.

Prison Fun Fact #44
There are more people in prison in California than there are in college in the entire United States.

Prison Fun Fact #89
Oddly, some people think warehousing delinquent youths has a negative impact on behavior and actually serves to make them exponentially more deviant and a threat to themselves and others. Sociologists call the phenomenon "peer delinquency training." Penologists have found significantly higher levels of substance abuse, school difficulties, criminal enterprise, and a thirst for random violence in adulthood for offenders detained in group settings versus those who were offered treatment on an outpatient basis.

Huh.

Prison Fun Fact #129
Who needs a tattoo gun to do a tattoo? Improvise, homes! Turns out you can do a tattoo with a sewing needle, or a ballpoint

pen with thread wrapped around the end, and India ink. No one in the history of the world has ever regretted getting either Fred Zeppelin or their cellie's name in huge block letters down their calf. I recommend a nice 18-point Helvetica Bold.

I get the cutie barista laughing the whole time she's steaming my Americano. I never get the cutie barista laughing the whole time she's steaming my Americano. Something vital has changed. A door has opened.

It's almost like she can smell Lacy Duplais on me.

Which means I am now a man. And apparently I am dangerous.

Actually, all we did was kiss.

But I do feel different.

Even as I slide into the booth where Elliot is doing the crossword next to a coffee mug the size of Cameroon.

"Wassup, Thunderdome?"

"Hey," he says, chewing his pen and rubbing his bald-ass head at the same time. His muttonchops are now in full flourish. His stubble is like wire carpeting. His expression is pure take-no-shit, shut-your-mouth, on a mission, shit-metal-cans-for-breakfast.

I no longer feel very dangerous.

"What's a twelve-letter word for *penchant*?" he asks.

El Hella. King of the crosswords.

"How do I know? *Fondness*?"

"That, my mathematically challenged friend, is only eight letters."

"*Partiality?*"

"Ten."

"*Whim?*"

"Four."

"*Inclination?*"

"Close. Eleven."

"*Soft spot?*"

"Two words. Cheating, plus not long enough."

"Ah, for fuck's sake. *Predilection?*"

He looks up and smiles. Actually smiles. And then pencils it in.

"Listen," I say. "I got good news and slightly less good news."

"You and Lacy?"

That throws me a bit.

"You saw, huh?"

He stares. "Everyone saw. You were practically massaging her tonsils. I thought you weren't interested."

"Yeah, I dunno. Anyway, that's not the news."

"What is?"

"I found a drummer."

He tosses the crossword. Finished, except for one long vertical.

"Seriously?"

"Yeah. He's from Balltown. Dropped out of Ball High last year to play online poker."

"Our drummer's a dropout?"

"I think it's more he dropped into some money. He's, like, a math genius or some shit. He's probably inventing solar energy this weekend."

"What's the not-so-good news?"

I sip my Americano. I clear my throat. I tear my napkin.

"He doesn't really play drums as much as he plays bongos."

Elliot's face drops, like Dad Sudden's sucked-in gut after the babysitter goes home.

"Bongos in a hardcore band? You're aware that we are not The Grateful Fred, correct?"

"I know, I know. But listen—"

"We are not REO Fredwagon, am I right?"

"Just listen. I really think—"

"Am I dreaming? Did I just wake up as the guitar player in Bruce Fredsteen and the Fred Street Band?"

"Will you *shut up*?" I say, way too loud.

People look over at us. He slams some coffee, spilling it down his chin.

"No way. I quit."

"You are not quitting."

"You're right. You're fired."

"I am not fired."

"You're right. But you're not in the band anymore. You're R&D. I just hired you on a no-benefits, minimum-wage temp basis to find a real drummer. And then to find your replacement."

"A bongo player could be our secret weapon," I whisper. "Just the sort of unexpected twist a smart band might employ to really stand out at Rock Scene 2013."

That at least gets him listening.

I lean over. "So we mic each bongo, right? Put on a bunch of distortion. The dude says he can play fast as hell. Says he's all over the things like a trip-hop octopus. We work it so it's all reverb and double-timed, so it sounds like he's playing a whole kit."

"Ridiculous. Totally hopeless. Zero chance it'll work."

I drop my neutron bomb. "No one's ever done it before."

El Hella wipes his mouth. He almost starts to smile.

"It's actually new," I say. "Sorta, kinda, a little bit new. When's the last time you heard something new?"

He does some quick calculating on his palm. "There hasn't been anything new in music since—"

"John Coltrane died."

"Nineteen sixty-nine."

"Forty-four years of stasis."

"Inertia."

"Status quo."

"Rote derivation."

"Boredom."

"Okay, okay, fine. We try him out. We see."

"There's just one other thing," I say.

"There's always just one other thing."

"Dude's name is Adam."

"So?"

"Actually, it *was* Adam. He legally changed it to Chaos."

"Chaos? Our drummer's name is *Chaos*?"

"Yeah. And it's like, okay, that's bad enough. But apparently you also gotta pronounce it his way."

"He's got a *way*? Rock star's got his own special pronunciation?"

"It's not Chaos. It's *Chowus*."

"Chow this!"

"I know. Believe me. But if you can get by that, he's actually pretty cool."

"You met him?"

"We Skyped."

"You Skyped?"

"Twice."

"Forget it."

"And he's right over there."

I wave my hand. Chaos walks over, smiling. He looks like James Dean except he's got that sort of prep-school dirty blond hair that curls behind his ears. He's wearing shorts, boots, a white T-shirt that says BLANK on it, a vintage button-up sweater that's supposed to look like Bing Crosby wore it in 1922 and probably cost three hundred bucks, the tiniest little wisp of blond mustache, and a corduroy suit coat. He should be on a sailboat with a golden retriever and a glass of sparkling wine instead of standing next to us.

"Hey, man," I say as he waits to be invited to sit.

"Hello, Richard."

"Ritchie."

"Of course. Wassup, rocker?"

"This is Elliot Hella. Dude I was telling you about."

Instead of shaking hands, Elliot puts his boots on the empty seat and leans back. His breath smells like a mixture of coffee and kerosene. "Who're your ten favorite bands, Chowus?"

Chaos grins. He rubs his chin like a mad scientist. "Um, okay, a test? That's cool. I dig it. The question is, do I name ten acceptably obscure bands so I come across as superhip? Or do I name ten bands that actually made some money, proving my commercial potential? Or do I name ten bands that are lovably semiuncool, thus proving that I am comfortable with my icono-clastic tastes and don't care enough to try to impress you, thereby impressing you?"

"You're impressing me, dude," I say.

El Hella just stares.

Chaos clears his throat. "The Stones, of course. *Beggars Banquet* to *Some Girls* with an emphasis on *Exile*, and in par-ticular anything with Mick Taylor playing lead. Then Roxy Music, just follow the nude album covers. Johnny Thunders. The first three White Stripes, even if, as a commodity, Jack has gotten way tired. Mastodon while driving, fucking, or fighting. Elliott Smith for the alone times. Pavement. My Bloody Valen-tine. Anything and everything Iggy Pop, especially and eter-nally the Stooges, but even the embarrassing eighties crap. Is that eight? No, that's nine. Let me toss the first Fred Zeppelin in there just for Bonham's cerebellum-abusing drumming."

There's a long silence. Elliot looks at me. I look at him.

"Did you just say Fred Zeppelin?"

"I did."

"Why?"

"I dunno."

We take a second to recover from the kismet.

"That's a good list, Chowus," Elliot finally says. "It's not my list, not even close, but, you know, I have to say it doesn't totally suck."

"Thanks, man."

"Yeah, dude," I say. "But you forgot My Chemical Romance."

Chaos laughs. "Whatever."

Elliot doesn't laugh. He stands up, all gorilla-agitated. His chair clangs to the side.

"What, you think Ritchie was joking?"

"Um, for real, or…?"

Elliot presses closer, hands clenched into fists. "I like My Chemical Romance, Chowus. In fact, they rule. And now I want to know what *you* think about them."

The other tables are all watching us. The whole café has quieted.

Chaos turns toward them and holds up one hand. He puts the other hand over his heart. "If you'll indulge me," he says in a deep, oratorical voice, "I'd like to deliver a few words on My Chemical Romance."

"Tell us!" say some girls at another booth, a couple even cute.

"Yeah, tell us," say some soccer kids, suddenly a congregation. "Testify, hippie!"

"You gotta give it to him—he knows how to work a crowd," I whisper.

Elliot waves me off while Chaos clears his throat.

"I think, when I think about them at all, I think *please* with the My Chemical Romance. I think *enough* with the My Chemical Romance. Um, what's the one word I can conjure that perfectly describes the My Chemical Romance experience? Oh, wait, I know: total dickless horseshit. Well, that's three words, but what I mean to say is, I hate them. That's what I think. In, you know, my opinion. Humbly stated."

The other booths laugh and cheer. Some people clap. A few people toss rolled-up napkins and Frisbee drink lids. The manager looks over the counter nervously, trying to gauge his next move.

"Fuck you. Chem Rome rules," some big soccer dude says.

Chaos laughs. "Did that guy really just say *Chem Rome*?"

Other tables laugh, too. Chem is shouted down, hard.

Elliot moves in, inches away from Chaos's face, all gorilla grill and granite chin.

And then smiles.

The smile.

"That right there is an A-plus answer."

"Righteous," Chaos says.

"Thank god," I say.

"Is the interview over?" Chaos asks. "We haven't talked salary yet."

Elliot walks away, calling over his shoulder.

"Ritchie's mom's garage. Saturday. Four o'clock. And don't forget your hippie-ass bongos."

He slams the door.

Chaos whistles. "That dude is, like, contents under pressure."

"You did good," I say. "Real good."

Chaos shrugs and picks up the crossword, then reaches over and pencils in the final answer, which is *Requiem for a Heavyweight*.

41

Yeah, there's a fight in the dayroom, and yeah, I go. Why? I'm not sure. The degree to which Undercard repels me is overridden by boredom. And fascination. Physical collision. Mindlessness. It makes me nauseated. It ramps me up. It's dog-level, pack-mind, barking because barking feels good. Lessens the hunger. Eases the fear. Lifts the tail. Unpuckers the arsehole.

Peanut is taking bets in cigarettes. Conner is on his stack-of-chairs throne. The bout is between a tall white kid, who stands like a pro boxer but is trembling, and a short black kid who doesn't even raise his fists. "Fight, already," Peanut says in his raspy voice. There're kids at the doors watching for counselors. Not much time to get the blood on. Peanut kicks the white kid in the back, who moves forward and starts punching the black kid, who doesn't even try to defend himself. There's hooting and cheering. The black kid goes down and curls up. The white kid punches and kicks him a few extra times, then raises his fists like vintage Ali.

Peanut collects cigarettes.
I want to puke.
Conner winks.
Peanut looks up, sees me standing there.
He winks, too.

A long pause. And then the pause ends.

"Ritchie?"

"What?"

"You wanna, like, make out?"

She's lying on my bed. I'm lying next to her. How did that happen? Here's how: I'm in the backyard mulching Mom's dead tomatoes. The wheelbarrow is heavy and I'm sweating my ass off. Her car just pulls in the driveway, no call, no nothing. I've got my shirt off, torn shorts, stank-ass yard Nikes.

She gets out and leans against the fence, watching me.

"What are you doing here?" I ask.

"Why, you want me to go?"

I open the gate and hold it, watching her shake on through.

Lacy Duplais is wearing an Indian uniform. Like, Native American. She's on the cheer squad, which somehow isn't the same thing as being a cheerleader. She's got the Pocahontas thing going, tight and turquoise and brown. There've been protests about it, some tribe holding signs outside football games. It's like, what, they got a problem with short skirts? They got a problem with the fact that the Sackville High Redskins stubbornly refuse to change their name or mascot even if it's totally mouth-raping their culture every time someone scores a touchdown and twelve girls in stripper/native wear start jumping up and down doing a tomahawk chop? Get a hobby, Native Americans, and stop asking us to take even one second to reconsider our institutionalized stupidity and gleeful hand in your genocide, okay?

In the meantime, Lacy's very, very short skirt is barely covering *toot toot beep beep* bad-girl fishnets. Way out of control. And her hair is now red. Punk-ass dyed red. Sweet, shy Lacy Duplais is changing before my very eyes.

"I bought the new Gaslight Anthem album yesterday," I say, which isn't true. Mostly because it sucks. Yesterday I bought Carcass's *Reek of Putrefaction* instead, which rules.

"I love Gaslight Anthem," she says. "Let's go listen."

"Let's do."

We smooth-roll up the stairs, Lacy giggling.

I double-check that the door is locked and suddenly we're on the bare mattress. Lacy lights a Marlboro Red.

"You smoke now?"

"Yup."

"Mom's not so big on it in the house."

"Is Mom home to lodge a complaint?" she asks, blowing smoke in my face. It's like the best scene from a bad movie. Or the worst scene from a killer movie. Her Pocahontas poncho is hiked way up and she knows it, pretending it's just how she's lying. I can see her underwear. I have prodigious wood. She knows that, too. We have a dumb fake conversation about some test, during the middle of which she puts her cigarette out on the cover of my English-assigned *Slaughterhouse Five*, reaches down, and grabs my package like a gearshift, cranking it into reverse.

"Yowp."

"You okay?" She looks worried. Actually worried. It's cute.

"Yes."

"You sure?"

"Yes."

And then she's on top of me. She's pressing herself all over me. I pull down her nylons with my toe. I pull up her shirt with my teeth. Her nipples are oval and brown. I put my hand in her underwear.

"Oh my god."

"What?"

She's so wet.

"Nothing."

Lacy puts her mouth over mine and sucks my tongue with desperation, like the alien that lives in her stomach just decided it prefers me as its new host. She levers her hips. We protract and equilateral, banging angles until there is approach vector.

I slide on a Trojan.

And then we are fucking.

Really for real fucking.

It's fantastic and totally surreal. I immediately grasp with utter clarity that every sex scene in every movie ever made is total horseshit. Nothing is smooth and easy. Stuff fits, but it's clumsy, too. Clumsy awesome. All I can think of is telling Elliot, move for move. Telling every guy in the hall. In homeroom. Screaming it in the streets. And then I think how not cool that is. Not for Lacy's reputation's sake, but because it will make me sound like a total First-Time Charlie.

Not a good look. Even though it's true.

Lacy's concentrating, biting her lip. Her stomach makes these squelchy sounds against my stomach that we both pretend aren't happening. Her expressions keep changing, like she's following along to music only she can hear. I am so fascinated that I no longer have to think about not coming. I could last forever. Just to make her make more faces. I arch my back and she inhales sharply, moving faster, hands on my chest. Her nails carve grooves.

She's close.

Inhale, inhale.

She's closer.

Exhale, exhale.

I am totally in control. I am a king. I am master of my domain.

And then I start thinking about Ravenna Woods.

For some reason imagining Ravenna Woods.

Transposing. Replacing. Confabulating.

No!

I try to make her go away.

Go away!

I close my eyes against her image.

Stop dancing!

I will her from my mind.

Put on some clothes!

She stays. I come.

Bang.

Twenty minutes later, we're in Lacy's Corolla heading into town. Fast-food run. She rounds a tight corner not nearly tight enough and we almost head-on into an F-150. She giggles.

I try to breathe again. "You're a shitty driver, you know that?"

"What are you talking about? I'm a great driver."

She blows through a yellow that's mostly red. A few horns beep.

"Careful."

She gives a mock salute. "Okay, Grandma."

There's a long straightaway. Almost no chance for her to hit anything. But not impossible. She pops a disc in the player, this lame old band called EMF. There're only two words in the whole song and they're singing them in fake Cockney accents, over and over, *You're unbelievable.* Except with them it sounds like, *Yuh uhn buh leaf aba.*

"Gonna have to butch up your music collection if you're diving in the deep end."

"What do you mean?"

I point to her dye job. "Um, the hair? The fishnets? Going punk means leaving this weak pop shit behind with the Christmas sweaters and the white denim."

She turns it up, singing along with the melody. It actually sounds good.

Yoo ur unnn beh leef eble!

"I thought punk was about not caring what other people thought."

"It is," I say. "But—"

"What if I'm the girl who dresses the way she wants, listens to whatever she wants, and anyone who doesn't like it can eat it? How's that for a rule?"

It's such an awesome answer that I have no response. So I change the subject.

"Can we be serious here for a second?"

She laughs. "Why not?"

"Why me?"

"What do you mean?"

"Why are you into me? I can't figure it out."

Lacy reaches over and scratches my neck, pushes my hair back over my ear. "Do you seriously not know how beautiful you are?"

"You've got to be kidding."

"I always thought it was a pose. Like, *oh, yeah, I have no idea.* But, you know, maybe you really don't."

I flip down the sun visor and look in the little rectangular mirror. The usual dickhead looks back.

"Whatever."

"You want to know what your problem is?"

"That I have zero interest in being told what my problem is?"

She lights a smoke and clenches it between her teeth.

On the floor is a Ramones disc, nestled among all the

wrappers and other garbage. I pop it in, and Joey's singing, *Now I want to sniff some glue!* as we pull into the drive-through line at Burger Barn. Lacy's telling me a story about something her friend's friend heard some other girl say about the first friend's sister that I am so not listening to, and then mid-yuk she hits the gas instead of the brake. The car leaps ahead and plows into one of the brick posts that hold up the big menu with the speaker on it. The menu shatters before toppling onto the hood. Cars behind us are either laughing or laying on the horn. The manager runs out, insanely pissed. His name tag says, HI, I'M CHAD CHILTON! He's got a goatee and the beginnings of a paunch.

"Take it easy," I say. "It was an accident."

"How do you hit that? How is it even *possible*?"

"Everything's possible, Chad."

"Did you not see it? It's painted orange, for god's sake."

"She got confused."

"Got confused or *is* confused?"

"Let's keep it professional, huh, Chad?"

He looks at me, sees Lacy about to cry, realizes I'm right, sighs, and points to the sign. "Can you at least give me a hand?"

Chad and I lift the menu, heavier than it looks, and prop it up so it can still be read. Mostly. He stares like if he refolded the cuffs of his dress shirt one twist tighter, the post would magically reassemble. Lacy is crying into her cell phone, on the curb in her little Indian outfit. Cars nose around, kids pointing and yelling. Old pervs slow down, checking out the big spread Lacy's throwing under her skirt. Finally, the cops come. Lacy gets a drunk test, passes, a ticket, fails, and they let her go. The cop keeps eyeballing me like it's my fault. I take a minute to silently hate cops an increment more than usual. Then some übersquare dude in a polo and loafers helps me push Lacy's car off to the side, which no one else thought to do.

"Thanks, man."

"Sure."

I'm standing there thinking how cool the dude is and how I should stop prejudging people by what they wear when he hands me a card.

Lawyer.

"Give me a call. There might be a way this is all the restaurant's fault."

I toss his card in the gutter and walk back over.

"I have to wait for the tow truck," Lacy says, mascara lining her cheeks.

"I'll wait with you."

She shakes her head. "In a minute my dad will be here. You shouldn't be around when he comes, you know?"

I know.

We don't kiss. She stands by the car. I stand all the way on the other side of the lot and call Mom to come pick me up. But Mom's not there, so Looper does.

"Thanks, man," I say when the Perfection van rumbles up.

Lacy gives a little half wave as we pull back into traffic.

"Hanging out with a strange brand of old lady these days, I see."

"What brand would that be, Loop?"

"Oh, you know, cute as hell, dyed red mop, dressed like Sacagawea, can't drive for shit, don't call me Loop."

I'm tempted to tell her I just got laid. I picture her expression. Would she be surprised? Pissed? Concerned? Proud?

"I like them spicy," I say.

Looper plays with her feather earring. "That right?"

"Yessir. *Muy caliente.*"

"You know what? So do I."

"Gross."

She laughs. "Yeah, sorry. I keep forgetting you're a kid."

I look out the window. It might be the nicest thing anyone's ever said to me. The weird thing is, I keep forgetting, too.

It's Saturday. I wait.

And wait.

And wait.

Finally, a car pulls up. A station wagon. Elliot's in the passenger seat, some old lady driving. I figure it's his mom, but it's not.

It's Angie Proffer.

Someone else's mom.

Mrs. Proffer squeezes Elliot's leg as he pulls his amp from the backseat, then peels away, giving me a half wave and a beep, *toot toot*.

I say nothing. Elliot says nothing. At least not for twenty minutes.

"Chowus is late."

"I know, Cougartown. Twenty-six minutes. Will you relax?"

"We don't have twenty-six minutes to waste, fuckhead."

"What is your malfunction, Bad Lieutenant?"

He bows up, clenching his fists. I step off my amp.

He goes boxing stance. I go MMA stance.

And then we rain blows and kicks down on each other in super slo-mo, talking like a poorly dubbed karate movie.

"I am now informing you we have but a single month in which to rope musical beauty together!"

"It is true! Despite your impure thoughts, that is undeniable!"

"Aiii! Rock Scene 2013 will not wait for slow rocks to grow doltish moss!"

"Ha! Revenge is a side dish that can be eaten both cold and hot!"

Elliot karate chops me in the neck, and I collapse in dramatic fashion.

"Just get out your guitar and be tuned up for when Chow Boy finally arrives, okay?"

I roll over and unbuckle the new hard-shell case I bought for The Paul. It's lined with this fake pink fur that smells like what some New Jersey lab thinks sweaty Catholic girls smell like. I also spray-painted SIN SISTERMOUTH on a bedsheet and hung it in the garage. There is, of course, an anarchy symbol underneath. I have no idea what anarchy really is, or wants to be, beyond the vague impression that it might mean mandatory wallet chains for all citizens. Or that I'll never have to bus tables again after the workers revolt. Or unite. Or hand out pamphlets. Or whatever.

Chaos drives a BMW converti. I know that because a BMW converti pulls into our driveway and screeches to a halt in a spray of gravel. He hops out, without using the door, looking like he just rolled in from a Newport regatta: madras shorts, a green Izod with the alligator cut out so you can see his left nipple, a deerstalker cap, and huge black Doc Martens.

"Are they unlaced?" Elliot asks, without looking up.

"They are unlaced."

He moans. "What in fuck are we getting ourselves into?"

"We are inching closer to genius, that's what."

Chaos gives me a bear hug, then shoots an imaginary pistol at Elliot. We retire to the garage while he sets up about three grand worth of equipment, flangers and tape loops and effects boxes. Chaos rocks three amps, two of them miked and then fed back into each other. Tiny mics are taped inside the bongos. He adjusts his stands and fiddles with his knobs and then looks up with a smile.

"You ready, cheesebag?" Elliot asks.

"I am ready, captain. Fire away."

Elliot chunks a chord and then muffles it with his palm. "Let's start with—"

"Oh, wait. One final adjustment."

Chaos pulls out a pipe. It's one of those scrimshaw or meerschaum or whatever deals, a big white carved pirate's head at the end of a black stem. He pulls out a baggie, stuffs the pirate to the rim with purple buds, and then lights up. He closes his eyes, blowing smoke calmly out of flared nostrils, then hands it to Elliot, who takes one tiny puff and practically coughs up a lung. I can't believe it. He hands it to me while trying not to collapse, but I won't even touch the thing.

"I hate pot."

"Everyone's got to hate something," Chaos says, taking another huge puff.

"I like my mind," I say. "I'm okay to see the world clearly."

"Are you?" Chaos asks, adjusting a pedal.

"What does that mean?"

"What does anything mean?"

"And thus, with one sentence, perfectly illustrating why I hate pot."

When Elliot finally pulls it together, he announces a rendition of "I Got the My-Girlfriend's-Been-Extraordinarily-Renditioned-by-the-CIA Blues."

"This better not suck, Chow Boy."

"I totally agree," Chaos says.

"So count it off."

"One, two, three, four."

We rip into the tune. The dual-guitar attack sounds like an F-16 strafing civilians. It takes Chaos a minute to catch up, but there's no bottom end. He's fiddling with knobs.

Fiddle, fiddle, fiddle, knob, knob, knob.

Elliot is getting frustrated. We vamp around on one chord, waiting.

Chaos holds up a finger, finally gets a bass signal, but then has to take off his shirt.

"Oh, for fuck's sake!"

Elliot is about to yank his plug, but I'm staring at Chaos. He's one of those guys with a perfect skinny physique, not an ounce of fat, an Abercrombie layout, like Iggy himself without all the broken-bottle scars. There's our draw right there, no matter how much we suck. The girls will be killing one another to get near the stage.

Chaos smiles, nods, and then pops into the groove. We let go of the vamp and race through the song's progression.

Within two bars it is immediately clear that he's a fraud.

Absolutely terrible.

Total shit.

Actually, that's not true.

The guy is a phenomenal bongo player. Right in the pocket, keeping up without breaking a sweat. Adding accents and layers. With all his effects and loops he sounds like about ten people, cutting right through our squall, meaty, propulsive. It's weird, for sure. It's different, for sure. But there's no question it's nine layers of completely, utterly awesome. Elliot and I keep looking at each other in disbelief, chugging away, playing twice as fast as usual. Chaos's hands are a blur over the skins, propelling us into better, tighter, more confident realms. We zip through our entire set in record time, except the last song, when Chaos finally begs off. "I am sorry, dude and dudette, but these fingers need a break."

He casually sits on the trunk of the Beemer and lights up again, sun on his tan shoulders, as if nothing amazing has just happened. He blows out a massive plume and smiles.

"So am I in, or what?"

"Fuck yeah," I say, and then look back at Elliot, who's changing a string. "I mean, you know, as far as *I'm* concerned. It's up to Smella Hella, too, though."

Elliot walks over, head down, hands in pockets. Chaos offers him the pipe, but Elliot declines, looking at his feet and sighing.

We wait.

And wait.

And wait.

Finally, Chaos starts fiddling for his keys. "Okay, that's cool. It's not working out? I understand. Thanks any—"

"You're in."

Chaos looks at me, winks, then gives Elliot a big hug.

No one in the history of El Hella has ever given El Hella a big hug.

He elbows Chaos away, but you can see it's almost with a shred of affection.

Five Things Our Band Needs (to win Rock Scene 2013):

1. ~~A name~~
2. ~~A drummer~~
3. A singer
4. A signature song
5. A collective embolism

"Okay, awesome," Chaos says. "Totally cool. Extremely excellent. There's just one thing."

"There's always just one thing," I say.

"If I'm going to be the third leg of this obviously musically transcendent kick-ass tripod, of this totally rocking-ass chart-crushing grindcore juggernaut, we have to make a smallish adjustment."

"Which is?"

Chaos gestures with the pipe. "My friends, we must come up with a better handle. With all due respect, Sin Sistermouth is very possibly the worst band name in the long and storied history of genuinely terrible band names."

I wait for him to laugh.

He does not laugh.

There is complete silence.

Even the birds and insects seem stoned.

"Fuck that," I finally say.

"Totally fuck that," Elliot says, rubbing his bald dome.

Chaos nods sagely. "It's been real, gentlemen." He quickly loads his stuff into the Beemer, backing up with a chirp. "But in that case I guess you dudes are just gonna have to find yourselves another drummer."

44

We're standing out at the basketball courts. Some other people are standing near me. I guess that comprises "we're." There's no actual basketball. A few weeks ago some twitch tossed it over the fence and that was that. Budget cuts or whatever. Maybe just spite. But no new ball. So people stand in groups. There's an old weight bench and some mismatched dumbbells. When no one's using them, I put in time with the iron. I can actually feel a little bit of chest developing beneath my shirt. Of course, when anyone else comes up and says, "I'm using this," I go stand by the three-point line like that's what I planned to do all along.

Which is where I am when Peanut comes up behind me. He's wearing a blue watch cap just like Jack Nicholson in *One Flew Over the Cuckoo's Nest*, except his voice is all syrupy Southern drawl.

"You down with Undercard, Sudden?"

"No."

It's the lamest possible response, but my mind has pretty much seized.

"That mean you holding bones?"

His breath is terrible. Like raw meat. Rumor is he's in for offing someone. Plenty of guys claim to be killers, but he's the only one I half believe. Especially since they say he strangled the dude with a shoelace.

It's too stupid to make up.

"I'm not holding shit."

"Didn't think so."

A car circles the perimeter of the fence, then speeds away. We both imagine ourselves in the backseat.

"Why you gunning for me so hard?"

"I was gunning for you, you'd surely know it."

"Then why do I always get picked to fight?"

"I like the way you fight."

"You mean the way I lose?"

He grins, shaking cornrow tails off the back of his neck. "People love to bet that great white hope. Hundred years since Jack Johnson and they still haven't figured out it's a great white hopeless. Also, I hear you talking with the lady."

For a second I think he means Looper.

"Who?"

"The doctor. Benway."

"Yeah, so?"

He says nothing.

"But I don't have a choice. I mean, doesn't everyone talk to her?"

"No."

"Don't you keep a journal?"

He looks at me like I'm a bug.

"No."

"Oh."

"Yeah, oh. You special, Sudden. Know what I'm sayin'?"

"I'm not special."

"You on the marquee for day after tomorrow. Name up in lights."

I try to think of a response. Refusal? Acceptance? A one-liner? I end up choosing tremblingly sincere. Or it chooses me.

"Do I have to?"

"Yessir," he says. "Got a premiere bout here; I can tell."

I can see kids watching us, counselors watching us, no one moving, no one doing shit.

"Oh, yeah," Peanut says, snapping his fingers by his calf. "Gonna be you and B'los. Bowing up and flat going at it."

"Fine," I say in the library, with a big upside-down art book I picked for cover, leaning back in my chair. Within seconds, Earl Paste, vice principal and dead ringer for a walking meatloaf, pushes my chair forward.

"No leaning back, Sudden."

"Yessir."

He adjusts his bulk.

"What're you reading there?"

I spin the book the right way and we both see it's a compendium of German graphic art innovations of the 1920s.

"Wouldn't have figured you for a Bauhaus fan, Sudden."

"No, sir, me, neither. But, you know, their first album is pretty good."

"Excuse me?"

My cell buzzes. It's Lacy Duplais. I don't answer.

"Nothing, sir. Just doing my best to expand my inexplicably limited horizons."

Vice Principal Paste clears his throat. "Who exactly do you think you're wise-assing here, Sudden?"

"Not you, sir."

"Never mind him, Mr. Paste," Elliot says, shooting me daggers.

"I'll never mind who I want to never mind, Hella."

"Yessir."

"And who are you?" he asks Chowus, who is wearing dress pants, wing tips, a sleeveless T-shirt, and a tan safari vest with a million pockets and zippers. In front of him is a volume of Shakespearean sonnets.

"Me? Just transferred. Adam Bahm."

"At Embalm?"

"Adam Bahm."

"Atom Bomb?"

Chaos spells it out. "A-d-a-m B-a-h-m."

"Transferred from where, Bahm?"

"Balltown, sir. Would you like to see my papers?"

Chaos starts to reach in his chest pocket. He's so convincing even I believe he's got them folded and waiting, despite the fact that it's a 98 percent certainty the only thing lurking there is his meerschaum pipe.

"No need, Bahm."

"Yessir."

Vice Principal Paste holds up one finger in warning, then touches his nose before waddling away.

My cell buzzes. It's Lacy Duplais. I don't answer.

"Bahm?" Elliot says.

Chaos shrugs. "Best I could come up with on the spur. My improv chops are rusty."

"How *did* you get in here anyway?"

"The door."

Elliot rolls his eyes and turns to me. "You're so asking for it, Sudden. Why give Paste such a hard time?"

"Why not?"

"Will you be cool, please? At least until Rock Scene? After that, you can be all the junior tough-ass you want."

"Can we get back to the subject at hand?" Chaos says. "The reason you called me? The reason I drove all the way over here?"

"Fine," I say.

"Fine what?"

"Fine, we are no longer Sin Sistermouth."

He leans back. "Good. Very good. Once again, you have secured the services of a kick-ass drummer."

"But now we need a new name."

"No, we don't."

"You got one?"

"I do."

"So what is it, Chowus?" Elliot asks.

"Close your eyes."

"C'mon, stop the bullshit."

"Close your eyes," he insists. "And really let it sink in."

My cell buzzes. It's Lacy Duplais. I don't answer.

Elliot and I clamp our lids.

Chaos takes a deep breath and says very slowly and very loudly, so pretty much every kid at every table and even Dice, who's leaning over the counter and flirting with Miss Flan, the librarian, looks up:

"Gentlemen, our new name is ... Wise Young Fool."

I'm in Mom's room, where the full-length mirror is. The audience is screaming.

Wise Young Fool!

I'm wearing just underwear and The Paul.

Wise Young Fool!

I adjust my package, do different stances, different pouty faces, different rock-god poses. I do the Keith Richards slouch, the Billy Zoom grin, the Chuck Berry duckwalk, the My Chemical Romance dickwalk, the Eddie Van finger-slam, the Hendrix teeth-pluck, the Joe Strummer low-slung, the Jimmy Page smack-daze. I raise one lip. I do speed scales. I attitude like Joan Jett's little brother, Mo Jett. I sling the thing over my shoulder and around my back like Rick Neilsen. I do the finger robot like Yngwie. I gaze at myself like crossroads Robert Johnson about to do a shot of poison whiskey. Then I stop screwing around and just straight-out pentatonic air-wail like my man Joe Walsh.

"Looking good, Ritchie," my reflection says.

"Thanks, Other Ritchie."

"You really can play that guitar."

"You, too, man."

I lean closer to the mirror. Condensation fogs part of me out. "Ritchie?"

"Yeah, Other Ritchie?"

"What do you say we show a little more leg, and then do a rendition of 'Chin Wag Chat' at four times its normal speed?"

"I say that's an excellent idea. Let's do it."

I count it off and then zip through the tune, mugging in the mirror, chunking through the heavy mosh part, adding little pull-offs and hammer-ons throughout. When it's over, I stare at myself for a while, giving sly little grins and pouty groupie faces.

My cell buzzes. It's Lacy Duplais. I don't answer.

"Other Ritchie?"

"Yeah, Richster?"

"Tell me the truth. Was that song any good?"

"It ruled, Rich. I wouldn't lie to you. It kicked some serious ass."

I smile at myself. A big white porcelain dazzler.

"You're a good man, Other Ritchie. You're a real man of the people."

"You, too. In fact, man, you're—"

"Who in god's name are you talking to?" Mom says, standing at the end of the hallway in her waitress uniform, which is covered in so much spilled ranch she looks like she just walked off the set of *Saw IX: Tied Up at the Salad Bar.* The look of horror on her face is way past the point of explaining.

At least I've got my underwear on.

My cell buzzes. It's Lacy Duplais. I don't answer.

"Seriously, Ritchie," she says in her best *no foolin' I'm really worried here* voice, "are you high?"

"Just high on life," I say, holding The Paul artfully in front of my crotch.

"I'm serious."

"Don't yuk my yum, Ma."

"Oh my god, yuk your what?"

"Don't judge. I'll never get ahead if I'm constantly lashed to the yoke of your judgment."

"Oh my god, yoke of my what?"

"I'm sorry I have to explain this, Mother, but in our new instant-gratification Internet world, a young man must have the courage to be peculiar, or he will drown in a vast ocean of pixelated mediocrity."

While she pauses, trying to digest that particular line of shit, I take the opportunity to blow by, stopping long enough to liberate the moo shu container in her hand, before sliding into my room and locking the door.

Ten minutes later, I realize my cell is in Mom's room, right where I left it.

Buzzing away.

47

Dr. Benway hits the buzzer that locks the door, so Meatstick can't hear.

"So you're saying this Peanut arranges gladiatorial battles in the cells?"

"In the dayroom."

She looks skeptical, wearing a cream-colored skirt, white blouse, and red striped blazer. Dressing down so as not to get anyone excited. I don't blame her, what with all the degenerates in here.

"It can't possibly be true."

"But it is."

"Then we need to do something."

"No, 'we' don't," I say. "And if I get questioned about it, I'll tell them I made the whole thing up."

"But why?"

"Why do you think?"

She plays with the buckle on her shoe, considering.

"Also, if you show my journal to anyone, I'll never write anything real in it again."

"Is that a threat, Mr. Sudden?"

I lean forward. She does a credible job of pretending not to flinch.

"You swore everything between us was confidential. You also told me I have trust issues. Well, here's your chance to be right both ways."

Dr. Benway sighs. "I just find it hard to believe, with the counselors on twenty-four-hour watch—"

"What, you think they don't *know*? That they don't dig the action? Shit, some of them probably place bets."

"Impossible."

"Listen, you're just a part-timer. You drive home at night. You don't see what really goes down in here."

"That's true," she admits.

"And you're crazy if you think you can just toss this back in the counselors' faces. Demand they 'fess up and apologize. Best case, you'll be transferred out before you can buckle your Blahniks. And then where does that leave me?"

Dr. Benway's eyes flash. For a second she realizes she's not in a Julia Roberts movie anymore. She's just a woman with a skirt and a night-school degree locked in a building with hundreds of feral boys and the tyranny of their desires.

"And so you'll fight with B'los?"

"I'm not sure yet."

"When?"

"Tomorrow night."

Her bottom lip settles, determined.

"I think I know a way to deal with tomorrow night."

"You just gonna snap your fingers and fix everything?"

"Fix? No. But maybe toss in a monkey wrench while I figure out what to do about the rest of it."

"Without involving me?"

"Without involving you."

Neither of us says anything for a long time.

"But if I stick my neck out I want one thing in return."

"It seems worth mentioning at this point that I have zero cash in my commissary."

She rolls her eyes. "I want you to tell me a story."

I laugh. "That's it? I'll tell you one right now. There once was a man from Rangoon..."

"A real story. Not about your band or school. Not about girls or cars. About your family. Your father, mother, and sister. Don't skimp on the details. Drop the attitude. Really dig in and make it worth my while. Can you do that?"

I consider for a minute. "I think so."

"You *think* so?"

"Yes. I can. But what's so important about them?"

"Your family?"

"Right."

"You're asking me what's so important about your family?"

"Right."

She shakes her head. "Well, that's exactly what we're going to find out, Ritchie, aren't we? At least if you tell it the right way."

48

The summer before Beth died, Dad Sudden comes home in his brown suit carrying the remnants of a bag lunch. He loosens his tie and turns off the television. His lips are shiny. His forehead is shiny.

"I have a surprise."

No one cares. My mother does not care.

"We're going on a trip."

I'm on the carpet, knocking out chemistry homework. Beth cradles her phone as if she were preparing to nurse it.

"What for?"

"It's time we acted like a family, that's what for," Dad Sudden says. Except it's not true. We're going on a trip because Dr. Harvey recommended it. Dr. Harvey sits in a chair while Mom tells him stuff.

"We all know things have been a little rough lately."

We did all know that. Beth coming home late, gone all weekend, silent and bitchy. Me locking my door, cranking tunes, refusing to answer when Mom knocks before bed, wanting to give me a hug with the arm that's not carrying a pile of folded laundry.

"So, anyway, I already bought the tickets."

"Oh, god," Mom says. "Where?"

"The Bahamas."

"Are you sure we can afford it?"

Dad Sudden gives me a wink. "We can afford it."

For some reason I sweat balls going through customs, like they're gonna find the forged Cézanne or weaponized anthrax I'd forgotten about in the bottom of my bag. But the Bahamian police, in their blue shorts and pith helmets, ignore us, white and pasty and colorfully clothed. They wave us through. I'm annoyed I don't rate more concern.

Beth and I share a room.

While we're unpacking, she runs through two quick cigarettes. I test the curtains, flush the toilet. She finds the hotel postcards and sits at the little desk.

"We've only been here an hour; what's there to tell?"

She doesn't answer. I get up and check the pay-fridge. There're two Beck's cans, three bags of cashews, chips, a Toblerone.

"Want a cashew?"

"No."

Beth writes one long sentence that starts in the middle of the card while slowly turning it, a spiral of words that snakes to the border. It's clever and stupid at the same time.

"Don't forget to leave room for the stamp."

She stares at the card. She has not left room for the stamp.

"Why do you have to be all *up* in my *shit* all the time?" she yells, and then storms into the bathroom, slamming the door. Two seconds later she comes back out, grabs a handful of postcards, her pen, the beers, and then slams the door again.

We spend the next day around the pool. Beth and me at one end, near some frat boys in their twenties. She's flashing all the oiled leg she can muster. I have *Tropic of Cancer* on my lap, fairly sure I am the only one, maybe in the entire world, who truly understands this book. Mom and Dad Sudden settle near the Jacuzzi, talking with an older couple, a hairy guy all elbows and knees, the woman frail, blue, shivering in the heat.

"We're gonna end up having dinner with those people."

Beth holds up *Us* magazine so it blocks the sun from her eyes. Also my face. "Why do you care?"

"I don't. It's just an observation."

She puts one finger in her ear. "Could you please not talk anymore?"

"I can't believe I bothered to begin with."

Beth holds her nose with two fingers. "Could you please maybe brush your teeth once in a while?"

Mom walks over, wearing a towel around her waist and a big woven sun hat that has BAHAMAS in purple cursive.

"Hi, guys. What do you want for dinner?"

"Don't know," we say in unison.

"Isn't the water great? It's so refreshing. I could swim in it forever."

"Yup."

"Can I get you anything from the room?"

"Nope."

"Well, okay."

"Okay."

She finally leaves.

"Did they *see*?" Beth hisses. I look over. The frat boys are busy yanking down one another's board shorts and ordering pitchers of crayon-colored vodka.

"I doubt it."

"If anyone asks, we can say Mom and Dad are a couple we met on the plane."

I raise an eyebrow.

"I'm twenty-five and you're twenty-three. The story is we're cousins who just happen to enjoy traveling together."

"That's the story?"

She eyeballs me over the top of her Wayfarers, a streak of white Banana Boat across her nose she forgot to rub in.

"Is there a problem?"

"No. It's just that one cousin seems to enjoy it a whole lot more than the other."

That night we eat with the old couple. Dad Sudden orders a third rum, his remaining hair sticking up in chlorinated tufts. Mom winks at me, bragging about how last summer I played third base on this team you didn't even have to try out for to join. Then Beth takes the reins, talking a bunch of giddy shit about cars, boys, and classes.

The old couple yawns in tandem.

"Yup, she's a pistol," Dad Sudden says, looking at me through rum goggles. "But at least she's not vegetarian."

I announced I no longer ate meat six months ago, making pompous statements about animal cruelty and evil farming practices, avoiding all stocks and tallows. I'm not sure why I have become so adamant. In truth, I don't really care. In a year I'll drop the whole thing and start in on bacon again, but I don't know that now.

"What are you going to order, honey?" Mom asks. "They have fish. Can you eat fish?"

"Fish is meat."

Dad Sudden scoffs, spearing a cherry from his drink. It falls off the stem and cartwheels down his white guayabera, leaving juice spattered across the front.

"Goddammit."

The old couple excuse themselves as the waiter rushes over, trying to clean it with a handful of paper napkins, just making it worse.

Beth starts to laugh. Mom starts to laugh. I start to laugh.

And for half a second it almost feels like we're a family, until that second is over.

The taxi tour begins at eight. It's an ancient pink DeSoto, pictures of smiling customers taped to the dash and seat backs and roof liner. They are uniformly smiling, sunburned, happy.

It's oppressive.

The driver, Livingstone, gives his tour spiel in a gentle, lilting patois. Dad Sudden's camera shutters everything it's told to.

We look at a few ruins, a few gun emplacements, a casino, and then stop at a deserted beach on the other side of the island. While my parents and Beth are swimming, I sit under a tree and watch the waves. My back presses against the layered bark, which hurts, so I press harder. After a while Livingstone gets out of the taxi and sits heavily beside me.

"Whas the mattah, young prince? You don' like ta swim?"

I shrug. "I just don't want to get wet and have to sit on my salty nuts for the next three hours."

He laughs. "Smart thinking. I prefer to stay dry meself."

My parents crawl out of the ocean, flopping onto their towels, shoulders red and raw and defenseless.

"How was it, my friends?" Livingstone calls.

"Beautiful," says Mom, in her clingy one-piece. There's sand in her long blond hair, which hangs in wet lanks. "I love it here."

"Whas not to love?"

"Plenty," I say under my breath.

"I know it," Livingstone tells me. "You think I want ta drive y'all around all day? But who it helps to say out loud?"

I eyeball him. "What, is that some kind of life lesson?"

"Yes," he says, and goes back to his cab.

We're almost at the hotel when the car banks into an awkward turn.

"Whoa there," Dad Sudden says, grabbing the dash.

Livingstone slows to a crawl, approaching an accident. A rented jeep filled with college kids has flipped over. A guy lies half under the hood, while two girls stand uncertainly on the tarmac. One of them is bleeding.

"Don't be lookin,' now, folks," Livingstone says.

Mom puts her hand over Beth's eyes. "Maybe we should stop?"

Livingstone doesn't answer, keeps driving, the sound of an ambulance in the distance.

"It's okay," Dad Sudden says. "Right? I mean, they're coming? The sirens?"

"That's right," Livingstone soothes, shifting into low. I look back. The guy under the hood seems to be staring at me. He's wearing a yellow tank top. His mouth is open. The taxi creeps around the final debris, broken glass spread over the tar so evenly it looks done on purpose.

I spend the last day by myself, down at the beach. There's a stable up in the hills. Ranch hands wearing old gym shorts and straw hats bring dozens of horses down to the empty strip and race them, weaving in elaborate patterns, hoof prints left in the sand like cursive. Afterward, they remove the rudimentary saddles and let the horses swim out, water churning, past the breakers. I am mesmerized by them, heads ratcheting through the surf, wet exhalations as they glide in a group. I begin to wonder if their noisemaking is not, in fact, some kind of language. *Turn left, turn right. I'm hungry. Man, is this water cold.* The horses spin around as a group, aim toward the beach. When they come in, the cowboys rub them down with old towels, roans and speckled grays steaming at dusk, corded with muscle, ignoring the whispers of their handlers.

It's nighttime before I make it back to the room. Mom pops her head in the door.

"Where have you been, honey? I was worried."

The cheap fluorescent light peeks around her cotton nightie, glowing through the material. I roll over.

"Beth? Are you awake, hon?"

Beth doesn't answer, either.

Mom closes the door.

The bedspread is bunched tightly around my feet.

I can feel Beth's eyes on my neck like ten-pound weights.

"I don't want to go home tomorrow," she says.

"I know," I say.

"The weird thing is, I don't want to stay here, either."

"I know," I say.

She reaches her hand across the bed. After a while, I hold it. We listen to each other breathe for the longest time, until I finally fall asleep.

49

I'm lifting weights beyond the three-point line. Curls, presses, more curls.

A kid I've never spoken to before rolls up. He's big, with freckles and a mullet. His name is Tench.

"Wassup, Sudden?"

"Not much."

"Gotta question for you."

"Shoot."

"You gonna back out?"

"Huh?"

"Undercard. Dayroom. Trying to figure out where to bet my bones."

"Oh. Right."

"Word is, you and B'los are boyfriends."

"Excuse me?"

"I bet on you, you refuse to fight, I still lose."

"Got it."

"So, are you?"

"What?"

Tench clenches his jaw. "Gonna fag out?"

I do one more set of curls, count seventeen-eighteen-nineteen, even though I'm really on seven-eight-nine.

"No."

"No, what?"

I dump the weights, just missing his toe.

"I'm fighting, okay?"

He smirks. "Now that's what I'm talkin' about! Feisty. Everyone figures white boy gonna fold. It's long odds on your skinny ass. You kick the Mexican piss out of that dude, I'm gonna clean up."

"Awesome," I say, and walk back across the court, hoping he's not following.

We're at the Pines, maybe fifty people, most of the soccer team still in their white shorts and cleats after a big win, someone springing for a keg. Fredtallica plays in a loop out the back of a car parked strategically below. Spence Proffer is pushing random people in the chest, spilling their beers. Three different girls tell me Spence told them to tell anyone who asks that he's looking for Elliot.

Three different dudes tell me that Spence told them to tell me that Hella is dead.

Fortunately, Elliot is home taking care of Lawrence. Or maybe in the backseat of a station wagon, taking care of Angie Proffer. Spence looks up at me like he can hear my thoughts, nods, grins, then knocks something out of a freshman's hand. The kid looks down glumly, says nothing, walks away. Spence picks up whatever it was and puts it in his pocket. I'm pretty sure if I weren't standing next to Young Joe Yung, he'd come over and put me in his pocket, too.

Lacy Duplais is here; she keeps trying to catch my eye.

I want her to and don't want her to.

Ravenna Woods is here; I keep trying to catch hers.

She wants me to, doesn't want me to.

Ravenna's standing next to the fire, fake-laughing at everything Kyle Litotes says. The party has barely started, and Saint Litotes is already half in the bag. He's got a big plastic quart of Royal Gate, pouring vodka in everyone's drinks, in people's beers, in people's sodas, everyone laughing, *Knock it off, Kyle!* Any other kid would have already gotten his ass kicked, but Clitotes is the golden boy. The soccer god. The dude who discovered the party at the very same time the party discovered him.

"That kid is a total wipe," Young Joe says. "Maybe I should have just let him choke."

I look over, surprised.

"Wow, dude. That's a very non-Joe statement."

He takes a sip of beer. "I guess sometimes I just feel like deep down I am an evil man, no matter what I claim or wear or shit-talk about, so why not let it all out? You know what I mean, Ritchie?"

I am fairly blown away, having always assumed a guy like Joe Yung comes by his positivity with zero effort, that his smiles cost him nothing. That maybe it's even genetic. I can see now how wrong I was. Some people actually put a lot of effort into restraining themselves. Or at least their worst selves. I should probably try it sometime.

"Young Joe, do I ever."

He nods. "The path toward righteousness is a long and difficult one."

"Agreed."

"But there's nothing says a righteous man can't pull off a harmless prank now and again, is there?"

"I guess."

Young Joe Yung's ever-present smile returns. "Follow my lead."

He walks into the middle of the party, winks, and then flops over like he's having a full-bore seizure.

A trio of girls scream.

"Holy shit," I say, and run over, make a big show of slapping his cheek and trying to revive him. Young Joe moans and groans, really hamming it up. I manage to drag him upright, one arm half around my shoulders, gripping the back of his belt and moving through the crowd. He's heavier than a mattress full of cement. He can't keep his balance. We spin around clumsily. Pissed looks are exchanged, but when people see it's Young Joe Yung, they tone down the complaints. He keeps veering unpredictably, sweat pouring off him in waves. The crowd parts like the Annoyed Sea, *Hey, hey, man, what the? Oh, wow, what's wrong? Be cool, dog. You okay, Joe Yung? Knock it off! Whoa!*

Young Joe has somehow manufactured mouth foam. His eyes roll back. He's speaking in tongues, in what sounds suspiciously like some kind of Dungeons & Dragons language. People are starting to freak. Joe finally spots his prey, takes two huge side steps, and logrolls Kyle Litotes. Litotes goes down with a yelp, face-first into wet leaves and pine needles, losing his vodka and staining his little soccer shorts. Joe rolls the other way and puts out half the fire with his neck. I bonk into Ravenna and, mother of god, does it feel good. My body is Silly Putty, absorbing the sense-memory of her skin. Lacy Duplais gives me a look. Joe blubbers more fake language, shit about orks and attack points, and then wipes out Litotes again, grinding him into the mud.

Some people laugh. Some give a fake cheer. Girls try to help Kyle up and keep slipping themselves. Six dudes help me carry Joe along the path, barking orders and being super responsible like they've been training as EMTs for years. We all finally stow him like a broken air conditioner in the backseat of the Saab.

"You want us to follow you, Sudden? Make sure Joe's okay?"

"Nah, fellas, I can handle it. But thanks for your help. You just might have saved a life tonight."

"Sure thing. Good luck."

I peel out and Young Joe sits up, gets in front.

"That," I say, "was hilarious."

He wipes his face. "I dunno. Actually, I don't think it was very funny after all."

"Are you *kidding*? You deserve an Oscar."

He wipes mud and leaves and squirrel shit into my upholstery. He wipes and wipes, and dirt just keeps coming off him.

"No, it was wrong. Even for Kyle Litotes. It was mean. I shouldn't have done it."

I nod. "It did kind of suck when those dudes all helped out. They were actually worried about you."

"I know," he says glumly. "But by then it was too late to stop."

Young Joe Yung is something I have never seen him before: way bummed.

I head over to Scumbies and treat us to veggie micro-burritos and coconut waters. We sit on the curb, chewing, as car after car pulls up.

"I keep being the person I always swear I will never be again," Young Joe says, mouth full.

"I know exactly how you feel."

He picks a bean off my pants and eats it. "You do?"

"You have no idea."

In the morning my phone goes off like a bomb. The ringtone is the Misfits, Glenn Danzig yelling, *"There are paint smears on everything I own, the vapor rub is lying on a table of filth!"* Pure poetry. Three times. I pull myself out of bed and flip the thing open.

"Who is this?"

She waits a minute. "Lacy."

"Lacy who?"

"Lacy fuck you, that's who."

"Oh, hi."

"Anyway. Are you listening?"

"Listening to what?"

"Kyle Litotes wrecked last night."

"Litotes got wrecked? Big surprise."

"No. His car did. Totaled it."

"Wait, are you serious?"

"He and a bunch of soccer heads were drinking beers out at the Pines."

"Yeah, I know. I was there, remember? You know I was there."

"Yeah," she says. "And then, when they decided to take off,

I guess he got tired waiting in line for everyone to take that left back onto Route Six, so he got cute and tried to gun it past them and lost control and slammed into a Dumpster."

"He's dead?"

"I guess he's alive, but everyone says he's messed up bad."

I put my head down on the counter. My whole body trembles. Behind my eyes, cars crash, whole lines of them, one after another.

Pure impact.

"Are you there?"

"Yeah, I'm here."

There's a long pause.

"We haven't, I dunno, talked for a while?" she says.

"I know."

"Are you mad?"

"Me? Why would I be mad?"

"So that's it, huh?"

"What?"

"How this works."

"How what works?"

Lacy hangs up.

Two minutes later she calls back.

"Everyone's going to the hospital at noon."

I picture the flowers and the solemn handshakes. I picture all the people crying, or making themselves cry because they feel empty inside, and then being hugged by moms and aunts and whispering Kyle's name whether they liked him or not, everyone staying stronger and more positive than everyone else.

212

Accident etiquette.

Grief 101.

There's no way.

I just can't do it again.

"So I was wondering," Lacy says, starting to choke up. "Would you at least bring me there?"

I should. I absolutely should. I'm a total jerk not to.

"Oh, man. I dunno."

"My dad won't let me drive anymore. At least for another five months. Besides, for some reason I just can't face going alone. Not today. Please?"

I let out a long stream of used air.

"I don't think so, Lacy."

"You don't *think* so?"

I'm about to explain when she hangs up again.

An hour later there's a knock at the door. I say a silent prayer to Wotan that it's not Rude.

It's not Rude.

"Kyle Litotes bought it last night."

It takes a minute to register that Spence Proffer and his neck are on my front stoop. He's enormous, all nostril, wearing jeans and a cut-off Molly Hatchet shirt and his stupid Italian horn necklace. His bulk is unnatural, like cinder blocks stuffed into a lawn bag. I wonder if it's possible he's smart enough to know where to get steroids, let alone what end to stick them in.

"He didn't buy it. I heard he was just messed up."

Proffer laughs. "Yeah, just screwing with you. He's only messed up."

"Only?"

"Only, like, permanent."

"What are you doing here, Spence?"

I wanted to call him *Proffer* but didn't have the balls to.

"I was at the hospital. With the whole rest of the school. Everyone crying on everyone else's shoulders. Noticed you weren't there. Thought to myself, that's weird, a big dramatic hospital scene and no Ritchie Sudden."

I know I should man up and toss him off my (mom's) lawn.

I gulp instead.

"So I figured I'd go see the king of sympathy. Have a little talk."

"A talk?"

"Actually, more like, hey, let's do some whippets. You got any?"

"No."

"Then let's go get some, son."

"I'm cash poor."

"You don't need cash for whippets, fag."

"I better not."

"C'mon," he says, smiling like a wolf.

A wolf with braces.

A wolf with braces that have things a wolf has recently eaten stuck in the metal loops.

I wonder for a second if I have the stones to shut the door in his face.

Turns out I don't.

He fires up the Mustang and leaves a patch forty yards long. We drive into town and take up two spaces diagonally in front of Scumbies.

Marshall Holt is at the register, this supermellow kid who graduated a bunch of years before us but still shows up at party spots to hang out by the fire. He's always wearing dark prescription glasses and a ponytail, chuckling genially and handing out free beers.

"Handsome Holt!" Proffer says.

Marshall looks at me like, *What's with the Odd Couple?* I shrug and follow Proffer down the aisle. There're two cans of Reddi-wip on the shelf. Proffer grabs both and pops the cap off the first, holding it at an angle and sucking in the nitrous. I can see his bell being rung, like a cartoon bear clobbered with a skillet, hippos in tutus dancing in circles around his head. He rubs his eyes and does it again, then hands it to me.

I bend the nozzle, which makes a little *pfft* sound, nothing coming out. "It's cashed," I say, trying not to sound too relieved. Proffer caps the second one, does the hit, and hands it over.

"I don't want it."

He slams it into my gut.

I press the valve and get half a rush. It's cheap and ugly, but for fifteen seconds blots everything else away.

"I'm calling the cops," Marshall Holt says.

"Go ahead." Proffer laughs, foam on his chin. "Just don't plan on ever going anywhere outside by yourself ever again,

215

okay, Marshall? I mean, go ahead and call them cops, but just don't plan on ever swinging by the Grove and trying to pick up on sophomores anymore, you fucking perv."

Marshall Holt puts down the phone. "You gotta pay for those Reddi-wips."

"Who says we aren't paying?"

Proffer kills off the second one. Some treadmill mom goes by and he tosses the spent can into her cart, then weaves back to the front and flings a handful of change at Marshall. "That about cover it, wuss? Or I still owe you tax?"

Marshall just blinks at us. There's an eyelash stuck to the inside of one of his lenses, magnified to the size of a slug.

Proffer grabs a can of lighter fluid and a steak, sticking them down his shirt, and walks out.

"C'mon, Sudden."

"Sorry, dude," I say to Marshall, then get in the passenger side. The Mustang roars to life. Spence guns across town, past the trailer park and the remaining farms, finally driving down a long dirt road. I have no idea where we are.

He grins through a mouthful of braces, neck flexing and unflexing on its own.

"You pork Ravenna yet?"

"Huh?"

He puts his hand on my thigh, not looking at the road. "Man, I see how she looks at you."

I knock his hand away. "Why the hell are you touching my leg?"

He puts his hand back where it was and squeezes. Hard. His fingers bore into muscle, through fascia, all the way down to bone. It's excruciating.

"Clowns like you always get whatever they want. Why you think that is?"

I don't answer.

"It's almost like you need someone to show you."

I don't answer.

"That you don't know how good you got it."

I don't answer.

He finally lets go and parks by a dirt path.

"C'mon."

I limp after him, mostly because I don't know what else to do.

He keeps spinning a KILL 'EM ALL AND LET GOD SORT 'EM OUT Zippo, then squeezes lighter fluid through the flame. It makes a mini flamethrower. He starts little fires here and there, aiming at trees and rocks and sometimes my sneakers.

"I'm going back."

"Pretty long walk home."

"I'll make it."

He steps off the path. "Check this out first."

There's a nest on the branch above us.

"Don't."

He squirts a jet of lighter fluid. The nest explodes into flames. A black bird rises up, screeching and flapping, then collapses to the ground, moving around some, but not for long. I turn to puke, but it comes out spit. Proffer tosses the empty can.

"That's all? I think I overpaid."

I stand there, waiting for whatever's next.

"So, listen, the other thing?"

"What other thing?"

"Reason I'm in the woods with your pathetic ass?"

"Oh."

"Your friend tried to bone my mom."

"Tried?"

"Tried."

"What friend?"

"Don't play stupid. She told me. And I'm going to take him apart. Chunk by chunk."

"He didn't. I don't think. I mean, it seems unlikely that—"

Proffer puts his finger over his lips, "Shhh," then pulls the steak from Scumbies from the back of his belt. The bloody juice has all leaked to the edge and is starting to drip through the plastic.

"I'm gonna go home and cook this bad boy up."

"Okay."

"You wanna come?"

His face is totally serious.

"Not today."

He shrugs and turns away, heading back up the path. I scoop some dirt over what's left of the bird. In a minute, the Mustang's huge engine roars. I walk back down the path. When I get to the lot, he's sitting in the car, waiting.

"Do me a favor, Sudden?"

"Uh, sure."

"You tell Hella that he is deader than fuck."

"I'll do that."

"Yeah, make sure you do."

Proffer slowly rolls the window back up, then peels away.

52

B'los and I step up to each other. We're surrounded by kids, but I can't see or hear any of them. There's no recognition in B'los's eyes. Like he's never seen me before. His pupils are black. I wonder if he stayed up all night like I did, thinking about this exact minute, or if he always knew he could just turn his brain off, go pure animal. Survive.

He pushes me in the chest. I push him back.

He feints, and I duck.

All the kids jeer and laugh.

He's fast. Faster than me.

He is going to beat me, and it pisses me off.

Not that it'll hurt.

Pain don't hurt.

Much.

What bothers me is how none of it seems to matter to him. The fact that I am not an asshole. That we are almost friends. The time in the library. He can still just plant his knuckles in my face, no problem at all.

I decide I am at least going to make him earn it.

But he has to hit me first.

If he swings, I am going to let loose.

Go feral.

If not, we can dance all night.

Peanut growls.

"Stop pussyfootin.'"

Conner laughs, throwing wads of paper down from his throne.

B'los closes in.

My fists feel like rocks.

Ready.

Part of me almost wants him to swing.

I stick out my chin, a dare.

Just as the circle parts and everyone fades toward the corners, pretending to be doing something else.

The counselors push through the crowd, carrying a DVD player and a stack of discs.

"Surprise movie night, and you assholes are fighting?" The Basilisk says.

"Aw, no one's fighting," Peanut drawls.

On cue, B'los puts his arm around me. I grin back.

"You guys girlfriends now?" Yunior asks, setting up the screen. Meatstick laughs.

"We were dancing," B'los says, busting out the Dougie.

"Showing each other moves," I say, busting out the Electric Slide.

"Whatever," Yunior says, pounding the remote.

"Y'all can thank Dr. Benway," Meatstick says. "She donated this gear."

No one says thanks.

Instead, they sit in a semicircle to watch. It's a movie about a huge St. Bernard named after a composer. It's the stupidest movie ever made. But it's a movie. Everyone laughs where they're supposed to, just because it feels good to laugh, even if it's not funny.

I can't believe Dr. Benway pulled it off.

I'm sitting there with a surge of love for her and her genius.

And then, right where the dog opens the washing machine with his mouth and tons of suds pour out, Peanut comes and sits next to me.

"How you doin', Sudden?" he whispers, all raspy in my ear. His breath smells like Doritos.

"Okay," I say.

"I know."

I can see The Basilisk watching us from the front, his arms crossed.

"Know what?"

"About you, son. And the lady doctor."

My body freezes. Solid.

"I didn't say shit."

Peanut leans in and smiles. I can't see it but I feel it.

"Did I say you did?"

"No."

"Then why you botherin' to deny it?"

Checkmate.

The dog farts. The dog barks. The dog saves a baby from falling down a well.

And then the credits roll and roll and roll.

Elliot rolls up on me, hard.

"Lacy Duplais can sing."

"Sure she can."

He's standing at my locker, nodding like a mynah.

"For serious. Chick comes up and goes, 'Hey, Elliot H, did you know that I sing?'"

"She called you Elliot H?"

"Says she's been in chorus for years. Says she wants to get with the band. Wise Young Foolio. I think it's a good idea."

"Uh-uh. No way."

"Dude, we need her, okay? Vocal-wise, you and me aren't cutting shit for mustard."

"Yeah, but I—"

"Yeah but you nothing. I already invited her. Gave her some lyrics to study."

"Just like that?"

"Just like that."

"I get no say?"

"Sure you do. Say yes."

"No."

"Have you seen her new red hair? It's wild. It's the perfect look. It's total album-cover action."

"Curtains don't match the drapes."

"Huh?"

"Nothing."

"Good, so it's settled."

"No, it isn't. It's completely unsettled. We only have two weeks left. There's no way she can learn all the songs by then."

"She thinks she can. Swears she's gonna live and die Wise Young Fool. Besides, we're practicing every day until go time. She doesn't work out, she doesn't work in."

"I can't believe this."

"To win Hollyrock you got to *be* Hollyrock, homes. Everyone loves a cute girl singer, especially judges and producers. They particularly love someone can actually sing on key. And since we don't have a pound of coke to hand out as bribes, she's our next best bet."

"True," I admit. "But—"

He waves me off. "Bottom line, if Lacy's got real chops, I'll switch to bass. Then we got ourselves a full lineup."

My jaw ratchets down to the tile. "You're not playing guitar anymore?"

"I dig bass. But I had to wait until you figured your way out of the maze. And man, you so have."

"What are you saying?"

"What I'm saying is that you fucking shred now, Ritchie. Haven't you heard yourself the last few practices? You play better leads than me. All that making out with The Paul? For once blood, sweat, and tears pays off for the lower classes."

It's the first time Elliot has ever complimented my guitar playing. In any way, shape, or form. Usually he just frowns and makes a face like he's about to pass a kidney stone.

"Thanks."

Five Things Our Band Needs (to win Rock Scene 2013):
1. ~~A name~~
2. ~~A drummer~~
3. ~~A singer~~
4. A different singer.
5. Not Lacy, Not Duplais

"Good. So it's you on guitar, me bass, Chowus Bongo Boy. We trade harmony, while Lacy overrides us both."

"Or rides one of us."

"Huh?"

"Nothing."

"Cowboy the fuck up, Sudden. We are about to take the next step."

"Into what?"

"Not into. Away from."

"Away from what?"

He holds out his arms like he's about to embrace all of Sackville. Or maybe the world.

"Saturday. The Black Widow's. Be early."

Ravenna Woods bobbles over as soon as Elliot is out of sight. She's wearing a tight black stretch dress. Every part of her is lovingly supported by every other part of her. I go to swallow, get it on the second try.

"Hey."

"Hey."

"I been thinking."

"About what?"

"You."

I fix my hair with one hand.

"Me?"

"How maybe we should hang out some."

I decide that if I wake up and this is a dream, I am totally going to stab my mind.

"Um, okay."

"Don't sound so excited."

"I am. I'm not. When?"

"How about Saturday? How about the lake?"

"I got practice Saturday."

She straightens her back and sort of shimmies with annoyance. It's like being slapped in the jaw with a sock full of dimes.

But her frown is what's really electric.

It takes in the world. And spits it back out. It knows exactly what's wrong with all of us. And just doesn't care.

"Practice what? Loser practice?"

"Ha. No, really. My band."

"What band?"

"I told you about us."

"You did?"

"Maybe not."

"So what? Just cancel it."

"Cancel it?"

"Cancel it," she says.

I'm listening. I'm actually listening.

My phone buzzes. *Buh-ringgg.* It's H.R. going, "*We will not do what you say or do what you want! No more!*" Three times.

"Hello?"

"Ritchie?"

Why did I answer, why did I answer, why did I answer?

"Hey, Lacy."

"You're pissed, aren't you? About the band."

"Getting right down to it, huh?"

"Would you rather play more games first?"

"No," I say. "And I'm not pissed."

"Liar. The question is, are you too cool to admit it, or too cool to care?"

"You mean about how you went behind my back?"

"Actually, I went over your head."

I press the phone against my cheek until I'm positive it's left a waffle pattern deep in the skin.

"Is this revenge for me not taking you to the hospital?"

"Are you kidding?"

"No, I'm bored. Can I go now?"

She laughs. "I still can't believe I fell for the whole Ritchie Sudden act. The sensitive loner. The angry poet."

"Fell for? Did I hang around *your* locker? Come to *your* house? Take off *your* pants?"

"I gave you my virginity, idiot!"

"And I gave you mine!"

There's a long pause.

"Wait, you did?"

"Um, maybe," I say. "Possibly not."

"Hey, you can't take it back now."

"I'm not. I didn't."

"But what about Beth's friend? Star Petrosky and her black tights?"

"That was nothing."

"Which means it was totally something."

"What business is it of yours?"

It's quiet for a while. She sighs.

"Listen, you're right that I pushed way harder than you did, okay? So I don't know what I expected or what I deserve."

"Exactly."

"But this isn't some ploy. I just want to sing. So when Elliot asked—"

"Wait. He said you asked him."

"Yeah, right. It would never occur to me that I could get between you two for a second, let alone a song."

"Does he know?"

"Know what?"

"What do you think? Us."

"Of course not."

"Good."

"I mean, you didn't...tell anyone, either, did you?"

"Like get drunk at the Beak and toss your name around? Brag about what a sex machine I am?"

"Okay, okay, sorry. That's not you."

"The bragging part or the sex-machine part?"

"Ha. The drunk part, I guess."

"Gee, thanks."

"So I'm coming on Saturday. Is it a problem or no?"

"I haven't decided yet."

"What does that mean?"

"It means I need a favor. You want in Wise Young Fool, you got to pay your dues."

"Are you serious?"

"Dead."

"Fine. What?"

I explain what I have in mind.

"Why don't you get Elliot to do it?"

"I can't."

"Why not?"

"I just can't."

"I don't know, Ritchie."

"It's a prank, Lacy. We get caught, it's detention at worst. You have to trust me. Do you trust me?"

"Not at all."

"But are you going to help me?"

There's a ticking on the line.

"I guess."

"I could kiss you, Lacy Duplais."

"You're an asshole, Ritchie Sudden."

"Well, even an asshole needs an assholette, so your timing is perfect."

"Whatever."

"I'll pick you up in the morning. Just don't wear anything black."

She doesn't answer.

"So are we friends again?"

"We were never friends."

"True."

"But I suppose I can put abjectly hating you on hiatus for a while."

"I'll take it," I say. "Just be ready when I swing by."

She is. We get to school even earlier than expected, sneaking down the hallway for a peek in the teachers' lounge. A bunch of them are having breakfast. Mr. Hmung and Vice Principal Paste and Miss Menepausse scoop up instant eggs. Dice is by the watercooler, trying to charm the new art teacher, who looks like a heavier, cross-eyed Susan Sarandon. She's laughing at his dumb joke. He's leaning closer and touching her wrist. Menepausse rolls her eyes and says something to Paste under her breath. He lets out a nasty little laugh.

"It's perfect," Lacy whispers, and she's right. Dice is fully occupied, practically bungee jumping down Sarandon's shirt.

We sneak into his classroom. I use bolt cutters duct-taped along my leg to snip the Master Locks. They open like butter. Then I use a mini pry bar on the spot welds. They pop like margarine. We yank all the components, pulling wires rudely from the wall, and hump them into the storage closet in the back of the room. I arrange them into a neat pile. Lacy slips a perfumed note from her pocket and lays it on top. She dials up a tube of Fiery Furnace and makes a lipstick kiss at the bottom. We sneak back out and tiptoe down to the boys' room at the end of the hall, changing into Chaos's brother Carlton's leathers. Carlton apparently races motorcycles in France or something equally impossible and exotic. I borrowed a pair for each of us, head-to-toe black, boots and gloves and two helmets with smoked visors. Lacy looks like a tough, if petite, dude. Ten minutes later, when the halls are full and Dice is in front of his classroom making jokes and spreading charm, we bust out of the bathroom and run full-speed through the crowd, yelling, "Look out! Look out!" while holding empty cardboard boxes. It clears a path the entire length of the hall. Kids watch us, mystified, and shy away, but no one seems too worried. Lacy and I bang out the rear doors and then curl around the side of the building instead of toward the parking lot. We yank off the leathers and dump them in the woods and then sprint back around front. Now I'm wearing khakis and a nice shirt. Lacy is in a pink dress. People are still buzzing about the two guys who just stormed through.

"Hey, did you see those dudes in leather?" I ask as we walk in.

Lacy's like, "Whoa! What the heck was that all about?"

There's a rising buzz of confusion and gossip.

Dice calms and shushes, telling people everything's okay, just go to class, no need to get wound up.

"Any idea who they were?" I ask.

"Nah," a few people say. "We were just wondering ourselves."

Lacy nods, and then says really loudly, "Well, whoever they were, I just saw them out in the parking lot loading a ton of stereo equipment into this jacked-up truck."

Dice turns white, zipping to his room in a panic. Two seconds later there's a torrent of swearing. Everyone packs in behind him, standing around the Teaching Tower, which leans to one side, looted, empty. It looks like Charlie Brown's Christmas tree.

Dice starts yelling. "Call the cops! Call the cops!" Then takes off in his squeaky loafers. Half the school follows, everyone pouring out the back door. Amazingly, there are no dudes in black leather in the parking lot. There is no jacked-up truck. There are no stolen components. Just a quiet, sunny day.

People start laughing and making jokes, punching one another's shoulders.

"Wow, man, looks like they got away."

"I can't believe someone just jacked Snake Eyes! Took him off clean!"

"Hey, Dice, you current with your insurance premiums?"

The look on Mr. Isley's face is beyond severe. It's molten. It's bloodless. He has zero pigment, eyes slit in fury. You can see chest flexing through his dress shirt.

235

"That's really a shame," I say, with utter sincerity. "Hey, guys, give Dice a break; that totally sucks."

"Shut up, Sudden."

"How'd you like to have *your* gear thefted?" I ask.

"Brownnoser."

Twenty minutes later, every cop in Sackville has the school on lockdown. They tape off the crime scene, and in a move of sheer genius, lift fingerprints from desks that already have fingerprints from every kid who graduated in the past ten years. Dice is sitting on a chair in the middle of it all, head in his hands, nodding while some detective who looks like he was born in wing tips and a trench coat jots in a little notebook. Lacy and I try not to look at each other as the rest of the teachers herd everyone back to class. An hour later, we're in the middle of *Computers Are Our Future*, when there's a round of yelling.

"I don't believe this!"

Some uniform finally got the bright idea of opening the closet door.

The note Lacy left taped to the equipment said, HA HA! GOTCHA! LOVE, MISS M.

An announcement roars over the loudspeaker. "Miss Menepausse, report to Mr. Isley's room, please. Miss Menepausse? Can we see you a minute, please? Right now."

Ten minutes later there's crying all the way down the hall. Denials are answered by barking questions. Every kid in school giggles while Dice and Miss Menepausse are escorted to Vice Principal Paste's office by two cops, the word *lawyer* dropped

like a cold meatball every third step. They send Dice's class to study hall, everyone in it letting loose a cheer. Which, conveniently, leaves the door to Dice's room open.

I look at Lacy and wink.

While she stands watch, I sneak in and lower the preamp, the speakers, the compressor, and the mixer out the window. When she signals, we zip around the building, grab the components, and put them in the woods next to the leathers. Then we just play it cool the rest of the day, go to lunch and our other classes, making sure a few teachers see us leave empty-handed.

That night, I pick Lacy up again. We cruise by school, which is totally empty, not a single car in the lot. It's a cakewalk to load the stuff in.

Safely across town, I pull behind Scumbies.

"That was crazy," she says. "I was scared shitless."

"I know."

"And then the look on Dice's face?"

"I know."

"Pretty freaking awesome."

"That's life as a rock star, babe. That's what it's like being onstage, the adrenaline, the roar of the crowd."

"When have you ever been onstage?"

"Well, technically never. But I spend a lot of time rocking out in front of my mom's mirror."

She laughs.

I lean over to kiss her.

I have no idea why.

Giddy with the rush of the perfect crime, I guess.

Or just wanting her to know that I'm glad we're cool.

Bad move.

Lacy turns her head and leans away, making a face.

I lay one on her cheek to avoid feeling like a complete douche.

"You were fabulous," I say, trying to cover. "You are now so part of the team."

Her eyes narrow.

"I earned my stripes, huh?"

"Totally."

"Well, I guess it was easier than spreading my legs again."

"Ouch!" Ghost Beth says from the backseat.

I look out the window. Some kids walk from Scumbies with

four cans of whipped cream. Two guys walk out with a case of beer. Three girls walk out with micro-burritos. It's weird how you never see anyone walking in.

"Yeah, and also?" Lacy says, as the mixer and compressor glint in the neon light. "Hilarious as that was? I thought you said this prank wasn't going to be illegal."

"I guess I lied," I say, thinking that Eyelied, She Lied would be the perfect name for a really shitty emo band.

56

"I didn't tell the whole truth," I say.

"Exactly what percentage of it did you tell?"

"Well, B'los and I weren't dancing; we just said that so we wouldn't get busted."

"I see," Dr. Benway says. I can tell she doesn't believe me. The counselors reported back. Everything in the dayroom was fine.

No problem. No fights.

Instead of rejoicing, it seems clear that she now thinks, officially and clinically, that I am full of shit.

"I mean, the movie deal? That was genius. Especially one as boring as *Beethoven*. Took the steam out of everybody. But somehow they know I told you. Or at least Peanut does."

"And how could he know that?"

"You must have said something to Yunior. Or The Basilisk."

"Sounds very complicated. And conspiratorial."

"Exactly."

"I promise you I didn't say a word."

One thing I've learned in life is that you should never try to convince anyone of anything. They're either with you or not. They believe you or not. After that, you're just digging a hole.

"You think I'm a total Bueller, don't you?"

"You are referring to Ferris, I take it?"

"No, Ted Bueller. Of course Ferris."

"What about him?"

"Like I made it all up. Undercard. The bouts."

She shrugs. "Maybe."

"Yeah, okay. And my bruises? Self-inflicted?"

"Maybe."

"Do you really think I'm that nuts?"

"No one knows what anyone else is capable of."

"Ah, yes. The central tenet of incarceration."

She raises an eyebrow. Either impressed, or her eyebrow itches.

"Well, I'm not."

"Not what?"

"Crazy."

"Good."

"All the voices in my head say so."

"You hear voices?"

"No, usually just a laugh track. My head can't afford a live studio audience."

Dr. Benway has food on her desk. What's left of her lunch. After she takes about a million notes and adds half a ream of paper to my file, she points her pen at it.

"Do you want some?"

I don't want her pity.
I don't want her handouts.
I don't want to touch anything of hers.
"I'm not hungry," I say.
And then wolf the entire thing down.

"It's tacos. Why don't you come on down and stuff your gullet?"

It's the second time Looper has knocked on my door tonight.

"I'm not hungry."

"Tacos," she says again, as if the allure were self-evident.

I turn off Talking Heads's *Fear of Music*. It's their only album I really dig. Musical disdain. Anti-chart. Anti-sales. Percussive as hell. Plain black cover. Not one iota of giving in to the forces of having to give a shit.

Looper pokes her square head in the door. "Smells in here."

I look around to make sure I haven't left a jerk-sock out. "Even if I knew what that meant, I have no response."

"You coming to dinner or what?"

"Is *I'm not hungry* suddenly Polish around here?"

"*Nyet.*"

"That's Russian. And why do you care? I'm sure you gals have private gal stuff to natter about."

Looper plays with her earring, lowering her voice. "Listen,

Ritchie. Your mom wants you at the table tonight. So why don't you pull your head out of your wise ass for a second and do something, just once, because she wants you to?"

I think about laughing. I think about slamming the door. I think about telling Looper to fuck the fuck off and mind her own business.

Then I get up and toss a shirt on, following her downstairs.

Mom's got the bowls all laid out: chopped tomatoes, ground chuck, grated American, iceberg, sour cream. Mexican food that not a single Mexican has ever eaten in their lives and wouldn't recognize as a taco if it were wearing a HI, MY NAME IS TACO! name tag. Mom's got makeup on. Looper's sporting new khakis. And possibly for the first time ever, lipstick.

"Oh, Ritchie, I'm so glad," Mom says.

We all sit down.

I fork a bunch of orange meat into the hard shell, which immediately gets soggy and splits down the middle. Looper grabs a pinch of tomato, a pinch of iceberg, and throws it on my plate. "Taco salad."

Mom laughs. Looper cracks a Stroh's and holds it up in a silent *cheers*. They're both sort of half grinning. They're either stoned or...

"What, you're getting married?"

"Nope." Looper laughs. "Still illegal in this state."

Mom doesn't laugh. "No."

"Thank god. I swear, you guys are freaking me out with the happy domestic routine."

"But there is something," Mom says.

I put down my fork. "There's always something."

"Ritchie, I don't know how to say this."

"So don't. Man, I should have known this wasn't just dinner."

Looper kicks me under the table.

Mom turns half a shade whiter than pale. "Well, the truth is, Looper and I..."

"What? Will you spill it already?"

"We've decided to try to—"

"Your mother and I are going to get pregnant," Looper says, raising her arms. "Woo-hoo!"

Mom turns red and glares at Looper, who shrugs.

"No way," I say. "You can't."

"Can't what?"

"Basic physiognomy? The, uh, total lack of dong?"

Mom turns purple. Looper looks like she wants to bury her fork in my neck.

"It's called artificial insemination, Ritchie. You ever heard of that?"

"Yeah."

"Well," Mom says. "I've seen a specialist. We've been going together. Amazingly, my eggs are very...healthy. I didn't want to say anything because, at my age and so forth, the success rate is not very high."

Looper squeezes Mom's hand. Mom raises Looper's hand to her mouth and kisses it.

"Are you serious? I mean, seriously, have you two thought this through?"

"Yes," Looper says. "Very much so."

"Um, okay, Mom," I say, my voice rising. "Let's just take things one step at a time. Assuming this wasn't an insane idea in the first place, given, you know, your previous success or relative lack thereof with the raising of children, excluding, of course, my own overall excellence and maturity, why would *you* be the one to carry it?"

"It?"

"Looper's ten years younger than you are. At least."

"I can't," Loop says.

"You can't, as in, *I have too many pools to clean* can't, or you won't, as in, *Think what that would it do to my figure.*"

Looper stares at her lap. "I'm not physically able."

"Oh."

I consider for a second acknowledging this fact. Maybe even being somewhat empathetic about it. But then don't.

"Well. Let's move on and envision a little mini Loop tearing around here, smashing into things and eating paint chips and juggling rusty knives. Who's gonna watch it?"

"Again with the 'it'?"

"Me, of course," Mom says, dabbing her lips.

"You? Like, *you* you, or a full-time, live-in nanny you?"

"Hey now," Looper says.

I try to contain the hysteria rising in my gullet, but it's not working. My cool is as gone as it's been in a very long time. I point at Mom. "But you're never here! You haven't been here in years!"

"That's not fair."

"Fine. So say you quit your job. Suddenly you're back housewifing. And this time you've got it dialed. What happens when she leaves? You really think Looper's in for the long haul?"

"Not cool," Looper says, more mildly than you'd figure. I jab her arm with an empty taco shell.

"Who exactly *is* this chick? Huh? She's not even a stepdad. A stepmom. She's just. You know. *Here.* I mean, is the Perfection Pools van parked in our garage for good?"

"When did being such a shit become so casual for you?" Mom asks, throwing down her napkin.

"I don't know. When did liking chicks get so easy for *you*? Remember Dad Sudden? All those years with a guy? What if you bun up, ready to knock out a kid, and then decide to switch teams again?"

Mom sighs. Her face is moist and streaky-red. She looks terrible. It's hard to figure what Looper sees in her. "I knew you wouldn't—"

"Wouldn't what? Understand? Like that's not a total cliché? Oh, it's just about me understanding or not, right? That's the real problem here? Me not being open-minded about your lifestyle? Okay, problem solved. My mind is now officially opened. I'm the alterna-kid poster boy. But, you know what? Me and my lifestyle never really got consulted, did we?"

I push my plate back. Grease lips off the edge and soaks into the tablecloth. I knock the chair over, get up, think for a second about the ridiculously dramatic scene I'm causing and how I could be so much cooler about the whole thing. About how maybe it's not so terrible after all. About how I'm sinking the dagger in less because I really care and more because for some reason being a judgmental dick is making me feel better, even though it should, by all rights, be making me feel much worse.

"Hey, you and Looper want to have Beth Two? Go ahead. Have Beth Two. Go through the whole thing all over again. Who gives a shit what I think?"

They're both staring at me, appalled.

It's weird.

I'm being appalling.

There is a certain logic to it. A certain pleasure.

It's also dirty. Sickening.

But, you know, in the end, I'm way too far in to stop.

So I cram an entire taco into my mouth, let the juice run down my chin, turn, and stomp up to my room.

It's quiet.

Really, really quiet.

I slam the door, lock it, and put on Agnostic Front, "Call to Arms." LOUD.

Vinnie Stigma lays down a vicious blast of rage.
And then he starts playing guitar.
I think about calling someone.
But I don't really have any friends.
Except El Hella.
And he doesn't count.

58

I'm in the library with B'los.

It's like nothing happened.

I don't say shit about the fight.

He doesn't say shit about the fight.

Might as well talk about breathing.

Someone donated a box of comics. The Basilisk confiscated all of them except one, saying they were too violent, even though twice I've seen him in his office with his feet up, flipping pages. The only one we were allowed to keep is some lame piece of crap called *The Adventures of Desktruktor-Bot and Manny Solo, Boy Mentor*. B'los takes it out of my hand, rips it into three pieces, then throws it in the garbage.

"There's a lot of junk goin' around. Peanut thinks you talked. Scuttled the bout. He and Conner are pissed. Might be they gonna make a run at your ass."

"I know."

"So did you?"

"What?"

"Talk?"

"No."

"You for sure?"

"Yes."

He stares at me, deciding. I don't bother trying to convince him.

"Either way, man. Nothin' I can do to help you out."

"I wasn't asking."

"Would if I could."

"I know."

He restocks a book.

"What you in here for anyway, Sudden?"

"Man, I killed someone."

"Get out."

"Offed his ass."

"For real?"

"Dude was asking for it."

"No shit?"

"Yeah shit. I'm just playing."

"Okay, though. Serious. What you in for?"

"The truth?"

"Yeah."

"The truth is, I don't really want to talk about it."

Looper wants to talk. I can tell. Mostly because she's sitting on the porch, Stroh's between her knees, waiting for me.

It's Saturday morning. I'm late for practice.

I put down my git case and lean against it. "What?"

"Was wondering if maybe you had a minute, bud."

"Don't call me bud."

"Okay, bud."

I stare at her. "I got practice."

"Practice'll hold, and you know it. Sit that fanny on down, huh?"

I'm tempted to turn and walk. But I like Loop, even if she is planning, through the nefarious miracle of modern chemistry and a lab geek with a fifty-thousand-dollar turkey baster, to knock my mom up.

"Tell you what, budette, you crack a Stroh's for me, you just bought yourself a Stroh's worth of talking time."

Looper reaches into her cooler, slid conveniently under the chair, and opens one, putting it on the little plastic table between us. I sit and pretend to take a sip.

"One."

"Yeah, yeah, and brush my teeth."

"Look," she says, and then bites her thumb. "Look, I don't even know where to start."

"Try the beginning."

She doesn't laugh.

"There's just no way for me to express some things to you, since I know exactly how you'll hear it, since I was sitting right where you are not too long ago. I mean, I know for damn sure I wasn't hearing anyone back then. So why should you be any different?"

"Come again?"

"Youth is wasted on the young, that routine. How you're doomed to make an ass of yourself until you're finally ready to listen up about a few things. But by then it's almost always too late."

"You got anything worth listening to, Loop?"

She nods. "Yes, I do."

"Will this listening entail descriptions of lesbo dorm sex by any chance? Hot girl-on-girl action?"

She sighs. "Doesn't it just bore you to tears to be such an unrelenting prick all the time?"

I think about it for a minute. "Yeah, actually."

"Okay." She grins and toasts, taking a swig. "Progress."

"Can you get to the point? I gotta roll."

She looks off into the backyard. "I played rugby in college. Don't know if I ever told you that."

"You did not, Loop. And I have to say, that's one of your best qualities."

"What is?"

"How you're never on and on about the glory days. No trophies around the house. No bragging about all the touchdowns you scored and cheerleaders you banged."

She laughs despite herself. "Yeah, well. Point of my mentioning rugby is to say how playing used to amp me up. Man, I loved hitting. I loved nailing someone at full speed."

"You do realize it's now entendre central around here, right?"

She ignores me. "Senior year, our first game, I'm so wound up I'm all over the locker room, kicking doors and stuff, positive I am gonna bust my hump downfield the first play and stick whoever catches the ball. Like peel back her scalp and plant her a foot deep in the turf."

I look at my watch. The one I'm not wearing.

"So it's raining. The field's a little sloppy. I unscrew my normal half-inch cleats and put on the one-inchers. This girl next to me, she's third string, freshman, doesn't even play. But she leans over and says, 'Hey, you're gonna blow out your knee if you wear those long cleats. The grass isn't wet enough.' I look at her like she's a moron. I say some dumb macho thing like *no guts no glory*. Then I go out there in my one-inchers, race downfield, make one cut, and BAM, there goes my knee."

"Ouch."

"Yeah, ouch. Full reconstruction. Never played again. Still hurts if I don't sit right."

There's a deer on our lawn. It's eating a shrub. Looper throws half a beer at it, missing by about twenty yards. The deer stares at us and keeps chewing.

"Point is, I've spent my whole life wondering why I didn't listen to that scrub. Why was I so arrogant I couldn't see she was right? Girl's probably a doctor or on a TV show or something now. But me and my about-to-be-thrashed knee knew better."

"Because if you did listen, you would have made the big tackle, impressed some scouts, and then turned pro?"

"Hilarious. But no. Because if I didn't spend two years having surgeries and rehab and Vicodin breakfasts, maybe I would have, you know, left town. Maybe not gone somewhere better in the long run, but somewhere different at least."

"I get where you're coming from, Loop. Seriously. Okay? Listening is a good thing. Certainty is foolish. Can I go now?"

"See, man, you mouth the words, but it's just the same old Ritchie act."

"What act would that be?"

"Tough kid dealt a tough hand. The young cynic. It's a con. You know it and I know it. And the reason I know is, I was exactly the same. Man, being eighteen, it's like being in a cave. You can't see outside yourself. And then, five years later, you're five years older with nothing to show but the attitude you leaned on so hard, and how it was all bullshit."

I start to wonder just how drunk Looper is.

"Uh-huh."

"Yeah, uh-huh. I guarantee in five years you're gonna have a crappy job and a crappy apartment, lying in bed while that cute little Lacy's snoring next to you."

"Snoring?"

"You'll owe on the rent, and the fridge will be empty, and you're gonna think to yourself, why didn't I tell my mom I loved her? Why did I have my head so far up my butt that I thought I was the only one carrying the water on how Beth died?"

I squeeze the beer can, spilling it across my lap and the floor.

"You don't even know me, okay? So where do you get off telling me you know anything about Beth?"

"Yeah, Ritchie, I do know you. I know you so well it hurts. I *was* you. And now I'm someone different. 'Cause I took the time to learn a few things. Or was made to learn them."

"Oh my god. Do you hear what's coming out of your mouth?"

Looper's eyes flare. And then she sighs.

"Yeah, I know. This speech, it's strictly from a movie. I mean, not what I'm saying, but that I'm trying to say it to you at all. It's hopeless."

I laugh. "For such a knob, you're actually okay, Loop."

"I am far from okay. And please don't call me Loop."

I stand, grabbing The Paul.

"Your mom's having a tough time, Ritchie. The fact that you act like she's a ghost isn't helping a whole lot. You're angry, sure. Maybe every inch of it is justified. I'm not saying you got to hold her hand and go shopping together. But maybe cut her a little slack. She's trying, just like everyone else."

"Listen to the pool lady full of advice," I say. "Like she's Donna Trump and not drinking away another Saturday morning. You got any other gems you want to lay on me before I go?"

"See now?" Looper says. "That's exactly what I...That's such a front I can't even start to be mad about it."

"*You* can't start to be mad?"

"You're such a hard case. Such a badass."

"Thanks for the beer, Loop."

"You can go fuck yourself, Ritchie. I'll be expecting a letter from you. Five years from now. When you apologize and tell me you remember this conversation and appreciate what I tried to lay on you."

"Yeah, but how will I know where to send it? You'll be three moms away by then, shacked up with someone else's vulnerable waitress."

Looper stands and grabs me by the wrist. She's ridiculously strong. She yanks me toward her and then shoves me back into the wall. These stupid little paintings of boats that Dad Sudden hung a million years ago crash around my feet.

"Ouch."

She does it again, this time harder.

It really hurts.

The last painting falls, breaking in the corner.

Looper raises her hand, and even midflinch I'm thinking, *She's actually pretty cute*. With her blue eyes and pixie haircut and stupid feather earring.

But she doesn't smack me.

She pulls me into her arms. And hugs me. Hard.

I just let it happen, my head on her shoulder.

I could cry.

She could cry.

Neither of us does.

Too much like out of a script.

After a minute, Looper sits back down, cracking a fresh one.

"Go to your practice, Rich-tard. And don't worry. No one has to know about it."

"Know about what?" I say, rubbing my head.

"About the fact that even total badasses need a hug every now and again."

60

I put the guitar in the back and fire up the Saab, taking a lei-
surely route, window down, whistling corny stuff like "When
the Saints Go Marching In" and "The Wreck of the Edmund
Fitzgerald." Around the corner from Elliot's, I stop whistling
and pull over. Through the trees, I can see them standing by
their cars. Lacy and El Hella laughing, set up and ready to go.
Chaos unloading his equipment. Half our songs aren't fully
arranged. Lacy doesn't know all the lyrics. There is no way,
absolutely none, that I can blow this practice off. The Saab hic-
cups. Chaos looks over and sees me. He waves. I put my forehead on the steering wheel, pound it a few times.

Go. Stay. Stay. Go.

"Hey, Ritchie!"

Do not, under any circumstances, drive away.

"Yo, Sudden!"

Pull the keys out of the ignition and toss them in the woods.

"Dude, we're waiting!"

I put the Saab in gear and leave a patch, speeding up before
I can change my mind. My cell immediately starts ringing.
Vrrring. I immediately start ignoring it. Which is hard, since

it's the New York Dolls going, *"That's when I'm a lonely Planet Boy, and I'm tryin', baby, for your love!"* Three times. Six times. Nine times. I can picture Elliot screaming into the phone on the other end. Throwing it against the side of the house, the thing smashing into fifty pieces of rage.

And it scares me.

But not nearly enough to turn around.

"Hey."

"Hey."

Ravenna is standing in her parents' driveway looking incredibly hot. She's got one of those white thigh-length baseball shirts on, the color and outline of her bikini nudging through, over little terry-cloth shorty shorts and sandals. Her hair dangles all the way down her back, glossy and black as a cliché about things that aren't really that black: night, kettle, Sabbath, ace of spades.

"Let's roll," I say.

She shakes her head. "You gotta meet my dad."

"I gotta what?"

"I'm not allowed to go unless you come in first."

"You're shitting me."

She just stares. Her bottom lip is insanely pouty.

After a while it becomes clear she is not shitting me.

"But look what I'm wearing," I say, looking down at what I'm wearing: khaki shorts, skull belt, ironic vintage Warrant "Cherry Pie" tour shirt with the sleeves cut off, no socks, and Israeli paratrooper boots.

"You look fine. You look great," Ravenna says, then hands me a pair of her brother's golf pants and a light blue Van Heusen button-down. "But put these on anyway."

The dress shirt has a little penguin over the heart.

"Fuck that," I say.

She leans over and kisses me, letting her tongue slip gently, like an advance scout, between my lips.

I kill the engine and suit up.

"Yes, sir, goodtameetcha, too."

We're on a porch out back, the kind that's screened off and has a bench swing and green AstroTurf carpet, no chance any fraction of outside might sneak in. Her dad is wearing green pants that match the patio furniture cushions. He has Ravenna's same pained, sarcastic expression etched into his jowly face. He has the same million-miles-away eyes hidden behind thick glasses. He and Ravenna are like the Chang and Eng of intimidation. Also, there are ducks everywhere. Wood, ceramic, plastic, stuffed. Ducks ducks ducks.

"You ever duck hunt?" he asks, and I'm not sure if he's kidding, the guy with a sly sense of humor maybe. But his stare does not waver. He's not kidding.

"No, sir, I have not."

"Huh," he says, nursing what looks like a Bloody Mary. It could be just tomato juice.

"But I do know a duck joke."

He raises one eyebrow. I start to sweat, wondering why in hell I just said that. Ravenna is now off in the kitchen with her mom, supposedly helping straighten up, but I know they're listening.

Her father pulls at the dark wiry hairs on his knuckles with his other hand. A magazine beside him is opened to an article about Iran—three pictures, three turbans, three beards.

"Let's hear the joke."

I clear my throat. Ravenna's mom brings me a glass of milk without asking. I take a sip and try not to grimace.

"Okay, so, uh, this duck waddles into a diner and eyeballs the menu. The specials are on the board, but the duck has lousy eyesight, and anyway, he can't read. The waitress finishes serving a couple truckers, tops off some coffees, and finally walks over. The duck says, 'So what's good today?' The waitress looks back at the cook, puts her hands on her hips, smooths her apron, and says, 'Burgers are good. Potpie's not bad. I don't really recommend the meatloaf. But it hardly matters, does it, since *we don't serve duck here*."

He doesn't laugh, doesn't even crack a smile.

"Ravenna says you hope to study prelaw next fall?"

Ravenna zips into the room, puts some crackers on the table between us, bending over to give me a panorama of décolletage, and winks.

"Yes, sir."

"Where are you applying?"

"Uh."

"Pepperdine," Ravenna says, putting her hand lightly on my shoulder. The pants I'm wearing are a size too big. The shirt is buttoned haphazardly. I am beyond a fraud.

The fraud me nods.

Her dad nods back.

"California, eh?"

I am only 26 percent sure that Pepperdine is in California, but am 97 percent suspicious that it's a trap and I'm about to blow my cover.

"The Golden State," I say.

"Good school. I suppose."

"Thank you, sir."

"Taken your LSATs yet?"

"Next weekend, actually."

"You roll double seven hundreds like I did, getting accepted will be no problem."

"Exactly my thinking, sir."

He nods. The wife brings him another Bloody Mary. Insects buzz safely from the other side of the screen. We sit there for a half hour and he doesn't say a single other thing.

Just looking at me.

And then the ducks.

Me.

Ducks.

Me.

Ducks.

Me.

Siouxsie and the Banshees blare from the radio.

"Yuck," Ravenna says, making a face. She snaps the dial, yawns, and stretches, the wind blowing her hair in intoxicating waves. Inviting waves. Hypnotizing waves. Medusan waves. Wavy waves.

My phone rings again. I have fifty-three messages, all within the past half hour. I turn it off.

"That was brutal," I say.

"What?"

"Your dad. He so hated me."

"No, he liked you. Totally."

"Oh, that's good. 'Cause I liked him, too. Totally."

Ravenna frowns. I decide it's wise to change the subject to almost anything else. So I do.

The lake is empty, as usual. It's a state park, but there's no beach, just the water and about a mile hike over rough terrain to get to it, which keeps most of the picnickers away. I know a path that leads to this real secluded place in one of the coves.

It's a nice hike, sun, birds, dappled green. I hold Ravenna's hand, helping her over rocks and logs. She digs the chivalry. We get to the sheltered opening and just talk for a while, sitting in the sun on a huge boulder overlooking the water. Everything feels right. Calm and easy. She laughs at my jokes. I laugh at hers. She tells me she's always thought I was cute. I tell her I've always thought the same.

"You thought you were cute?"

"Ha. Yeah, I've had my eye on myself for a while now."

"What about Lacy?"

"What about her?"

Ravenna stretches coyly. "Isn't your girlfriend going to be angry that you're out here with me?"

"Lacy is most definitely not my girlfriend."

She nods with approval, then leans over. We kiss. Her mouth tastes like frozen strawberries. I nibble her lips. Soft and then sharp. It doesn't seem real.

Am I actually touching Ravenna Woods?

I am.

Am I actually groping Ravenna Woods?

I sort of am.

In fact it's almost like watching footage of some other lucky prick, except it's me. There's so much of her, I can't decide what to concentrate on. It's like those scenes in all the vampire books where the starving but humane vampire loses control, full of lust and blood and bloodlust, almost draining his willing human. After a while she laughs and gently slaps my face.

"Slow down, Speed Racer."

I try to hide my disappointment. I also try to hide the part of me pointing frantically toward magnetic north.

Ravenna steps away, toward the edge of the rock, and does a little dance, putting on a show. Not a stripper routine, but something slower and classier. Something French and cinematic. It seems vaguely illegal. Against science. Flouting natural law. She hums off-key, weirdly composed, totally un-self-conscious. Or maybe she just dances for guys a lot. Either way, it truly is a thing of mystery and wonder. I'm proud that I can step back and take a second to admire it dispassionately.

Especially when it ends with her slowly taking off her baseball shirt.

"Wow, awesome bikini," I say. The bikini is like a Band-Aid and two rubber bands, tiny, azure. I can see the almost-invisible downy hairs that run up her back and thighs.

"Who needs it?" she says, then winks, removing her top with a flick of the wrist. The totality of her is finally lo and thusly revealed unto me. It's like Christmas morning. Angels are playing trumpets and orchestras are blaring hosannas to the gloriousness and gorgiosity made flesh.

I'm staring.

I know she knows I'm staring.

She likes that I'm staring.

She knows that I know she likes that I'm staring.

"Are we gonna swim or what?" she asks, dipping a toe in the water. I figure it's not too smooth to pull off my shorts for a full-frontal, *Oh, won't you take me down to Crowbar City, where the grass is green and the girls are pretty*, so I sort of turn to the side, yank them down, zip by her, and dive in. It's the perfect temperature, clean, clear. Fish dart and curl, startled. I kick out and float on my back, breaking the surface like a periscope, my manhood dappled by a thousand eager wavelets.

I want to tie a flag on it and steam back into harbor.

"C'mon in."

"Don't rush me."

I wonder what it's like to have sex underwater. Movie-awesome? Or clumsy, mossy, and difficult? Ravenna stands

266

there, enjoying my scrutiny. She does a little sashay and then finally dives with a heavy splash, ripples concentric as I submerge beneath them. When I come up, expecting to see her head bobbing, it's not there. None of her is.

She's been under for a long time.

I swim back, call her name, treading water, rotted leaves between my toes.

"Ravenna?"

The water is calm. I shiver, confused, getting ready to yell, when I notice a flash of pink up in the foliage. I swim back in, clambering up the mossy rock with difficulty.

"Ravenna?"

She's behind a bush, crouched and turned away.

I pull the shrubbery aside, reassuring myself it's just some dumb joke. Like maybe she's going to leap up and ravish me standing. But she doesn't leap. She doesn't ravish. Instead she turns, holding herself. Bleeding.

"Hey, what the hell?"

The sharp planes of her face are screwed into a red, teary mess. The sarcasm is gone. The haughtiness is gone. All that's left is pain.

And it's strange, but in that look, the edges of her mouth turned down, anguished and alone, Ravenna is distilled into her perfect self. It's like she's made of glass; I can see clear through her and back. I can't believe I never noticed before. It's not the body or the face, the tortured slope of her shoulder that's the source of her allure. It's the acceptance that an elemental discomfort is the natural way of things.

"Hit the rocks diving," she mutters. "More shallow than I thought."

I look down.

Her nipples are badly scraped. The skin around them is torn and curled. Blood thinned with water runs down her stomach and into her bikini bottoms, beading there before continuing to her ankles. It's like the final scene of *Carrie*. I'm not sure if I should touch them or touch her. She stares at her feet, holding herself with crossed arms. I reach out and she pulls away, really crying now.

"Do you want some leaves?"

"Leaves?"

"Like, you know, as a bandage?"

"Oh my god."

"Or cold mud? To act as a...a..."

A crossword pops into my head. Twenty-three down. A nine-letter word for *soft, moist mass, typically of plant material or flour, applied to the body to relieve soreness and inflammation.*

"Poultice."

She grabs her shirt and starts down the trail. I realize I am still naked. My body seems particularly pale and lame. I yank on my shorts and catch up, holding her elbow and guiding her over rocks, listening to her little yelps of pain with each step. It takes forever, but I finally get her in the car, trying to make her comfortable.

"It's going to be okay."

"No, it really, really isn't."

I lean over to kiss her but she pulls away, showing me her cheek.

"What can I do?"

"Just get me out of here."

"You got it. Home or hospital?"

"Home."

"You sure you don't need, uh, stitches?"

The look she gives me could quarter a horse.

I jam the key in the ignition, crank it hard.

And then do it again.

And again.

The Saab won't start.

Ravenna puts her face in her hands and begins to sob.

"I'll deal with this," I say, then pop the hood and fiddle with some wires. I have zero clue what any of them do or are for, conjecturing as to their possible purpose or guilt. I push a couple knobs, yank a few belts, blow on battery terminals. The piece of shit still won't start.

HORROR.

I get out again and think about who I can call. Elliot?

HORROR.

Looper?

HORROR.

Lacy Duplais?

HORROR.

I finally decide, punching in some numbers.

"Yeah?"

I explain the situation.

"Is bad."

"Can you come?"

"I come."

Half an hour later, Rude pulls up in a decommissioned tow truck.

"Where the hell did you get that thing?"

He gets out in a black beret and leather cape, peeks in at Ravenna, and whistles.

"And so? Very nice."

"Uh, Rude?" I say. "She's bleeding, not deaf."

He puts the T-bar under the tires, then lifts the front end.

"You must ride in cab with me. Is illegal, sitting in car on tow bar."

I explain to Ravenna.

"No way. I'm not moving. Or riding *anywhere* with him."

I walk back over to Rude. "We're staying in the Saab."

He nods. "The domestic violence is very ugly thing, Ritchie."

"But I didn't—"

He holds up one hand, cutting me off. "I do not wish to hear. You ride in Saab, keep heads down. If cops are pulling us over, I am not covering for you. Okay, O.J.?"

Neither of us says a word for miles, facing at a forty-five degree angle like we're about to blast off. I check my phone. One hundred and seventeen messages. Ravenna also doesn't say a word when we pull into her parents' driveway, and she doesn't say a word as she slams the door, walking pigeon-toed into the garage.

I get in the cab with Rude, who is staring at Ravenna's ass.

"Very, very nice."

"So are you going to call Dad Sudden after you drop me off?" I ask. "Report in and tell him all about it?"

Rude jams it in reverse, gunning back into the street. The Saab whips around behind us like a can on a string.

"I do not call your father. I do not report."

"How come?"

Rude thinks for a minute, as if trying to decide the best way to translate.

"Today, I think, you are officially man. Is no longer his business."

61

I'm coming back from the library. Suddenly people in the hall-way are clearing out and making space. For a second I think it's for me. Then I realize Peanut and Conner are following behind.

"Hey, Mouth! You talking to anyone today?"

Ten feet behind.

"Yo, Mouth, you reach out and touch someone yet?"

Then five.

"You make a love connection?"

Then three.

"All that talking, you must be out of anytime minutes."

I keep walking, arms held across my chest, pigeon-toed in fear.

I don't turn around.

The worst thing you can do is turn around.

"Warriors," Peanut sings in his Georgian accent. "Come out and play-ay."

They follow me all the way around the side of the building.

"Warriors, come out and play-ay-ay."

I finally make it back to the units.

"Busy making friends?" Meatstick asks.

I stand next to him like we're leaning against the wall outside 7-Eleven.

"I have no friends."

"That's too bad. "

"Nah, it's easier. Cleaner."

He grunts. "Had myself a little date last night."

"Again? With who?"

He doesn't answer, just winks.

"The Meatman still gets around, huh?"

"You better believe he does."

We stand there with our hands in our pockets. Kids walk by, but none of them meet my eyes.

"Had enough of the stroll?" he asks.

"Yeah, I think it's time to hit the sack and watch a little cable."

He laughs, leading me to my box and slamming the door shut.

I lie on the bunk and try to sleep, while all down the hall, Peanut's voice echoes.

"Warriors, come out and play-ay-ay-ay."

62

Elliot is sitting on his couch, noodling on this old beater bass half-assedly. He runs through the Sly Stone tune "Stand!" and then plucks away at something I'm pretty sure is the Stooges's "Loose" but could just as easily be some new pussy John Mayer thing; you can never tell with the bass, especially one that's such a colossal piece of *merde*. Lawrence is in his chair, nodding to a phantom orchestra since the reel-to-reel has come to an end, spinning aimlessly, the leader making a tiny slap with each revolution.

The house smells like rice pudding and diapers.

"I got your messages," I say. "All of them."

Elliot won't even look up, practically speaking to his boot.

"Dude, you missed practice."

"I know."

"Chaos was there. Lacy was there."

"I know."

"Question is, where was your lame ass?"

"You wouldn't believe me if I told you."

He chuckles grimly. "Let me get this straight. Your play is gonna be to act like it's no big thing?"

"I'm not acting."

"You said you'd be there. You *promised* you'd be there. I mean, I guess what I'm wondering is, does your word stand for anything at all?"

I stare at his bald dome while he zips through this weird overtone scale, milking it for all its impending doom.

"I'm sorry."

"Do I give a fuck about your sorry? No. Does your sorry change anything? No."

"Sorry is as sorry does," Lawrence says from across the room.

Elliot finally looks up, eyes flat and angry. "So why'd you blow us off, Little Runaway?"

"It's sort of private."

"*Private!*" he says, turning like he's talking to an imaginary jury. "Everyone knows there're no secrets in a band!"

"Privacy is an unreasonable expectation in most circumstances," Lawrence agrees.

It's two against one.

So I take a deep breath and just tell them. All of it. From ducks to Rude.

When I'm done, Elliot sits there shaking his head. "You're *so* lying."

"Nope."

"You blew off practice to be with Ravenna Woods?"

"I did."

"For her."

"Yes."

"For that stuck-up wanna-Britney, fat-ass money-tease?"

"Her ass is so not fat. But yes."

Elliot stands and kicks a chair. It slams into the wall, leaving a chair-shaped outline in the Sheetrock.

"Uh-oh," Lawrence says.

"Listen, Hella Crazy," I say. "You're seriously starting to get all Charlie Manson about this. It was just one practice."

"Just one practice," he says softly.

"And, I mean, fine, it'd be great to win Rock Scene 2013. I definitely want that guitar. But, like, *so what* if we don't? It's a stupid contest by a stupid company with stupid bands. Okay? Get a handle."

Elliot sits down and puts his face in his palms. I think he's just trying to communicate, in a new and quiet way, how furious he is. Shaking with anger. Ready to explode. About to kick me in the neck, toss me into the wall.

And right then, right there, the whole world slides sideways, slowly changing color.

From sepia to all black to lily white and back.

Because Elliot Hella is crying.

"Are you seriously *crying*?"

He looks up, shrugs. His eyes are red. His bald dome is blotchy and flushed.

"No."

"You are. You totally are! What in the *hell* is going on around here?"

"Nothing."

"I thought you said no secrets. You just said zero secrets!"

He wipes his eyes. "Fine. I'm failing out of school, idiot."

"That's not good," Lawrence says.

"Oh."

I'm quiet for a second.

"Yeah, it's really terrible and all, but, um, wait, who gives a shit?"

Elliot nods. "About school? No one. So what? I'll graduate from the school of punk instead. I'll get a degree in mosh. But everyone else at Sack High is going off to college in a few months. Off to Paris for a year. Off to their hedge-fund internships and cooking schools and institutionalized learning facilities. Meanwhile, I'll be right here in Sacktown. Which, you know, is fine. As long as I'm here with my band."

"I hear you."

"My *full* band."

"Yeah, yeah."

Elliot leans in, all chin and bad breath.

"I don't just want to win, Ritchie. I *need* to win. Hell, I'm gonna be ladling pasta for the next four years. You think I don't know that?"

"So it's about the money."

"No, it's not about the money! Or even showing up Flog and Angelo. What I really want is..."

And you know what? It's amazing. Because even up to this point I have no idea what it is that my best friend really wants, no clue at all how he's gonna finish his sentence.

"...what I really want is that Hollyrock slot."

"Oh my god. Are you kidding me? *That's* why you've been such a hard-on the past two months?"

Elliot stands up, bald head bobbing over his enormous torso. "Yeah, why not?"

"Well, let's see. Because reality TV is beyond stupid? Because they only want the morons and pretty boys and guys with fourteen-pack abs? Because there is zero chance we could ever actually get cast?"

He shoves his hands in his pockets. "We could."

"You might as well catch a red-eye to Vegas and blow your wad on slots. You might as well join a cult and wear a robe and wait around for the Rapture. I mean, the odds are practically infinitesimal."

"Infinity is a disproven mathematical concept," Lawrence says.

"I know how far out it is, okay?" Elliot says quietly. "But it's something. It's a chance. You don't see any other chances hanging around, do you? Any life-changing piñatas ready for me to take a stick to?"

"No, but—"

"But nothing. So, yeah, it's embarrassing. I want to be a star. I admit it. A superstar. I want people to know who I am and have a special trailer and an assistant. A hot assistant. I want toys and lunch boxes and posters and a freaking action doll that looks exactly like me while not looking one iota like me."

"That's so not punk."

Elliot laughs. "*Punk's* not punk, you fan boy. Punk hasn't meant anything since 1977. Punk is just a word for angry losers to describe what they wish they were and what they're glad everyone else isn't, so they have something to feel special about."

I put my head in my hands. It's too much to process. It's like being told that the coolest person you've ever met in your life believes in the Easter bunny and voted for Mitt.

"So now the cards are on the table, Sudden. I need to know right here, right now. Are you in or not?"

Lawrence has fallen asleep again. The house seems even smaller and more worn than usual. Elliot stands there in his Clash shirt, brown eyes hard, stubble and squat legs and raw attitude and sweaty desperation.

"Yeah, I'm in. All practice, all the time."

"You sure?"

"I'm sure."

He nods, exhaling, genuinely relieved.

"Okay, enough Oprah. Let's play."

I pull out my guitar and start tuning it.

"Can I ask you one question, though?"

"Shoot."

"Ravenna really messed up her jugs, huh?"

I nod. "Bad, dude. Way bad."

He scratches his chin. "So, okay. Given the tragic wrecking of the Tit-tanic, you get a pass."

"A dispensation from the Pope. Cool."

"Good for one usage only."

"Yeah, yeah."

He plucks a few strings, starting to count off "Anarchy Is Panicky."

I follow with a wash of sheer noise.

And then right before he sings the first line, El Hella leans over and says, "I'm serious, though, Yoko. You sure as fuck better be at the next practice. Like, not even a single second late."

So it turns out that Kyle Litotes isn't going to be paralyzed. In fact, word is he's up and walking around, miracle this, miracle that. He's totally alive and functioning, the only downside being that apparently his head's not quite right. And from what I hear it's never going to be right again.

I call Lacy.

"Hey, it's me."

"I know," she says. "Don't even ask."

"Ask what?"

"I'm not doing any more pranks. Or should I say felonies?"

"I just want to talk."

"It's way too late for that, Charlie Rose."

"Will you stop with the tough-guy routine? I know you're mad, but we both know you're not *that* mad. Let's pretend a month went by and we had a big fight and said really mean things to each other and then made up and now everything's cool, if not a little tender around the edges. Because that's what's going to happen anyway. We might as well save us both the time."

At first she doesn't laugh, but then she does.

"Fine. So what do you want?"

"A truce. An understanding."

"What happens in Sackville stays in Sackville?"

"Exactly. We're two adults. We had a consensual moment. It's no one's fault."

"*Fault?*"

"Okay, okay. We each benefited equally from the charms of the other."

"That's slightly better."

"So we're cool?"

"Yeah, I guess."

"We're bandmates?"

"Sure looks like it."

"Has anyone ever told you, Lacy Dûplais, how hip and well adjusted you are?"

"They have now."

I clear my throat. "The thing is, it's not—"

"If you say, *it's not you it's me*, I'll scream."

"Don't scream."

"But since we're being all honest, Ritchie, why don't you just admit what's going on?"

"And I know what you're talking about because…"

"You're obsessed with Ravenna! You'd rather live in some fantasy, not just about who you want to be with, but who you *are*. And the reason I can't stay mad is it's been obvious all along. I'm the idiot for thinking you'd ever change."

HORROR.

"Speaking of change?"

"Yeah?

"The other reason I called is, I was wondering what's going on with Kyle Litotes."

"Why?"

"I was just...I dunno. Sort of worried about him."

"You? Worried about Kyle Litotes?"

"Yes. So will you tell me what's up, already?"

Lacy is friends with Brittany Lowe, who's friends with Aubrey Pike, whose cousin is Nia Wayne, who is besties with Tiffany Skip, who is Kyle Litotes's on-and-off girlfriend.

"Well, Brittany says Aubrey says Nia says that Tiffany says Kyle's so messed up you wouldn't believe."

"Oh, man."

"Yeah, Brittany's all on and on about how Tiffany says she goes to the hospital and he's there—it's Kyle, but it's not Kyle. He's like a little kid now. He talks slow and acts all innocent, except out of nowhere he'll grab her ass and be like, "Let's fuck," right in front of his mom and grandma, and then suddenly he's playing with a napkin for an hour like it's the most fascinating thing ever invented."

"Oh my god."

"I guess he spits and bites and picks his nose and has screaming tantrums. She says it's not him anymore, it's someone else, but what can she do, break up? I mean, that would make her the biggest bitch in Sackville history. But she says she cannot spend one more minute in that room watching his mother watch *Wheel of Fortune* while Kyle tries to feel her up behind a towel."

"Wow."

"I can barely stand retelling it," Lacy says. "Let alone if it were me."

"Let alone if you were Kyle."

"You know what, Ritchie?"

"What?

"I'm so on the verge of saying something supercheesy right now, like, 'Hey, we have no idea how lucky we are.' "

"But it's true," I say. "We totally have no idea."

The question is, do I mean it?

I run a quick internal diagnostic.

Turns out I do.

"Coming from a cynical prick like Ritchie Sudden? That really stands for something."

And with that, Lacy Duplais hangs up on my ass.

Ravenna Woods leans against my locker. Her sad face seems infinitely sadder than usual, the corner of her mouth turned down instead of up.

"My dad is making me transfer to Killington-Holloway."

She's wearing a yellow sweater. You can clearly see the thick square bandages where her nipples should be.

"He didn't really buy my explanation that I wiped out in field hockey. He's all, *Where's your sports bra, then? Did you scrape right through it?* And then all the way to the hospital he keeps repeating, *That's it.* I'm all bawling like, *What's it, Daddy?* but he wouldn't answer. I guess Killington-Holloway is what it is."

I want to hold her hand. I want to make her tea. I want to kiss behind her ear. I want to ask if her father has any plans to sue me.

"So how are they?"

She stares for maybe five minutes straight.

"*They?* You mean my freaking tits?"

"Yeah, sorry. I mean, you know, are you okay?"

"Did you not just hear me say that my dad is making me go to private school?"

"But that's sort of cool, right? Like, don't the Kennedys go to Killington?"

"Maybe a million years ago. Now it's all dictators' daughters and Russian mob kids."

"That's crazy. When?"

"I start Thursday. Today's my last day here."

I think how weird it will be not to have Ravenna around. What a grim, gray place school will become. And how it's pretty much entirely my fault. How from now on every guy at Sack High will hate me with a singular passion, the sort of hate usually reserved for ayatollahs and pedophiles and blink-182.

"We should throw you a bash."

Her face creases along its most sarcastic fault. "Wow. Yeah, thanks. How thoughtful. Hey, can it be a pool party? Or, even better, maybe down by the lake?"

"I'm really sorry."

Ravenna Woods looks at me from behind the severe blackness of her eyes.

"You know something? You really are."

That night Mom's actually home from a shift. She and Loop and I have mac and cheese with extra cheese.

"What's new at school?" Looper asks.

"You know. Fires. Explosions. A mild smallpox outbreak. Some trench-coat kids with guns and bombs. Also, a friend of mine is transferring to Killington-Holloway."

"Impressive," Mom says. "What's his name?"

"Ravenna."

"Ravenna?" Loop says, winking at me. "Sounds exotic."

Mom kicks Loop under the table.

"So anyway," I say, "I was just wondering, since she's going and all, just an idea, nothing set in stone, if maybe there's enough in the ol' Sudden bank account so maybe I can transfer to Killington-Holloway, too?"

Mom looks at Looper.

Looper looks at Mom.

Then they both start laughing. They lean back, holding their stomachs, and howl. They're laughing so hard I have to reach over to keep the platter of macaroni from wiping out onto the carpet.

After ten minutes they finally stop, dabbing at the corners of their eyes with napkins.

"So, I take it that's a no?"

Which sets them off all over again.

65

I wait for my turn at the pay phone.

His wife answers. The operator comes on, explains where the call is coming from, tells her it's collect.

The wife hangs up.

I try again.

It rings and rings and rings.

I try again.

Pick up. Put down. *Click*.

Dudes behind me start to jostle.

I try again.

This time Dad Sudden answers.

There's a pause, but he accepts the charges.

"Richard?"

"Father?"

He clears his throat, chuckling a little. "I was going to say 'Can I help you?' but I suppose I'll spare us both that lazy platitude."

Good old Dad Sudden. Using nineteen words when four will do.

"Actually, you can help me."

"I see."

"I'm in trouble."

"Again?"

"No, not again. In here."

"The facility."

"It's called juvie, Dad. Why pretty it up? At any rate, I'm still working off my sentence."

"What kind of trouble?"

"Well, there're these two kids. Essentially, they want to kill me."

"Murder-kill, Richard? Or blacken your eye?"

"This isn't boarding school, Dad."

"Yes, well. Which is it?"

"I'm not sure."

He sighs. "You've made your own bed on this one, haven't you?"

"If you're going to toss around the helpful clichés, I think I'd prefer 'Don't do the crime if you can't do the time.'"

A child yells in the background behind him.

A delinquent yells in the background behind me.

"Would you really like some advice?" he says.

"Yes."

"Go to the warden. Ask to get yourself transferred. It's called protective custody. It may mean a stretch in solitary, but if you can prove you're in danger, they most likely will be amenable to moving you there."

I rest my forehead against the cold metal of the phone. Dad Sudden has seen way too many Burt Reynolds movies.

"Yeah, running is one option, I guess, even if we had such a thing as a warden or solitary or anyone who's used the word *stretch* since they finished editing the last Dirty Harry movie. But to be honest? I'm starting to feel like it's the whole reason I'm in here to begin with. When I should have turned around and faced things, I ran."

"I'm sorry, but I don't know what that means."

"It means Beth."

His voice lowers. I can hear inklings of pain down in there, from maybe the only place he can't pretend is all boarded up.

"What about her?"

"About the night she died. About the party. There's stuff we've never talked about."

"So why bring it up now?"

"Because I've been sitting in here thinking. Which is about all you can do in a cage. Except when it's too loud to think at all. And so you just sit."

Some kids in line roll their eyes, sigh, waiting their turns.

"What will going over this again prove?"

"I'm not trying to *prove* anything, Dad. And we've never gone over it at all. That's the whole point. I'm just saying, the night I got arrested? It wasn't an accident. In fact, I did it on purpose."

"So what do you want me to do, Richard? Call a lawyer? Have them reinvestigate the incident based on a sudden burst of guilt from a young man who's finally taken a little time to consider something besides himself, mainly due to the fact that he's currently incarcerated?"

Unbelievable.

"No," I say. "I don't want you to call a lawyer. I just want you to act, for even one short second, over thousands of miles of fiber-optic wire, like you actually give a shit."

I can hear Dad Sudden's new wife in the background, talking. I can hear her bitchy voice, nag nag nag.

A child starts to cry again.

"I've got to go. My son is—"

"Yeah," I say. "You go take care of your son."

And then the prick hangs up.

We're halfway through "I Will Bequeath You All My Duplicity and More" when I fully and completely come to terms with the fact that Lacy Duplais is good. Now that she knows all the songs, she's really, really good. Her voice is hard and raw, a little like Rod Stewart's, but not abrasive. Eyes closed, playing to the packed bar of her mind, I can almost see a phantom audience sway, hanging on every word. She actually hits notes and holds them, confident. She smirks and winks and shakes her sexy little hips. She works it without too obviously working it, all tight shirt and leather mini.

Wise Young Fool might not be the Stones, but it's hard to say we're not at least legit.

After a few tunes, I go out to the Saab and unload Dice's equipment. The preamp, the speakers, the mixer, the compressor. Elliot doesn't say anything, just starts hooking the stuff up. Chaos doesn't say anything, goes out to his Beemer, comes back with a file, and removes all the serial numbers.

We sound even crisper. We sound even tighter.

The PA is booming and clear.

Thanks, Dice!

Meanwhile, I can feel the whoosh of air from my Reverb Deluxe every time I play a bar chord. I've just gotten this new ultracool-rhythm thing down tight, no longer cheating on the upstrokes. It adds another layer to the song, *chunka chunka chunk-ah.* The roar of us is ungodly. I can only imagine what Lawrence is thinking while he chews on his spoon.

Behind me, Chaos is all over the place, his two bongos plus now he's added big timbales and these other African shaker things while he stomps out delay-chorus poly-rhythms that make us sound like Santana at Woodstock in double-time run through a defectively amplified wood chipper.

It's *awesome.*

Also, Elliot, as it turns out, was born to play bass. He's thumping away on this huge Fender Precision fretless that he pried away from his brother Nico, totally in the pocket, working his neck back and forth like a chicken and making *boomp boomp boomp* sounds with his lips. And that leaves Lacy, right out front with her flaming red Mohawk. Yeah, her Mohawk. Way out of control. She's a hotter Annabella from Bow Wow Wow. She's a hotter Penelope from the Avengers. She's a hotter Cherie from the Runaways. Elliot's giving her clues just in the way he pops a note, when to lay low, when to come in roaring. She reads my lyrics sometimes off a piece of paper on the floor, but she's done her homework, has most of them memorized. Amazingly, my words sound good. They make sense and have a point and don't just rhyme. Coming from between her lips they seem to have a whole new depth, purpose, sexy subtext.

Lacy looks at Elliot. Elliot looks at Lacy.

The song ends.

We don't even talk, no jokes, no bullshit, just start the next one.

Elliot looks at Lacy. Lacy looks at Elliot.

Chaos counts off the beat for "Truckasaurus Rex Bites a Chunk Outta Yore Neck," *one, two, three, four,* and I come in hard with a wash of distorted madness, like a thousand electrified axes chopping down a thousand cherry trees. I am a buzz saw of cerebellum-reducing cacophony while Lacy Duplais twirls the mic in one hand, pure style, soaking in the love of an imaginary crowd.

Chaos and I are sitting outside in the grass during break. His eyes are clear and calm. His hair curls behind his ears. He's wearing a sheepherder's jacket and huge cargo shorts. He looks like he just stepped out of a catalog for wine racks and thousand-dollar shoes and Cuban cigars and ointments made from endangered rhino horn.

I have decided not to say anything about the fact that, as I walked over to flop down and let the short blades tickle my neck, I saw Elliot pinning Lacy against the wall of the garage, her legs around his waist, their mouths locked. I stood there rooted in place like a total dipshit. She opened one eye, winked at me, then closed it again, going back in for more.

"Intraband romance," Chaos says, somehow knowing anyway, "can be a tricky thing."

"It's a disaster. It'll never work."

"Although they appear to fit together quite well. From architecture to temperament."

I sigh. "Young love is the stuff of a million lousy songs. Maybe we'll add a few fucking ballads and start doing bar mitzvahs.".

"Fucking ballads, or ballads about fucking?"

"Is there a difference? If they screw, we're screwed."

"Are you jealous?"

"Jealous of what?"

Chaos just smiles, then pulls out his pipe, packs a thumb full of buds, and has it lit in one motion. He tries to pass it over.

"Sorry. I'm against anything that clouds my thoughts or purpose or vision."

"How about something that heightens and augments your vision and purpose and thoughts?"

"You do your thing; I'll do mine."

"Yeah," he says, "but what *is* your thing?"

It's a good question. Women? Making music? Writing songs? Hating the world?

"Man, I'm clean by choice. Willing to accept the pain of existence un-numbed. I want to feel everything from good to bad to worse. Unlike you, I am prepared to hold my hand over the candle."

He grunts. "Have you considered the possibility that masochism is just another high?"

It bears considering. Just not very much.

"Drugs are for losers, hippies, and experimental poets."

"That's a hard line, my friend. That's a dogmatic take."

"If you mean a dog that protects your yard, plus an automatic that fires hollow points, I agree."

Chaos shakes his head. "You know what your problem is, Señor Sudden?"

"No, man, I don't."

"You're like a rich kid complaining about the menu, and then leaving a lousy tip. It's boring. I think you should consider, from now on, always leaving an overly generous tip no matter what you think of the world's service."

In the distance a car revs its engine. Children laugh, riding bikes. A bird wheels and caws. Or maybe that's Lacy.

"You know what, dude?" I say.

"What?"

"I'm going to majorly surprise you here."

"Please do."

"I think you're right."

He laughs and sparks another bowl. "Self-discovery is the most powerful intoxicant of all."

"Chaos, let me ask you something."

"Shoot."

"Your folks still together?"

"No, sir. My pops split when I was, like, born."

"And mom?"

"Divorced, remarried, redivorced. Playing the field at the moment."

"Any luck?"

"Some guy name of Rodney stops by now and again, hangs out for breakfast, asks about my classes."

"Interesting, interesting."

"You doing a survey, Sudden? You the census man?"

"Nah, just curious if all us products from broken homes got something in common."

"Like what?"

"Like a tendency to be awesome."

Chaos squeezes my shoulder in a poised and reassuring and totally manly way, like we're two aging fraternity brothers meeting for Scotches after the funeral of a guy we never really liked.

Then we both go back into the garage, ready to tear through the set one last time.

67

Dad Sudden finds the Buick online, the thing low and slow and heavy, a total grandma ride, perfect for a girl inclined to pay attention to everything but what's right in front of her. Like turning, braking, or signaling. The whole first week that it's in the driveway, before it's even legal, Beth's turning the steering wheel and hitting the signals and making *vroom vroom* noises like a little kid. She picks out the perfect bumper stickers: BIE-BERETTE (ironic), MONDALE '84 (retro), and PERVERT THE SUB-MISSIVE PARADIGM (no clue).

She finally gets it registered on a Saturday. The insurance takes twenty-four hours to kick in. To prepare for the maiden voyage, she's out in the driveway trying to get rid of the grime and smell and random stains the guy who sold it insisted were just a Formula 409ing away. I'm inside watching *Behind the Music: Sammy Hagar*, the episode where Sammy has decided jamming out is way more fun sober. He's just replaced Diamond Dave, cock slinger and Jack Daniel's guzzler extraordinaire, as lead wailer in Van Halen, and immediately gets busy talking the rest of the dudes into going Straight Edge. He talks about what a douche Diamond Dave was and how he, Sam, finally sees the true direction the band needs to head in, a direction that involves keyboards and songs about mountain biking. So instead of continuing to be this iconic LA strip-metal behemoth, Van Hagar starts recording horrible power ballads, the kind of insipid mall-chick chart rock that makes you want to eat your spleen and run screaming into the night. So, yeah, way to go, Sam. Forget drive, you can't *spell* fifty-five, either.

"Oh, crap, Ritchie," Beth yells. I ignore her until she does it again, louder this time.

"Help!"

I sigh and pause Sammy.

"What?"

"Just come, asshole!"

I jog outside, thinking maybe she's been crushed under the back wheel after putting it up on blocks to clean the tire treads with an old toothbrush, but she's just standing there covered in dirt, rags sticking out of her pockets, head bowed.

"This better be good."

Beth holds out her arms like a spokesmodel on *The Price Is Right*. I lean over and take a closer look. The Buick's paint job was hardly new and sparkling to begin with, but it was relatively rust-free and unmarred. Not anymore. The thing looks like it caught a bad case of Detroit clap. Big white splotches span from bumper to bumper, ugly swirls like polka dots run from front to back.

"What the hell?"

"I just polished it," she says, gesturing with one of those big sponge buffing gloves. "I put the stuff on, and now it won't come off."

"What did you use? Battery acid?"

Beth hands me the can, yellow with a yellow top. I turn it over. Lemon Pledge. It's furniture polish. She spread the stuff in layers and then let it roast in the sun while vacuuming inside.

I try not to laugh. "Did you think the longer you left it on, the cleaner it'd get?"

"I dunno. Maybe."

Apparently whatever toxic composition makes your mahogany sideboard look like it's dipped in spit reacts poorly with auto paint, because swirls of Pledge are now baked into the finish.

"Ritchie, do something."

I go and get the hose, hook it up, find a spray nozzle, and crank it on high, really scouring a two-foot section of the quarter panel. When I pull the hose away, it's done nothing at all. Except make the disease look glossier. Shit is permanent.

"Can you fix it?"

I read the warning label on the can. It basically advises you not to huff the fumes if you have any intention of graduating from community college. Also that it's a bad idea to spray it directly into your eyes. It says nothing about disfigured Buicks, which can only mean even the Pledge legal team didn't think anyone would ever be dumb enough to soak down a car with their product.

"You realize this is only for wood, right? Like, indoor furniture?"

"It says wax! I was waxing the car!"

Beth throws the giant sponge glove at me, kicks the passenger door, putting a nice dent in the center of it, and then starts to cry. There're so many jokes I could make about dumb blondes and how many Beths it takes to change a lightbulb. I could really lay it on thick about how all the kids at school were going to laugh their asses off when they spot her spotted bucket pulling into the lot like a rolling measle.

But I don't.

Instead I walk over and put my arms around her. I tell her it doesn't matter. I lie through my teeth and say it actually looks sort of cool. That it's art. That no one in the history of Sackville High has ever had a car anything like hers, which is true, and if nothing else, she's a genuine original.

Her bottom lip trembles.

"At least now it has a nice lemony smell."

She laughs. The tiniest little bit.

"I mean, it's only a car, right?"

"Right," she says, laying her head down on my shoulder.

We stand there for a very long time.

Ring. Tone. Ring. I snap the phone open, Ian MacKaye going, "*You tell me you like the taste, YOU! JUST! THINK! IT! LOOKS! COOL!*" Three times.

"Hello?"

It's Ravenna.

"Who is this?" I ask.

"Hi. It's me. Calling from a pay phone in the dorm."

Ravenna has been at Killington-Holloway for five days.

"Oh. Hey. Why a pay phone?"

"My dad canceled my cell. Punishment. You know."

"Right."

"So, anyway, Ritchie Rich, why don't you get in your little shit-brown Saab and come on up for a visit?"

"You want me to visit you?"

"Don't sound so astonished."

"I have to admit I am fairly astonished."

She sighs. "Well, I still don't really know anyone here."

"Give it a full week."

"Everyone thinks I'm a friendless loser."

"There's no way they think you're friendless."

"I miss you, Ritchie, okay?"

"Um, okay."

"So I need Sackville to represent."

"To *represent*? Wait, remind me again. Am I talking to Salt or Pepa?"

"Besides, you owe me one."

"Don't you mean I owe you two?"

"Okay, fine, I'm hanging up now."

"No, you're not."

"I'm not?"

"Let me guess. You just called everyone else you know. None of them can make the drive. I'm, like, what, twenty-sixth on the list?"

"Twelfth. But so what? I'm still calling, aren't I?"

"Hard to argue with that."

"So come already."

Mom and Looper are downstairs watching Mom and Looper movies, which means either a middle-aged lady thinks she's too fat but hates to diet or some older dude almost has a coronary on Viagra and everyone in the ER makes nonstop boner jokes until the credits roll.

They're actually laughing down there.

"Fine, but I'm bringing Chowus."

"Who?"

"Our drummer."

"The Abercrombie boy? Why?"

"Your various Killingtons and Holloways will recognize him as one of their own immediately. And thus, by association, I will feel less like a mere footman or commoner."

"Good thinking. Bring Chow Us."

In study hall I mention I'm heading up to Killington right after school. Meb Cavil says she wants to come. Fine with me. It seems wise to arrive in hostile territory with a woman in tow.

Then Young Joe Yung says he wants in, too. He's wearing overalls, a raincoat, and shit-encrusted rubber Wellingtons. His dreads are even dreadier than usual. I figure it's never wise to arrive in hostile territory with an enormous grass-fed, free-range hippie in tow.

"I dunno, big dog."

"Occupy Killington-Holloway!" he practically yells. "I'll start a tent city on the quad! I'll gather signatures! I'll solicit donations! The one percent needs a taste of me!"

Chaos, who now comes to Sackville practically every day and sits around with his feet up, not attending classes, has a huge grin on his mug.

"They do, man. They seriously need a taste of you."

Young Joe laughs, and then Beenie Sloat shows up with a Tupperware full of quinoa and raw vegetables. They squat over it and go to town.

"Ravenna's gonna kill me," I say.

"Ravenna killed you a long time ago," Meb says.

Vice Principal Paste comes walking by, sees Chaos, and gives him a little salute.

"Mister Bahm."

Chaos salutes back.

"Morning, sir."

"Wait, how did you get in here again?" Beenie Sloat asks, ancient grains tumbling from his mouth and down his shirt.

"There's nowhere Adam Bomb can't go," I say.

"True." Chaos laughs. "But mostly I just use the door."

The windows are down because it's nice out, and also Joe Yung smells like homemade yogurt. Meb tells us funny stories about all the creepy pervs who come into the lingerie shop she works at, Veronika's Answer, pretending to buy sexy items for their wives but really dying to wear them under their Brooks Brothers at the big meeting the next day. Also about how all Veronika's stuff is made in Indonesia with huge vats of ruinous chemicals that tend to give people rashes between their folds, who then are mostly too embarrassed to limp back in and ask for a refund.

"Mostly?"

"Those are the days I earn my minimum wage," Meb says. "No doubt."

We all have to show ID to the security guard at the gate. He gives the serious eyeball to Young Joe Yung and insists we sign a "Guests' Comportment Agreement" before he'll let us onto campus. It's definitely Chaos's Beemer that put us over the top. If we'd rolled up in the Saab, Homeland Security would have had Young Joe hog-tied and waterboarded before you could say, *They hate us for our freedoms.*

There's a long, winding road through heavily pruned pines.

305

Between them are animal-shaped topiaries, squirrels and swans and rabbits. At the head of a horseshoe is a massive Catholic basilica, all spires and crosses and trumpet-y cherubs. Fanning out from its sides are rows of dorms, immaculate brick and whitewash rectangles, each named after a president, general, or random carpetbagger who donated a few million to the research lab. All in all it's like Harvard but smaller, nicer, and with fewer hedge funders clogging the quad with tweed.

We find Ravenna's dorm, but she's not there. Her roommate, a tall, elegant redheaded chick with a French accent and calves you could slice bread with, has about four hundred books open across her desk. She says Ravenna's out back in a way that you can tell she wishes Ravenna would stay there permanently.

We head down the rear stairwell, which opens onto a concrete patio, and there's Ravenna. Smoking a long, thin cigarette with about ten other kids puffing away in a circle around her.

What a difference five days make, because Ravenna Woods is transformed. What once was mere Sackville überhotness is now something rarer and more refined. Her oddness has become pure exotica. She's wearing clothes so fashionable they have no label. Like they're made from some material you can only buy by appointment. Standing there full-smirk, arms crossed, blowing a plume of smoke up into the ivy and gables, she is now the most willowy-beautiful woman I've ever seen in my entire life, and that counts TV. She looks like royalty. She looks like antiquity. She looks like you wouldn't think twice about storming a castle, fording a piranha moat, and impaling half of Saxony on the tip of a rusty broadsword just for the right to throw her over your shoulder and spend the next ten years wrapped in tresses and trembling legs in the hopes of planting just the right combination of xx and xy to make a perfect crowned heir.

Or something.

Anyway, the posh school agrees with her.

Ravenna spots us, lighting up like a bank of kliegs before realizing she should, in fact, play it cool. The new girl needs to tamp the townie past. Keep her utter trust-fundlessness on the down low. Even so, she's all, "*Dudes!*" garnering looks from the harder-core prepensteins, who would never use a word like *dude*, even on a ranch. She sees Young Joe, frowns, blushes, recovers, hugs us all anyway. Everyone lights a new smoke. Even outside it's like being trapped in the exhaust pipe of a '72 Fiat sportster. Some people say hi, but pretty soon close ranks and start talking among themselves again. Chaos dives right into the middle, doing secret handshakes, the Skull and Bones, the show dog, the requisite Hilfiger-y ass-sniffing, immediately at ease. Meb and Young Joe stand to one side, talking to each other as if they were actually interested. I pull Ravenna into a slightly darker corner and give her a hug.

She holds me at arm's length. "Thanks so much for coming."

"Of course."

"And bringing...him."

Young Joe Yung laughs at something Meb says, big and horsey and raw. He's wearing a homemade T-shirt that says, I'LL VOTE REPUBLICAN WHEN YOU PRY THEIR ENTITLED VACU-OUSNESS FROM MY COLD, DEAD REASON.

"How could I not?"

She rolls her eyes. "You look good."

"It's only been a hundred and twenty hours."

She laughs. "Seems like years. Like I've been out at sea practically forever."

I don't tell her how different she looks. She knows I know. Her haircut is better, simpler, all style. Her makeup is so perfect it almost seems like she's not wearing any. The anger is still there, but simmering way beneath the surface, smirk abated, knife dulled.

She's totally home. In the middle of a mausoleum to wealth and the unbearable whiteness of being.

"How're things back in Sackville?"

"Widely unchanged. On a Level of Suck, I'd say holding steady at an eight-point-five."

"Good, good."

"How's your roommate? She seems like a lot of fun."

"Oh, she is," Ravenna says, but she's no longer really paying attention, glancing over my head, worried that she might be missing something in the inner circle. She meets my eyes, but all her ambient energy is concentrated on whether the (right) Killington people are watching her talk to The Mysterious Visitor. And if so, are they impressed?

They're watching, but they are not impressed.

Which means I'm already a diminishing return.

I squeeze her arm to bring her back to earth.

"So you smoke now, huh?"

Her eyes refocus. She stamps out her cig on the concrete and lights another.

"Yup."

"And how are the twins?"

She looks down at her chest and smirks.

"Healing nicely, thank you."

With that, she drifts away. So much for the big reunion.

"So what's with you two?" a girl next to me asks. She's thin and birdy, hair almost white, skin beyond white. She looks like a Russian princess who died of hemophilia a hundred years ago.

"Who?"

"Ravenna. The goddess. You obviously know her."

"Biblically? Is it that obvious?"

"Ha. No, I was thinking more like periphcrally."

Ravenna looks back over her shoulder at us, as if she heard but doesn't care, imperious. Her smile is a masterpiece of giddy calculation.

"I'm Sigourney," the Russian says.

"Hi."

"You might as well just give up."

"Excuse me?"

"You may have had the inside track in Smalltown or Hangtown or Farmtown or wherever you guys are from. But here? Her? Ha! Do you even want to *know* how many rungs down you already are?"

"Yes."

"You sure?"

"Yes."

Sigourney lowers her voice to a crude and dirty whisper. "Okay, she's not even sleeping with a professor at Killington.

No, that would be too cliché. She's sleeping with a professor at the college across the river instead."

"In five days? No way."

"Way."

It sounds like the usual gossip, but I don't entirely doubt it.

Sigourney nods, enjoying the misery in my eyes. "The guy's forty-five and has three kids. He picks her up in a Benz. They've gone to eat in the city twice already. He wrote a book about Teddy Roosevelt or something that was on the bestseller list."

"So boring," I say. "So obvious."

Sigourney slips her arm into mine, like we're about to stroll along the Thames. "But enough about her. Let's talk about me."

"What about you?"

"Why be coy? Jensen Partman's my father."

I almost do a spit-take, then cover it by pretending to sneeze. Jensen Partman is a famous indie director. He shoots movies that make no money but still make careers. Jensen Partman made *Give It All Away, Sheila Blue*. He made *Winter Into Spring Into Winter Again*. He made *The Trial of the Brooklyn 9 and Other Travesties*. Big-name actors constantly beg to be in his films, but he tends to cast nobodies and make them somebodies. He's, like, so totally my hero.

"Nope."

"Yup."

"That's such a lie."

"It's so true."

She reaches into the pocket of her little blazer and pulls out a school ID. It says SIGOURNEY PARTMAN, right there under her picture. I hook my arm back around hers with greater enthusiasm. "Well, Miss Partman, what do you say you and I go sit on that stone wall over there and spend the rest of the night saying bitchy things about your classmates under our breath?"

"I thought you'd never ask."

And so, we kill an hour watching Ravenna and her court, giving each one a nickname. Ears Earrington the Third and Gavrilo Princip and Fuzzy Zoeller and Lil' Miss Stalactites. Not to mention Chelsea Girl and Ivanka Lump and Ernie Madoff and The Winklevoss Twins. When they finally finish smoking enough to kill off three container trucks full of transplanted lungs, we pile into someone's Mercedes personnel carrier. It takes us to a café in town, a small town that's surprisingly blue-collar and a café run by a staff that clearly loathes and resents the fortunate sons of Killington-Holloway. I want to hang a sign around my neck that says, I'M ONE OF YOU. I'M UNDERCOVER. DON'T HATE ME. But everyone else ignores the staff with a cappuccino-fueled obliviousness, talking shit-dialectics, talking about Mary Cassatt and Dvořák and Robespierre and everything else half read on the current syllabus. I don't say much. Partly because for the first time in my life I am around people who are all as smart as or smarter than me and who are at the very least more well-read, steeped in the classics and twentieth-century political theory and various old-world debating techniques. The usual off-the-cuff cleverish misanthropy I tend to coast by on is like a packet of NutraSweet to these people, cheap and fake and not worth dumping into their extra foam. Chaos, on the other hand, is full of laughs and has been five-slapping with the lacrosse types for hours. Meb met some nerdy Indian kid with a posh accent, the dude leaning extremely close to her as they do the knee-hand shuffle under the counter. Young Joe Yung hums contentedly to himself while forking up an enormous salad, and Ravenna is in a booth, making eyes at a big blond dude who is either the secretary of state's son or the pride of the Young Astronauts Program.

She never looks over at me, not once.

It's suddenly crystal clear what I'm really here for.

And it's not coffee and a bagel.

Payback's a bitch.

69

It's morning. Loud and hot and pointless, like every other morning.

Except today's different.

Today it's going down.

Payback.

I can feel the bitch in my bones.

I walk to breakfast; no one's talking. I sit down at the center table, and all the lames clear out. It's just as well. I eat a lot of eggs, really pack in the protein. Keep up my strength.

There's no reason to look around; I can feel the stares.

There's no reason to listen; I can hear the whispers.

B'los nods. I don't nod back.

I just keep eating. There's nothing else to do.

Except marvel at how all the counselors seem to be in a good mood.

In my mind I whip through the Dorian scale. I mentally play a progression in D-minor, which is deep, complicated, ominous. Then I bust out the tritone. I go up and down the fretboard, showing off. I do finger tapping; I wail in high E. I play in a shuffle pattern, so I sound like the bass player for Buddy

Holly who gave up his seat to The Big Bopper in the plane that crashed an hour later and killed everyone on board, including Ritchie Valens, who no one knows the name of, except me: Waylon Jennings.

Music died the day the music died.

Their plane went down, my plane's going down.

It's morning. Loud and hot and pointless, just like every other morning.

El Hella is officially in a good mood. He signed up Wise Young
Fool for the Sackville High talent show, figuring it'd be the perfect run-through for Rock Scene 2013, and now the time has
come. Perform or perish. Put up or shut up. Bring it or wing it.

Actually, that was a joke.

Elliot is not in a good mood. He's a nervous mess, sweat
pouring off his scalp, biting his nails, haranguing each of us
over little pointless details until Lacy takes him behind the
piano stand and whispers in his ear, soft soothing phrases I
imagine are mostly about bunnies and naps and warm milk.

It's a Friday and the last two periods of classes are canceled, the whole school packed into the assembly hall all rowdy,
since not only has the weekend arrived, it's about to be kicked
off with free license to hector, harangue, and mock with zero
mercy or compunction a bunch of talentless talent acts. It's like
tossing raw strip steaks to a mob of starving raccoons.

We're in the front row, where all the acts wait until they're
on. By some fluke we're actually going last, top billing, which is
cool but means we have to sit through the entire lineup first.

Dice, the usual emcee, refused to participate this year as a protest, since school insurance declined to replace the equipment stolen from his Teaching Tower due to "egregious carelessness and possible insider involvement."

Which means that Mr. Bramblety, all rayon and comb-over and querulously high-pitched voice, is announcing Myra Volt. She comes out and sings a number from *Cats* to an utter smatter of applause and sarcastic meows.

Then this crazy little dude Liam Pope comes onstage with a boom box, hits play, and walks back off. It's this cheesy eighties song "Rock Me Amadeus." No one knows exactly what to make of it. There're boos and whistles. Just as Mr. Bramblety is about to pull the plug, Liam runs back on in a giant cardboard pastry costume, the thing covered with fake white frosting, and starts singing at the top of his lungs, "Rock me, I'm a Danish!" He dances around for a while, tossing about three bags' worth of sticky buns into the crowd, and then cartwheels off to huge applause. It's pretty inspired lunacy, and I'm clapping as hard as anyone else.

Then Tedd Lester, earnest as a dress sock, drags his acoustic guitar out and does a strummy number about nuclear war and Vladimir Putin and how we could make friends with the whales and the Arabs if only we could find a way to be a little less exactly like we are. He gets light applause mixed with a rumbling undertone of *suck-ass*.

Judy Sweacher comes out in a purple dress and reads a poem that rhymes *Duracell* with *chanterelle*, and then *acne* with *attack me*. Zero reaction. Stunned boredom. Not a peep throughout the hall.

Some sophomore kid does a few magic tricks, screws most of them up, but pulls off a winner at the end when he makes Miss Menepausse disappear in a cardboard box. A huge cheer erupts at the idea that Menepausse may not be returning from the mystical ether, followed by a resigned and disappointed hiss when she actually does.

Finally, Young Joe Yung is up. He comes out barefoot, in a kimono (possibly just a bedsheet) covered with Aramaic symbols. Joe Yung does a combo of yoga and karate dance moves to the accompanying music his new girlfriend Tantra knocks out on a gong and finger cymbals. Tantra, who he met behind the lunchroom at Killington-Holloway, looks to be about thirty-five. Young Joe finishes his dance and then announces as an encore he will eat meat for the first time in two years. Huge cheer. He says, however, that he will not digest it, because his body is now impervious to all animal flesh. Confused cheer. Tantra walks over holding a plate with a big raw sausage on it. Young Joe ties string around the center, holds it up for everyone to see, dangles it high above his open mouth, and then swallows the banger in one gulp. Hooting and laughter. Joe does a bit more dancing, a few side kicks and leg sweeps, and then suddenly starts to look sick. He's reeling. He's gagging. Tantra tries desperately to keep up with her gong. Joe holds his neck like he's been poisoned, on the verge of collapse, then reaches down his throat and yanks on the string, pulling the sausage all the way back out, completely intact.

Sheer bedlam. Pure love and hilarity from the audience. Yells of *Encore!* and *That's what I'm talking about!* and *Now do a Quarter Pounder!* echo around the hall. Mr. Bramblety tries to calm everyone to zero avail.

Finally, Young Joe and Tantra bow, kiss, bow, wave, and then we're on.

"Last up tonight," Mr. Bramblety says, reading off a cue card, "is White Young Spool."

"Wise Young Fool, fool!" Elliot yells.

This only confuses Mr. Bramblety, who drops his cue card, coughs, turns red, reannounces us as "Widely Used Tool," forgets to turn off the mic, cringes at the screech, and waddles away.

And then it's real.

We are plugged in.

Staring at the audience.

Staring back at us.

There is pure, expectant silence. There is the fine, fluttering high of adrenaline, of cheap glandular accelerant, of the opportunity to either conquer the city or burn up in the atmosphere like chunks of exploded cosmonaut.

"Kick ass, Sudden!" someone yells.

People giggle nervously.

There are hoots and whistles.

At sound check we narrowed it down to three possible songs:

"I Will Crush You Like a Bug and Then Reanimate You With the Hugeness of My Love"

or

"Communism's Candle on Socialism's Cake"

or

"Rhyme Faster, Lame Victorian Poetaster"

In the end Elliot won out, and we went with "Communism's Candle." Of course, it's a song in which I have many complicated parts, two solos, and backing vocals. I practiced it all night long, forward, backward, sideways. My fingers know the positions intuitively; my voice knows the timbre cold.

Even so, I'm terrified.

I close my eyes and then Chaos counts it off.

It amazes me how the totality of us magically floats through insulated cables, rising out of speakers cranked to maximum volume. There is singing. There are notes, notes, notes, followed by a bass-y, rumbling twang. We're ragged but sort of all on the same beat.

It's clumsy, but it works, beginning to build.

Beginning to coalesce, beginning to crush.

I sweep in with a massive crest of distortion.

Just as Elliot's amp begins to short out.

The bottom end comes and goes with bursts of static. I try to match it, but it's too random and I end up playing gibberish. Lacy strains to find the pocket. Her mic is too low. She's lost beneath it all, singing the wrong verse. Elliot comes back in, goes out again. Lacy starts the chorus too soon. Suddenly, it's bongo bongo bongo, the whole world drowning in bongo. Chaos realizes and pulls back. He gives me the thumbs-up as one of his stands falls over. It crashes to the floor and rolls off the stage, dragging cords and mics with it, releasing a hellish squall of pure white noise. Lacy looks like she's about to cry. I signal for her to keep going. She's forgotten the words, numbly saying the same thing over and over, *Oh, you pretty things. You pretty vacant things.* Elliot's bass comes back in again like a slap in the neck. He's in the wrong key. My fingertips are sweating.

I didn't know that was possible.

The song is over before it even started.

I'm holding an open G.

The final overtones of the final chord fade from my amp.

An audience full of students blinks in stunned silence, with a thousand-headed frown.

Mr. Bramblety signals for the curtain, but it doesn't move.

There's not a single clap.

Not one.

The Paul begins to feed back.

I lay my hand over the strings.

And our noise mercifully stops.

71

Elliot refuses to talk to any of us the next day. Lacy doesn't come to school until lunch, and even then she's wearing a baseball cap and dark glasses, maybe even a fake nose. Chaos walks around laughing at all the shit-talk, slapping five with the worst offenders, acting like our implosion was all on purpose, some sort of performance art. But he gives me a look of murder when we pass in the hall.

"Don't eyeball me, Adam Bomb," I say. "You don't even go to this school!"

That afternoon I sit on the porch, closing one eye and then the other, which makes the lawn flip back and forth like a deck of cards. We're supposed to practice, but since Elliot isn't talking to anyone, who knows?

Rock Scene 2013 is in seventy-two hours.

Cold drips of terror run down my legs.

Warm drips of boredom bore into my spine.

And then my cell phone explodes.

The ringtone is Donald Fagen warbling, "*It was still September when your daddy was quite surprised to find you with the working girls in the county jail!*" Three times. I'm sure it's Elliot about to tell me to get my ass in gear.

But it's not Elliot.

"Hello?"

"It's Sigourney."

The Russian princess.

"Who?" I ask.

"Um, remember? From Killington-Holloway?"

"Oh, yeah, of course."

"I'm having a party tonight. At my house. Actually, my dad's house. In the city. Want to come?"

I'm too crushed. Depressed. Ruined.

"Well, that's very cool of you to ask, but I'm pretty sure I have practice."

"Ravenna will be there."

"Oh, yeah?"

"She broke up with the professor."

"She did?"

"Yup. Said his legs were too wrinkly."

"I see."

Sigourney laughs and gives me the address.

"So come on over."

I should. I totally should. Ravenna. Me. In the city.

Screw Wise Young Fool.

"Thanks. I owe you one."

"You don't owe me anything. Just don't wear a shitty band shirt with the sleeves cut off, okay, townie?"

In the driveway, the Saab is dead. Completely and utterly.

HORROR.

I walk to Route 302 and stick out my thumb.

A few hours later, I get off the train and stroll across the park, through the middle of a big open meadow full of sun tanners and Frisbee players and scruffy dudes cooking pigeons on makeshift hibachis. The address Sigourney gave is for a massive brownstone with a doorman. The guy announces my name through an intercom. The elevator is all mirrors and plated gold. Inside, there're about thirty kids, mostly dudes, slacks and vests and Oliver Peoples, young American Psychos in training. Ravenna is in back wearing an incredibly tight pink dress. She's lost weight, all the Sackville baby fat melted clean away. Her curves are more studied, European, dangerous. She sees me, sees right through me, goes back to her conversation.

"What can I get you?" asks a dude with his French cuffs rolled up, standing behind the stocked bar. You can tell he's been whipping up sloe gin fizzes at his parents' dinner parties since he was eight.

"Mountain Dew," I say. "Rocks."

He makes a face, pours me a club soda.

In the corner, a bunch of guys in their crested school blazers are shopping for drugs. They're dialing numbers out of some kid's address book, all louche and striped-tied, feet up on a coffee table full of *Vogue*s, credit cards and

BlackBerrys ready. Technology. But they're not having any luck.

"I can't believe Mama Hurricane's not holding," one kid keeps saying over and over.

Ravenna laughs at a joke that probably wasn't particularly funny, shifting weight from one incredibly high heel to the other. She's so beautiful it makes my spine hurt. She's wearing glasses, obviously just for show, but they totally work, making her look like the intellectual and gravitational force at the center of an infamous circle of feminists, cultural critics, and NBA wives.

The Loudons and Hamishes and Brinkleys stare at her as well, imagining what they'll never have and can't pay for, speed-dialing their dealers instead.

Sigourney comes over in a black velvet cape. She's so pale her veins are visible four inches deep, like a laptop schematic. "Hey, Ritchie."

"Hey."

"Way to dress up."

I look down at my sweater (ill-fitting, too big) and corduroys (bought for school last year, rust colored, never worn).

"You bet."

"Ravenna's here."

"Yes, she is."

"Now's your chance."

"Chance for what?"

Sigourney smiles too wide, and in the sparkling light of her fake-friendly eyes it's obvious why I've been invited.

Did I actually think we were friends?

Could I possibly be one iota dumber?

She's counting on me to roll in, be gauche and loud and hilariously blue-collar, maybe make a scene, provide a little drama for her party.

"It won't work," I say.

"Have a drink." She turns to talk to some guy who looks like a Medici. "It's early still."

My cell buzzes, Robin Zander going, "*She's tight, she's giving me the go, she's tight, she's giving me the high sign!*" Three times.

I mute it and walk around to the back of the massive apartment where, no shit, some of the sets from Jensen Partman movies are installed. Three walls are covered with stuff I recognize, half a coffee shop counter from that scene in *Killing of a Short-Order Crook* where Harry Dean Stanton empties his pistol into the waffle guy, and the neon facade of the dance club where Julia Roberts and Raul Julia make out in *Her Name Is Clyde*.

I'm leaning over, about to run my hand along the fake chrome stools, when someone goes, "What makes you think it's okay to touch that?"

Without turning I say, "What makes you think I care what *you* think is okay?"

Ravenna laughs. She takes my hand.

"Howdy, stranger."

"Hi."

"What's new?"

"Oh not much. Unless you count how I hear you're getting it on with a college professor."

"Oh my god. Let me guess. Everyone's favorite hostess told you that?"

I shrug. "Maybe."

Ravenna finishes her martini and sets it on the piano, a Bösendorfer that has to cost at least sixty grand. "It's possible there are people here who don't have my best interests at heart."

I grab the glass and wipe the water ring with my sleeve. "It's possible there are people here who have no hearts at all."

"Does that include you?"

I think about it. "Maybe, but at least I'm filled to the rim with soul."

"Well, you've got to have *something* to offer the devil down at the crossroads."

It occurs to me for the very first time that the real reason I've liked Ravenna for so long, despite her looks, is because of how whip-smart she is. She's funny like me. She gets what I get. The orange juice concentrate of my cynicism mixes with the ice-cold water of her sarcasm, making a frothy and refreshing beverage. It further occurs to me that I am an unredeemable tool for not realizing it sooner. And that the best possible way to make it up to her would be to just leave her alone.

"Speaking of which, I better get back to Sackville. We're supposed to practice."

"Elliot Hella still pulling your leash?"

"Woof," I say. "Grrr."

She plays with an earring, leans against me. "What is it you're really getting back to, Ritchie? Have you ever asked yourself that?"

I laugh. "No, but at least now I know what passes for profundity up here at Killington-Holloway."

She stares, hard, the corners of her mouth curling downward in their painterly way, snatches of conversation swirling around us.

"...I'll try being nicer, if *you* try being smarter..."

"...use *much* at the end of a sentence much?..."

"...you're like binge and purge but without the binge..."

"...it *sounds* like English, but I can't understand a word you're saying..."

"...if I *wanted* to take a girl with a mustache to the prom, I would have *asked* a girl with a mustache to the prom..."

"...your dad's the ambassador to Bahrain. Buy your own cigarettes..."

"...I can't believe Mama Hurricane's not holding..."

It goes from funny to sad to depressing and stays there. It's like a scoop of sherbet. A palate cleanser. I know I should leave, but I want to say one last thing. I just don't know what that thing is.

"So, are you coming on Saturday?" I finally ask.

"Coming where?"

"Rock Scene 2013. The biggest night of my life."

"Tonight is the biggest night of your life."

There's no need for her coy smirk, but it rears its head anyway, in full lipsticked glory.

"It is?"

"Do you want it to be?"

While I'm trying to think of a smooth answer, she leans over and sticks her tongue in my mouth.

What else am I going to do but bite it?

I mean, hell, it's so totally in the script.

It's sometime around two. Everyone has left, including Sigourney, who went to get pancakes with a bunch of guys who claimed to be Whiffenpoofs, and never came back. Ravenna and I are in some room whose shelves are lined with practically every good book ever written, in archival vellum wraps and mint dust jackets. There're first editions of *Naked Lunch* and *Notes of a Dirty Old Man* and *The Dharma Bums*. There's an original copy of William Blake etchings that has to be worth a million dollars. We're sitting on an ancient leather couch. It smells of cigars and cognac and sweaty jodhpurs, like it was shipped from some officer's club in colonial Burma in 1892.

Ravenna's mouth is locked on mine. Her tongue swirls clockwise. My tongue, a natural contrarian, swirls counterclockwise.

We meet at a quarter to six.

Communion.

It's really kissing.

Movie kissing.

Deep kissing.

Which I've never actually done before.

Touched someone and genuinely cared that she touched me back.

I'm not entirely sure how to handle it.

Ravenna can sense my confusion, because she puts her hand gently behind my neck, palm cool and soft, and holds it there.

It's the kind of thing that could only happen to a better, smarter, sexier me.

Except it's happening to this me.

Which, you know, is an amazing feeling.

Suddenly being that guy who winters in Biarritz.

Who chairs the charity ball.

Who always tips the valet.

And every full moon, hires a peasant girl to wax his chest.

That guy strokes Ravenna's hair.

That guy strokes her thigh.

That guy leans back and just keeps leaning.

I wake up near dawn.

In a bed the size of an aircraft carrier.

I get up and find my clothes, late for school. Ravenna is awake but pretending to sleep. She knows it and I know she knows I know it.

Last night was last night.

Today is today.

It is what it is.

Except it isn't.

"Come here," she says.

I roll back under the covers and pull her close to me.

We poke and squeeze and giggle and whisper insanely

329

smart things in each other's ears. I am somehow aware that this behavior is way older than either of us. We're playing tennis instructors in Paris, comparative lit professors in Rome. She bites my lower lip and tells me to have a good day. *Maybe this is love*, I think. Maybe all it takes is the welling feeling that I am luckier than any other fucker on earth. That there is someone beneath me wrapped in sheets that smell like cinnamon and salt and pitted fruit, breasts and sex unfolded, hair wound across the pillow like a conquering flag, who wants me to stay enough to admit out loud that she wants me to stay.

And then the alarm goes off for the third time.

Ravenna slaps my ass, rolling over and closing her eyes.

In the kitchen there're fresh croissants. And grapes and mangoes and pomegranate juice and coffee so strong it could dissolve a barrel full of mob informants. I drink it while running my hand along each one of Jensen Partman's sets.

Downstairs, the doorman looks surprised but does a credible job of hiding it. He instantly knows what happened and neither of us can quite believe it, but the look on his face says he's bored with the sons of the rich—if only because he, too, should have had the chance, at least once, to stroll out of a brownstone with the smell of teen daughter and furtive cocktails wafting around his neck like an Hermès scarf.

I hand him five bucks.

"What's this for?"

"It's a tip."

He shoves the money back in my pocket. "Don't be a wiseass."

330

There's a honk and a beep and a screech, some homeless dude railing away about the end of the end.

"I wasn't," I say, but the doorman's already gone, helping a woman out of a taxi who's holding a dog that is literally smaller than the word *yap*, the thing tucked under her arm like a dinner roll, barking for every last thing it's worth.

72

In the bathroom I look in the mirror.

It's bolted to the wall, made of soft metal that barely reflects an image through the thousand tags and curse words and Nazi symbols etched into it. I open my mouth, try to speak, give my wavery face some advice, can't.

Lunch is theoretical, because my stomach is locked.

I go to the library, but it's closed. No one will look at me, meet my eyes. Groups of kids stand there, Josés and Ralphs and Garys and Laphonsos. They kick their sneakers together, talk in low voices.

B'los isn't around.

There're no counselors around.

A bunch of kids are gathered at the end of the hall, in front of Dr. Benway's office, hands in pockets. No one says anything, but it's obvious they're not going to let me pass.

There's nowhere else to go but outside.

The basketball courts or the dayroom.

Why put it off?

I decide on the dayroom.

A group of kids follow me in. Five of them.

A bunch of mopes who do favors for Peanut and Conner.

Waiting for me to try to run.

I'm not going to run.

There's a series of shrill whistles, a signal.

They're saying shit, laughing, calling me names.

They can smell blood. Taste blood.

I can't turn around, won't turn around, don't turn around.

I press my face into a corkboard with notices for GED classes and yoga classes and crude anatomical drawings, vaginas as imagined by three-year-olds, cartoon dicks that A-Rod could bat cleanup with.

It highlights, in its subtle way, the elemental stupidity of everyone and everything.

Behind me, the stage is ready.

The dayroom is packed.

The doors are open.

The audience is primed.

The talent has arrived.

And not a minute too late.

I'm late and have to go to the office for a detention form.

"You're already missing the assembly," the secretary says.

"What assembly?"

She gives me a look like I just crapped her mattress.

I walk down to the auditorium. The door creaks and every-one turns, glaring.

Dice is up onstage. There's a poster next to him, just like the one they had for Beth. The main difference being that it's a picture of Kyle Litotes, and he's not dead. Dice gives a real heartfelt speech. About how great a student Kyle was and how much he, Dice, loved Kyle and gazed deeply into the pool of his unlimited potential. How Kyle was too special for words, too talented for fate, too determined for luck, too sexy for his shirt. Essentially word for word what he said about Beth.

Except Dice didn't kiss Kyle.

Didn't force himself on Kyle at a party.

Didn't make out with Kyle, grabbing his shoulders while he tried to pull away.

I hear a song in my head, one that I often do. Mostly

because I made it up. I've never shown it to Elliot, because it's not a song for Elliot.

It's a song for Dick Isley.

I usually picture it being sung by someone named Tiffani or Brittney, a midtwenties plastic blonde trying to corner the teeny market. I see her wearing a plaid schoolgirl skirt and sports bra, dancing on the desk in front of a classroom.

In front of a goggle-eyed Dice.

Who's pretending to be professional, disinterested, shocked.

But is so, so into it.

Brittney or Tiffani or Tammi or Misti pops a lollipop in her mouth and then leans over and sings, to a sultry backbeat, with male dancers behind her:

I think we're alone
Like we were meant to be
Just us in the classroom
In applied credit biology.

Oh, I think we're alone now,
Teacher man,
Take off that tweed jacket and
Show me your hand.
Lay me across your
Desk, desk
Pop quiz me
Yes, yes
I'll give you my apple and

You give me your
Best, best.

Oh, I think we're alone
Now and forever more
Bell rings the end of days
Laughing in the corridor.

It's just me and you
And the things that we do
It's just you and me
And everything you've yet to see
So much to teach.
So much to learn.
So far to reach.
So easy to burn.

We're going up in an academic
Con-fla-gration.
We're going up in an honor code
Vi-o-lation.
We're going—

Dice takes a breath, interrupting my reverie. He wipes a tear, then talks about how cosmically unfair it is that Kyle won't be going to college.

"There will be no college for this fine young man."

How tragically unjust that Kyle will not be cashing in his scholarship—which has already been revoked—or pursuing further athletic glory.

"Sadly, athletic achievement is now a thing of the past."

He concludes that Kyle made, in the blink of an eye, a mistake in judgment that he will pay deeply for the rest of his life.

"These tiny, random decisions are often vast and irrevocable."

Students are then advised to be unusually understanding this morning, because Kyle isn't always in control of his language and his attention can wander.

"He may not appear exactly as you remember him."

Also, no flash photography; the lights hurt Kyle's eyes and may disorient him.

"So stow your cameras and cell phones, people."

Dice begins to clap. "Students of Sackville High, please give a very warm hand for one of our own, Kyle Litotes, and his mom, Myra!"

Kyle and his mom get a standing O.

She leads him out to the podium. It gets still and quiet. Even the most sarcastic pricks are listening, no one cracking wise. People are scared. They're freaked. Because, essentially, here's this kid they all know backward and forward, this kid they've gone through year after year of math classes and gym classes and study halls with, but it's not really him anymore. It's Kyle, but from the fifth dimension, like one of those movies where a space slug bores its way into the president's ear and takes over.

Now the president's skin doesn't really fit right, and he starts eating lightbulbs and passing all these crazy laws, but the Secret Service guys let it go because what are you gonna do, the space slug won the electoral college outright.

The mic feeds back. Kyle bonks it with his forehead and giggles. When he finally talks, it's way too slow. It's like he's underwater. And not only because his mom has to keep leaning over and wiping his lips with a hankie.

Kyle gets his sea legs and starts talking about drinking and driving and how bad it is. How sorry he is. How glad he is to be alive. People are nodding. Girls are crying. Tough kids are wondering if maybe it really is time to take a long look at themselves and their six-pack Friday nights. But others are shaking their heads, thinking, *Yeah, dude, we get it; everyone knows what the smart move is as far as getting behind the wheel hammered. But, on the other hand, we live in this shit-ass town, don't we? I mean, we live in the middle of nowhere and the roads are paved cow paths and there's no bus system or anything, so if you want to go somewhere, you got to drive. And if you drive somewhere at night, there's a good chance someone's got a few beers to knock back. And so there's a good chance you're going to be drinking and driving, unless you go to the movies or mini golf or some other square shit with the Saving It for Marriage team or the Anti-Masturbator's League. It's just, like, unavoidable.*

I know Beth thought it was unavoidable.

I know she took her chances, plenty of them.

And then I'm thinking, *Hey, there's another speech Kyle could be giving.* It's a speech about being a hotshot. About having to show off in your car, or on the team, just to prove what a hilarious dude you are all the time. About how the Litoteses of the world only find the moral of the story after the story brings them to their knees, but the moral was nowhere to be found when it actually mattered, because they buried it under all the ways they were busy taking advantage of their advantages.

Clitotes wasn't sorry during Beth's assembly.

He was texting his friends.

Kyle loses his place. His mom prompts him, but he gets confused, and then says, *Shit fucking shit!* at the top of his lungs. About eight times. People start to laugh despite themselves. Someone says, *Right on!* Kyle waves, says, *Motherfucker dogballs bitch* about nine times, and then Dice sweeps over and wraps it up. Everyone stands and gives Kyle another ovation. All these girls in expensive sweaters are crying and guys are looking at their feet and I'm standing, too, just clapping away, giving it up like I mean it for Kyle Litotes.

And the thing is, I really do.

Because no matter who he was before, he's this Kyle now.

And no matter who I was before Beth, I'm this me now.

And this me wants to take Kyle out for a hot dog and some onion rings and tell him I understand.

That no matter how much of a douche he was, he was probably just scared of getting left outside the ring of cool. And it mattered so much that he wasn't able to muster the strength to be a better person. Not everyone has the strength to be a better person. We're all trying to pretend that not being our worst selves every minute of every day is easy.

It's so not easy.

And also that the only person in the whole school, maybe the whole world, who has no excuse for ever being his worst self ever again is Dice Isley.

We practice for four hours straight, running through our set eight times. Elliot is talking again, but he's so intense, there's almost nothing to say. His eyes bulge out of his head like they're ready to pop. He snaps at every little noise. He even yells at Lawrence. All of us are so freaked out that we play like we're in a studio recording with Charlie Parker. No one flubs, but there's no groove, no swing, no joy. It's pure math, beat calisthenics, rote discipline. Chaos finally begs off, saying his fingers can't take it anymore, and splits in the Beemer. I pack up my stuff while Elliot sits on a milk crate in the corner.

Lacy sits on his lap, talking to him quietly.

Rubbing his neck.

Just like Ravenna rubbed mine.

Except totally and completely different.

On Friday morning we blow off school, practice for six hours, and then all pile into the Black Widow's Renault.

"Is this for real?" El Hella asks. "I'm not driving all the way out there if someone's pussing out at the last second."

"I'm in."

"Yup."

"Me, too."

An hour later we roll over the dusty gravel outside Spider Webb's Tat Emporium. There's a big sign in the window with a fist giving the world the middle finger. Underneath it says, MANAGEMENT RESERVES THE RIGHT TO TELL YOU TO GO SCREW.

The place is empty, art over all the walls, real fifties stuff like hula girls and screaming eagles and Betty Boops. In back there's a desk with a dude standing behind it. He's beyond grizzled, a bearded old crank with an Aunt Jemima bandanna, gray ponytail, and not an uninked inch on his arms, legs, or neck. In other words, exactly what you'd expect Spider Webb to look like.

"You the Spider?" Chaos asks.

He doesn't bother to answer, inspecting his ink guns. After a while he looks up, sizes us up, frowns.

"I can't do you if you're drunk."

"We're not drunk."

"I can't do you if you're under eighteen."

"We're all eighteen."

"I can't do you if you have hepatitis."

"No hepatitis here."

"Crabs, maybe," I say, "but no hep."

Elliot laughs. Lacy elbows me in the spine. Spider rubs his eyes in a way that makes it clear that the weight of both life's experience and the immutability of youth's colossal dumbass-edness is presently crushing his very soul. "Yeah, fine, whatever. One of you delinquents get in the chair before I change my mind."

Elliot goes first. He gets WISE between his shoulder blades, the letters all filled with these cool Escher-like geometric patterns.

Chaos goes next. He gets YOUNG between his shoulder blades, each letter bursting into a different-colored flame.

I go next. And get FOOL between my shoulder blades, the F and L shaped like bent metal, bolts and rust and spot-welds at the joints.

Lacy, her dyed red hair slicked up into a mean and pointy Mohawk, gets a pretty cool Godzilla plucking a stand-up bass on her calf. Underneath, surrounded by musical notes, it says NEVER THE WISER. When she cries out, Elliot holds her hand, kisses her forehead.

The concerned boyfriend.

It's astonishing.

And sorta cool.

Maybe he's human after all.

When the Spider has finished his last spiky flourish, we pool our cash to pay and amazingly come up with fifty extra. So Chaos goes back for seconds and gets a mug of coffee on his biceps. In the steam, rising off the swirling java, are the words ALL IS CHAOS in cursive. Spider does it in such a way that you don't even realize they're words unless you look really close.

It's true art. The work of a master.

"It should say *All Is Chowus*," Elliot says. Lacy laughs too hard. Spider Webb doesn't laugh at all.

We're checking out our new ink in the full-length mirror when two biker-moms come in and push past us like they're regulars. One gets a shamrock on her ankle, the other a pink unicorn. We're standing there watching, until the Spider tells us to fuck the fuck off already.

So we do.

Ring. Gring. Gring.

It's Saturday morning. I mute the phone in the middle of Stiff Little Fingers going, *"Inflammable material is planted in my head, it's a suspect device that's left 2,000 dead!"* Three times. I don't know about my head but there's a serious pain between my shoulder blades, the skin sore beyond belief. It's either from my new ink, or the fact that Ravenna spent most of the night using me like a cheap pair of skis she was grinding through moguls on.

Afterward, we spooned up on the tiny dorm bed.

"Hey, did you know you have *Fool* tattooed on your back?"

"Um, yes, I was dimly aware."

"Can I ask why?"

"Wise," I said. "Young."

"You lost a bet and someone had to be the fool?"

"Nope. I wanted to be the fool. In fact, I almost had to fight for it."

She drew me closer, pressing her sweaty stomach against my sweaty back.

"But why?"

"Because I'm not afraid of the fool. I embrace him."

"Embrace who?"

"The idea that I know nothing. That I never will. That people who think they do are delusional. That the only thing you can genuinely know is the vast expanse of what you will never understand."

She bit my arm. "If I wanted to screw a philosophy major, I would have used *a priori* in a sentence out on the quad."

We took turns laughing and then fell asleep at almost exactly the same time.

Twenty minutes later the phone goes off again. It doesn't seem to bother Ravenna, who snores as softly as possible, the noise a milk-sotted kitten might make. Her roommate, on the other hand, sprawled on the other bunk with tissue stuffed in her ears, looks up, pissed.

"Hello?"

"Oh, god, Ritchie."

It's Lacy Duplais.

"Who is this?"

"Not now, asshole. He got Elliot."

"Who?"

"Spence Proffer."

"Got him? What do you mean, *got* him?"

"It's bad."

"Where are you?"

"The hospital."

"In Sackville?"

"No, the ER off the highway."

I jump up, yank my pants on.

"Where are you going?" Ravenna yawns. "I thought we were getting breakfast."

"I know, but I can't."

"Wait, so you're *leaving*?"

"Yeah, babe. I'm sorry, it's just..."

She sits up. The sheet falls to her waist.

"Just what?"

"Elliot. He—"

"Whatever," she says, showing me her palm like a traffic cop. "Run back to your boyfriend. Run back to Sackville."

"Where I belong?"

"Where you obviously want to be more than here."

"I don't have time for this."

"Zo go, already!" the roommate yells in her French accent.

Ravenna and the roommate start going at it. I duck out and run down to the Saab, which for once, starts on the first kick.

Lacy meets me by the nurses' station. She's all teary and shaky and freaked out. Her Mohawk has lost its stiff and is listing badly to one side. Her skull is unbearably cute.

"Elliot's sleeping."

"Tell me what happened."

She kicks at an insurance form someone dropped.

"So we were running through vocals and then took a break,

just sitting out on the lawn having a smoke. This car screeches up. A Mustang. Proffer's drunk, yelling shit about his mom. What is this about his mom, Ritchie?"

"I, uh...I got no clue."

"I mean, that's crazy, right?"

"Totally."

"Then Spence takes off his shirt and starts throwing punches."

"Oh, man."

"Yeah. I was screaming. I couldn't pull him off. He wouldn't stop until two neighbors came over with shovels. There was blood everywhere."

"I should have been there," I say, my throat catching. "I should have..."

Lacy Duplais puts her arms around me, and I hug her tight.

"How bad is it?"

"Bad."

"I want to see him."

"I don't think—"

"Hey, is that Fuckhead I hear out there?" Elliot yells.

I let go of her and run into the room. Elliot's on a metal bed, under a blanket, some cuts and bruises, smiling. There's a big scab in his hairline. One of his eyes is swollen pretty good. That's it.

"What the hell, man? I thought you were all messed up?"

He waves my comment away. "Nah, I'm fine."

Lacy's right behind me, grabbing my arm. "No, that's what I was trying to tell you. I meant—"

"Meant what?"

"I *meant* I was trying to pull Elliot off Spence. Before the cops came."

I look at grinning El Hella. Bruised El Hella.

"Wait, *you* kicked Spence Proffer's ass?"

"Yup."

"No way."

"Apparently so."

"But . . . how?"

He shrugs. "I dunno. Side of beef ran at me. I swung the bass."

"You clocked him with your bass?"

"Yeah. Caught him good. He went down. But then he got up."

"Oh, shit."

"Yeah. He punched me a lot. But I guess I punched him more. To be honest I don't really remember." He makes a *grrr* sound. "I went animal."

"He went animal," Lacy confirmed, rubbing Elliot's arm. "Like, seriously Rottweiler."

"So . . ."

"So you should see Spence. He's three doors down."

"Get out."

"Get in. He's there." Elliot makes a weird face. "Maybe not alone."

"Huh," I say.

"Yeah. Huh."

I head down the hallway. It's true.

Spence is in the same kind of bed Elliot's in, except he's out cold. Or just asleep. He's got a drip in his arm, the other one in a cast, bandages wrapped from his torso to his neck.

On a chair next to him is Angie Proffer, a little teary-eyed. She looks up. "Are you a friend of Spence's?"

"Um, yeah," I say. "I'm Todd. We go to Sackville together."

"Thanks for coming, Todd."

"Of course. How is he?"

She rummages around in her pocketbook and pulls out a pack of smokes. Her hair is blond, dirty, pulled back in a ponytail. She has dark eyes, Spence's angry nostrils, a weary face, nice legs. She looks like she knows exactly how fucked up every single thing in the world is, and then some. She lights the cigarette. There's a NO SMOKING! sign right behind her head.

"You're not going to turn me in, are you, Todd?"

"No, ma'am."

She nods. "Spence will be okay. Broken arm. A few ribs. Possible concussion. Some bruises. He'll be here over the weekend, at least. The doctors say nothing permanent."

"Great news. But what happened?"

She stares, haloed by light coming in the window. "Spence seems to have picked one fight too many."

It's my turn to nod.

"Ever since his father left? He's been so angry."

"Yeah."

"His father was no saint, you know?"

"I hear you."

"Anyway, it finally caught up to him."

"So, no pressing charges?"

She frowns. "I don't imagine so. The police used the phrase *mutual combat*. Besides, believe it or not, they've got a great insurance plan at the restaurant. So at least this is covered."

"Terrific. Okay, well, I gotta—"

"You're Elliot's friend, aren't you? The one in the band?"

I consider lying, don't.

"Yeah."

She stubs out her smoke. "You can go now, friend."

I run back to Elliot's room, hug him and Lacy until they both tell me to lay off.

"Oh my god, dude, you are so my hero."

"Nah," Elliot says, turning pink. "Just protecting my own, you know?"

Lacy kisses his cheek.

"You mean the band's equipment?"

Lacy gives me the finger.

"To be honest, I actually feel a little bad for ol' Spence."

It pops out of my mouth before I know what I'm saying. I immediately recognize it as empathy, unfamiliar but potent.

To my surprise, Elliot says, "I know what you mean."

"You do?"

"The only thing that guy had going was invincibility. And now all he's got left are bruises."

We all sort of muse on that for a minute, chewing the

profounda-cud, and then the nurse comes in and says it's time to sign Elliot out.

Our Band Needs ~~Five Things~~ Nothing:
1. We got a bass player who kicked Spence Proffer's ass. What does your lame band got?

77

Four kids rush me.

Instead of facing them, I run over and grab Conner by the pant legs. He's so surprised he just sits there watching. I rear back and yank him off his throne. He comes crashing down onto the floor with a yelp.

No one moves, stunned.

Conner lies there, holding his head.

He actually looks scared.

Or maybe just insanely pissed.

Both, definitely.

I scramble up the stack of chairs, to the top of his throne, almost losing my balance. When I turn around, it feels like I'm towering six miles above the crowd.

They're looking at me, looking at each other, not sure what to do except slowly move in.

I spread my arms and raise my chin.

"Get him!" Conner yells.

Peanut has something at his side, metal.

It flashes in the thin light.

The throne is surrounded.

I am surrounded.
But then I do something really,
totally,
and completely crazy.

I open my mouth.

And start to sing.

It stops them all cold.

78

"Okay, so we're meeting at my place at six, right?" Elliot says in the hospital parking lot. "Then we'll pack up the cars and all drive to the Question Mark to load in?"

I shake my head. "Don't need the cars. I got that covered."

"What do you mean, you got that covered?"

"Trust me."

Elliot looks at Lacy. She shrugs. "You want to come back with us? Run through a few last vocals?"

"No, I got something to do."

El Hella frowns. "Today of all days, what else you got to do?"

"Pick up Ravenna. She's coming to the show."

Lacy's eyes go dark. "I'll get the car." Elliot hands her the keys and she walks off.

"So that's where you been all week, huh? I thought you were becoming Jim Morrison's ghost."

I tell him about Sigourney. The sets. The apartment. The sex.

"I should have known. Jesus. I should have known by that look on your face."

"What look?"

"Um, Ritchie Sudden no longer furious at the world and all its faults? Ritchie Sudden being understanding and kind? Ritchie Sudden, suddenly neck deep in *amor*. Ha!"

I can feel my cheeks burn. "She's not what you think. What *I* thought. Ravenna's actually pretty amazing. For one thing—"

He holds his hand up. "Don't bother, dude. If it'll make you play better, go get your chick. I'm all for it."

"Really?"

"Really."

"So does Lacy make you play better?"

Elliot doesn't even blink. "Without question."

Lacy Duplais, improver of men, pulls up in the Black Widow's Renault. "Can we go, already?"

Elliot grins. "What's she pissed about, you figure?"

I can't tell if that means he knows Lacy and I slept together or that he has no clue Lacy and I slept together. That he's cool with it or not cool with it. That he's going to tell me or not tell me. That at some point I'll have to 'fess up or deny. That it will forever be a problem or something we'll just bury.

Actually, Lacy probably told him first thing, before they even kissed, because she's smart and cool and honest.

Unlike me.

"Girls, man."

"Yeah."

Elliot lowers himself gingerly into the passenger seat. "But whatever you do, don't be late."

"I won't."

"I mean it."

"So do I."

"I am not even remotely fucking around."

"Spence-slayer? I promise I will never, ever do anything to make you mad again."

He nods, satisfied.

"Don't. Be. Late," Lacy says, giving me the hook-horn metal fingers, and then squeals away.

The guy at the security gate, a big blustery dude in a red uniform, is not feeling my act. He sees steam coming from under the hood of the Saab and shakes his head no.

I don't have time for blustery. I don't have time for red uniforms.

"I'm going in," I say.

He pretends to consult his clipboard. He does not raise the gate.

"There is no way I am not going in."

"That's a double negative, son."

"Listen, man, I have a huge gig tonight. This is important."

He shakes his head no again, but I can see his resolve beginning to crumble.

"What kind of gig?"

"Rock and roll, dude," I lie.

"Really?"

"How can I bust out my best chops if my old lady's not backstage?"

He laughs, sighs, wipes his neck, and then waves me through with two fingers.

I've got four hours, tops, to get Ravenna dressed and ready before roaring back to Sackville. I picture all the dudes at the show seeing her with me. On my arm. The crowd parting. The insane jealousy. Every single guy there wondering why they never learned to play guitar. Why some guys get the hottest girls and others are left to learn science and shit.

Me and Ravenna: the first couple of punk.

I park and hotfoot it across the quad just as her roommate bangs out the dorm's front door. She gives me an evil smile, says something under her breath that sounds a whole lot like *blind leading the blind*, without a trace of a French accent, and keeps going.

"Real good to see you, too," I say. "Have a great weekend."

My hand's on the knob when Ravenna herself floats out. Behind her is this guy I half recognize. It takes a second to place him, but then I realize he played the teen mechanic in *Return of the Starfighter Squad*.

Sigourney's brother. Jensen Partman's son.

Has to be.

He's small and finely featured, almost prettier than he is ridiculously handsome.

"Oh, hi," I say, like a cow up on a hook, hit between the eyes with a beef hammer. In the span of one afternoon Ravenna has managed to seriously trade up. Or maybe she's been doing it since the party. Bait and switch. Lever and fulcrum. Donkey and carrot. With every breath, things make a little more sense. Or maybe a little less.

"What are you doing here?" she asks, both sides of her mouth curled upward. I've never seen that before.

"Um, picking you up for the show?"

"What show?" Starfighter says, genuinely curious.

Ravenna yawns. "He's in a band."

"Are they any good?"

"Not really."

"That's too bad," Starfighter says, sounding like he means it. He hooks his arm in hers.

"Ravenna?" I say. "Seriously?"

"Oh, grow up, Ritchie."

And I do.

In that second I really, really do.

"What happens in Sackville stays in Sackville," she says. "And so should the people who live there."

They walk away with these impossibly long and perfect strides, laughing like drawings from a *New Yorker* cartoon, so classy and unperturbed, so utterly at home in themselves, that I can only stand there and admire it.

Halfway back across the quad, I sit on a bench and consider crying. I mean, hey, why not? But it just won't come. Puking also seems possible, but not that glamorous. So I rest my head on my shoulders for a while instead. Students stream by, laughing, joking. No one stops. No one asks me what's wrong. No one puts an arm around my shoulders and invites me back to the dorm for a hot toddy.

I want to get drunk.

I want to get in a fight.

I don't want to do either.

Not too far away is a girl studying on a blanket in the grass. I walk over to borrow a pen, then lie on my back, far enough so that she won't call security, and write. It's a song. Or a poem. It all comes out in one torrent, one breath, one exhalation, like breaking the surface and spitting out water for air. It's cheesy. It's lyrics. It's not epic or tough or cool.

It's honest.

It's the first thing I've ever written that's honest.

Which means it's the best thing I've ever written.

"It's called 'Teach Me to Reach Me,'" I tell the girl while returning the pen.

She looks confused.

"I said I was just borrowing it, right?"

She goes back to her *Petrochemicals in Contemporary Society* textbook.

And then I start to run.

The Saab won't turn over.

HORROR.

It won't even make a noise.

I jog down to the gate and ask the guard if he's got any jumper cables. He gives me a look like, *Exactly how far are you prepared to push it in this life, son?* I decide to just leave the piece of shit in the lot. Rude can come get it if he wants it. But not before I release the brake, put it in neutral, and push it down the grade a bit, where it rolls sideways and nestles against the rear bumper of a red Mercedes convertible with the vanity plate PARTMAN1, blocking it in.

On the bus back, I notice this Asian girl. She's sitting alone, totally cute, dark eyes and tiny smile, lips pursed. She's looking down at her lap, fiddling with a cell phone. Her hair is long and straight. I can practically see my reflection in it. She's the anti-Ravenna. She's a human being. She's not perfect and she's not glowing. She's just there, occupying her own space. I can see the warm blood pulsing around inside her, instead of Freon.

I tell myself to go over and say hi. Not to pick her up, just to have a real interchange. How's it going. Here we are, both alive. Communication between the genders. Between the races. Between the species.

A stop goes by.

Then two.

I walk over and plop down beside her. She looks at me warily. I know the people in the seats all around us are listening, dudes watching my play, but I like her smile and so I get encouraged.

"Hey, look, I hardly ever do this. You know, approach some random girl. Not that you're, you know, random...I just mean I'm actually pretty shy and mostly just want to be left alone, so I try to extend that courtesy to others. Especially female others traveling by themselves. Ha ha. But I saw you sitting here and I thought, I don't know, you look interesting. Beautiful, definitely, but more interesting. That's where my head is at these days, you know? My priorities. Connect with people who actually have something to say. I mean, I'm not smooth, I'm not giving you some bullshit line, but I was looking at you and thinking about my parents, how you meet someone. And end up on a date. And before you know it you've moved in and bought a couch and suddenly you're together for life. Or at least until you get divorced. You entwine your existences. Or you go out to dinner and it sucks and you never see each other again. How weird and random it is that maybe the person who's your perfect mate is a few rows away and you never said anything. Because you were too nervous to speak up. I mean, I know that sounds ridiculous. I'm not saying you and I...I mean, no pressure here or whatever. It's just that, wow, it's been a tough morning for me. And then, there you were..."

She doesn't say anything.

"Listen, I'm really sorry. I know I'm babbling, but I just came over to, you know, invite you to a show. I'm in a band. Called Wise Young Fool. We're playing tonight and, I dunno, I thought maybe you'd want to come."

She finally opens her mouth.

I wait.

And then she goes:

"Ting bu dong. Dui bu qi, wo bu hui shuo Yingwen."

All the dudes on the bus start laughing their asses off. I mean, seriously breaking up at what a knob I am. A posse of *vatos* are pointing at me and throwing shit. They're bumping knuckles and fiving highs.

I get up and go sit in the back of the bus and think hard about how badly I want to have never existed.

How much I just want to sweep myself up and throw myself away.

How I have a little less than an hour to make the show.

80

I spread my arms and sing "Teach Me to Reach Me."

Softly at first, rising in increments.

And they actually watch.

The whole dayroom.

Having already rushed the stage, they take the time to check it out.

Conner still lying there on the floor, looking up.

Peanut, his eyes dark but confused and amazed, the metal at his side.

And I sing.

I sing them a song about Ravenna Woods.

Breaking whatever heart I pretended to have.

Breaking clichés about my heart in half.

As smooth as I can.

As raw as I can.

Vulnerable.

I run through it twice, don't hold anything back.

No pose, no pretense.

Just soul and a snap of the fingers.

Just a song.

That I have memorized.

Because I've been singing it in my head, on my bunk, staring at the ceiling, for months.

And because I believe every word:

Please,
    Go ahead and
    Show me every way you're not
    Exactly who I knew you were
    All along.
    Fooled myself, lied and denied
    Just to lie beside you,
    Just to hide inside you
    Every stroke a betrayal of
    Anything I ever claimed to be.

To teach me
    You got to reach me
    Something I don't know how to allow.
    Breaking through to the other side
    Grab a seat on the liar's ride
    Angry words over angry chords
    You're a leather jacket I can't afford
    A layer of lipstick
    That has no taste
    Every minute we're not fucking
    A total waste

Thought I was using you
    Thought I was cruising you
    But I'm the one who
    Watches while
    You walk away.
    Laughing as if
    You had something
    Worth saying to say.

You got to reach me
    To teach me
    'Cause I already knew how not to care.

You got to teach me
    To reach me
    'Cause you were never really there.

Never really there.

Never *really* there.

Never really *there*.

I take a cab from the station, tell the driver to please hurry. It's this ancient Sikh guy with a turban. He scowls the whole way, dark and pissed and bent forward, going ten miles under the speed limit. When we finally pull into the driveway, I realize I don't have enough cash.

"Hey, man, I'm really sorry, but I'm a little short on the fare."

He eyeballs me hard in the rearview.

I sit there and wait for him to freak out.

Call the cops.

Beat me with his cane.

"That's cool," he finally says, and takes what I've got.

"Really?"

He strokes his mustache. "Bro, I been there."

I almost cry.

I almost kiss him.

I don't do either.

Not a second to lose.

Mom and Looper are in the kitchen and Mom is all drawn and weepy-eyed. The TV's on behind them, but there's no sound. I walk in and they stare at me. I know whatever it is, it must be horrible. Elliot? It has to be Elliot. He was hurt worse than we thought. An aneurism. The hospital called. I'm about to turn, without a word, and run straight to the ER, when Mom smiles.

She turns sideways and Looper puts her hand on Mom's tummy, rubbing it clockwise.

She hands me a Polaroid.

Except it's not a Polaroid.

It's a sonogram picture. It's a little being, a little thing hunkered there on its side, about the size of a lime. A tiny little foot.

Amazing.

Terrifying.

"Is it a girl?"

"Nope."

"A boy?"

"You have a third suggestion?" Mom asks.

"A boy," I say. "Huh."

"A brother."

"An as-yet-unnamed Sudden male."

"Except he's named," Looper says.

"He is?"

"Lincoln."

"Link?"

"Lincoln Richard," Mom says.

"Link Sudden," I say. "Kid's gonna have to be a badass to live that down."

"He'll have a good teacher," Mom says.

I shake my head. "No way. The only thing he's getting from

me is Barbies and chocolates and soft pillows. The tough-guy routine officially ends here."

Mom hugs Loop.

Mom hugs me.

Loop hugs me.

"I need a favor," I whisper in her ear.

She doesn't even respond, just palms me the keys.

I pull up at the Black Widow's in the Perfection Pools van and everyone cheers. Even Chaos cheers, loading his bongos into the hold. Elliot exhales hard, rubbing his wet scalp in disbelief.

"Cutting it a little close, eh, Sudden?"

"Dude, you would so not believe the day I've had."

Something in my expression is *fuck yeah* convincing.

He just nods.

Lacy does a scissors kick, howls, laughs. She looks amazing. In full purple leathers, no less. Her Mohawk matches her outfit, even purpler, with jet-black tips. She's smoking hot. I tell her so.

"Easy there," Elliot says.

"Thanks, Ritchie," Lacy says, kissing me on the cheek.

She's glowing. She's beaming.

Elliot is amped and absolutely ready to rock.

Chaos is Chaos.

We all laugh, giddy.

I am cranked on a pure nervous high.

"Wise?" I say. "Highly debatable. Young? Certainly. Fools? Right down to the last man."

Lacy puts her hands on her hips. "Down to the last woman. And this woman is proud to be a fool."

"Too right, too right," I say, locking eyes with her. "I'm sorry."

She knows what I'm sorry for, knows exactly what I mean.

"That's the last piece!" Chaos yells, slamming the bay doors. "Let's go."

"To hell or to Hollyrock," Elliot says.

And so we do.

Parking space: check. No problem.

Huge bouncer dude in front: check, we're on the list, Wise Young Fool. "That's you?"

"That's us."

Sound check: check. Pro gear, pro sound guy, crisp and clean and full. Dice's compressor is plugged into Dice's pre-amp, fueling The Paul, right out front where anyone can see. A dare. Go ahead and say something. Besides, mother of all that's both metal and holy, The Paul is now insanely *loud*.

Press: lots of local reporters, cameras, cords, equipment. Also, some slick dudes who are obviously part of the *Real Godz of Hollyrock* crew.

Backstage posse: connected scenesters, club guys, bar owners, promoters, velvet-ropers, and various minor deal makers.

Emcee: tight black pants, tight black shirt, too cool to live. He looks like he just walked out of a catalog for steak cologne, except he's got a goatee. "You lames have twenty-five minutes exactly. Don't go over. I'll introduce you, and then the clock's running. After, if the crowd is limp, you're done, period. If by some chance they actually dig it, I'll signal you back on for an encore. Then you got an extra five to really flaunt your shit. Got it? Once I signal off, you're off, period."

Other bands are loading in, everyone eyeballing one another up the yang, chests out, showing off leather and ink. Elliot hands us each a piece of paper.

"Learn it. Live it. Love it."

SONG LIST—Wise Young Fool RockSceneTwentyThirteen

1. Ignition Bloody Chrysalis
2. The Big Book of Little Genocides
3. Necro Feel You Up
4. Archer Fires Arrow, Flesh Takes Point
5. Today's Duplais Display
6. Mack the Spoon

   If encore: Disguster

83

I stop singing.

I'm out of breath and out of words.

For the very first time ever, the dayroom is dead silent.

The chairs creak below me, wobbly as shit.

I'm ready to jump down, see what's coming.

Whatever it is.

But I don't have a chance.

Because someone yells, "Five-O," and then the doors clang. Meatstick and some other counselors rush in.

Everyone turns, pretending to play Twister or sullenly eyeballing their sneakers.

The counselors see Conner on the ground and figure there's a fight. They see Peanut, who tries to ditch his shiv, standing over him. Not metal. Plastic. A Colgate medium bristle, sharpened to a mean point. Yunior zips over like he knew it was there all along, grabs Peanut, and wrestles him to the floor. The Basilisk grabs Conner, who doesn't resist, and they drag the pair of them out of the room.

It's like a breeze coming in off the sea, washing away the industrial stink of the city and the sour thoughts of small men.

Maybe that's a bit much.

But things do seem to change in the room, a slight shift.

I climb down.

And slowly begin to unstack the chairs.

The legs clang together, vibrating.

The metal pads click against the floor.

I can feel eyes on my back, but I don't hurry.

When I'm done, for the first time in eighty days, there is no throne.

It's been deconstructed. Decommissioned. Deflated.

I turn and start to pass the chairs around, sliding them toward different kids. They just stare. Or flinch.

I keep sliding them.

All of them.

One stops in front of B'los.

He shrugs and actually sits down.

So some other kids do, too.

A bunch of them sitting.

Not standing.

Comfortable.

Not posturing.

Reclined.

The hierarchy of plastic furniture.

Is a hierarchy no more.

Ass to seat.

Ass to seat.
Ass to seat.
Ass to seat.
A place to rest and put up your feet.

It's an amazing thing.

The Question Mark is packed to the gills. People are pouring out the front, out the windows, shoved against every possible inch of wall. Astonishingly, half of Sackville High is representing, plus packs of teen dudes we've never seen before. Rocker girls of every stripe laugh and pose, single, spoken for, slutty, shy. Püre Venum fans glare at people the other bands have brought. Cleverly, and like the promo kings we are, we've brought no one but ourselves. Or maybe it's just that we have no friends. In any case, we catch a break as they draw numbers from someone's Slash top hat for playing order.

We go on second to last.

The first four or five acts are all different: a hippie jam thing, a singer-songwriter type with backing harmonies up the yang, a Krautrock/electronica hybrid with turntables and weakass rapping, dudes doing classic-rock covers somehow under the impression they're doing originals, and some super-screamy arty deal with slides projected in the background and a lead singer who wears nothing but bunny slippers and a diaper.

The crowd takes it all in stride, everyone's posse going nuts when required, but no one seems blown away on the whole.

Diaper Dan warbles through a final coda and takes a bow.

There're cheers, but not enough for an encore.

Emcee Badass makes a few announcements, says to tip the servers, talks up the sponsors, tells a few jokes to zero laughs, and then says our name.

Finally, finally, finally Wise Young Fool clambers onto a real stage.

I shoulder The Paul.

Look out into the lights.

The crowd is wound up. Sweaty and pissed and drunk and doubtful and expectant. A mob. A pack of hyenas. A murder of crows. Ready to tear meat off the bones of lameness.

I swallow a sudden rush of pure, unadulterated fear. It's like one of those freezing-cold swigs of milk you can feel all the way down to your kneecaps.

Lacy gets right up on the mic, says some sultry lines. A few dudes in the crowd whistle and then Chaos counts it off. There's a wash of noise I am somehow part of, dead-handed. The first song is pretty much over before I even realize we're playing.

Did I screw up?

Did I nail it?

Do they hate us?

I take a second to desperately wish we'd practiced a million more times. Or that I was home on the can playing scales. Or that I had chosen watercolors of horses as a hobby instead of stupid guitar.

And then something magic happens. We're halfway into "The Big Book of Little Genocides" and I'm just not scared anymore. Suddenly I don't care. Or I do care—so much it hurts—but have come to the realization that my caring has no effect on the outcome either way.

I smile and look up.

Lacy is killing it, the crowd with her, watching every move. She shimmies, voice all husky. She shakes leather bootie, oozes presence, head thrown back, belting it out.

My hands choose that minute to fully reanimate. The neck of The Paul seems to shrink; the strings become super fat.

We segue into "Necro Feel You Up," chord chord lick lick hook, and here comes my solo. I rest one foot on the monitor, stick out my crotch, and lean over the crowd like a million guitarists have done at a million concerts with varying degrees of cheese since the dawn of time, spitting blood or biting the heads off bats or just wanking the whammy bar in a collective understanding of the language of spectacle.

The girls in front, low-cut and crazy-haired and remarkably fluent in this language, go crazy, screaming their lungs out. I spool out about a million notes, bend the shit out of my strings, hammer on and hammer off, mostly cheapie tricks but they work, and then step back for Lacy's chorus with half a beat to spare. El Hella slides right into my spot, pressing his teeth against the mic like he's gonna swallow it whole. The two of them sing in a tight harmony they've obviously been practicing on their own; I've never heard it before.

It's fucking great.

Beautiful, even.

They follow each other around in circles, rising in a wave.

It's the kind of small thing, when added to a bunch of similar small things, little accents and fills and ideas, that turn an okay song into something exceptional.

And they nail it.

Dice's compressor redlines, compensates, and then it's over.

We go real commando punk style, no stupid patter, count off the next one right away: and one and-a two. We do "Archer Fires Arrow," pull out all the stops, die-cast our name into the metal plates of the collective skull. I crank my volume pedal and a wall of distortion collapses onto the heads of the willing. We hit the bridge, I fingerpick a solo that copies the melody of Lacy's vocal, and then out.

I blink once, twice, and we're playing "Today's Duplais Display." I go from jangly fills into another solo, sort of just aping the chord progression, rude and tasty, some longhairs nodding in appreciation in the back. Outro. We quickly retune. Lacy asks the crowd to give it up for the guitar player. There's a roar I refuse to look up and acknowledge, mostly because I've forgotten that the guitar player is me. Then Lacy reminds everyone not to forget to vote for Best Band, suggesting us as a wise choice for young fools.

The crowd laughs and then cheers.

I lean over for a sip of Sprite. And spot Dad Sudden. Out in the middle of the audience. Come to see me, like a scene from a shitty movie, the father passing the baton, watching his son with pride now that he's become a man.

Even if he had no part in the man becoming anything.

380

But then I blink and it's not Dad Sudden at all, just some pudgy dude with a smile and a beer and about six hairs on his head. He raises his bottle and whoops.

And then "Mack the Spoon" is chugging along hard and fast. By the end of the first verse, like a blooming flower or a blooming fist, all these dudes are moshing in front of us, slamming shoulders with rhino force, lipping off the stage and then back into the twirling mass. They're out of control. Sheer madness.

Elliot slap-funks a bass solo thing.

Chaos *bam-pitty-bam-pitty-bams*.

And it's done.

We put down our instruments, cheer, cheer, cheer, whoo whoo whoo.

The four of us press together backstage, everyone dripping sweat.

"Holy shit."

"I know."

"Wow."

"I. Know."

Crowd noise shifts into overdrive. Emcee Badass gives us the nod.

"You guys ready?" he asks with 367 percent more respect than he gave us twenty minutes ago.

Then we're back for the encore, first band to get one.

Cheers, whistles, a broken bottle or two.

A fair amount of bedlam.

I shoulder The Paul like an old army buddy at closing time.

"Disguster" begins. It's really sort of a vanity vehicle for

381

me, superfast mini-chords over thumpa-thumpa rhythm and Lacy-moan, into an extended distortion thing where I essentially pretend to impregnate my amp. In the meantime, Elliot and Chaos build and build and build until finally the whole thing breaks like a wave of corrosive sludge.

Lacy looks at me and winks.

I almost drop my pick but don't.

Voice and noise and timbre and lust and fury waft through me, up from the bottoms of my feet and out the top of my skull, like a cartoon gusher, an oil derrick out on a lonely Texas plain just booming with groove and crude.

There is just something, man, about being in front of a bunch of people, people watching you do your thing, enjoying it, this note, that note, and you're sort of controlling how they feel with sound. It's a cliché, sure, it's everyone's rock-star fantasy for a reason, but here you are *really* doing it, and it's just so bizarre and excellent and fulfilling, deep in the narcotic, adulatory part of your cave-brain, that you don't ever want to let it go.

The song is basically over and we're just vamping around, hunkered in the pocket. The stage dudes keep signaling it's time for Püre Venum. So, of course, Elliot starts the progression again. I step on my wah pedal and wank wank wank this eighties arena solo just for laughs. They go genuinely apeshit below me, literally drunken primates flinging excrement and warring over control of a stand of banana trees. The stage dudes are really pissed now, screaming at us to wrap it up. Emcee Badass slashes his throat with two fingers like, *Cut! Cut!* Elliot nods at

Chaos as if to say, *Oh, hey, sorry. Sure, of course*, but instead doubles down on the walk-up and *whoops*, we're going around the progression one more time. It's a colossal F-U, but the crowd is so with us they don't have the balls to pull the plug, and I'm just improvising shit, atonal, faster and faster and faster until it's way past common sense or logic, verging on release or madness, and then finally, mercifully, Lacy sings the last line for the fifth time.

And we are offstage.

I am herded into some room in back, beaming like I've just won a free toaster. A guy in a motorcycle jacket passes around beers and says, "Make sure no one sees you underage fuckers," and then it's one glad hand after another.

"...but yeah, you deserve it; you guys rocked the..."
   "...Wise Young Fool so rules, I mean..."
   "...hey, man, nice Hendrix action..."
   "...hi, I'm Sarah..."
   "...whew, cool, so okay..."
   "...wow some solos, especially the second..."
   "...hi, I'm Wendy..."
   "...drummer is freaking original, I mean, whose idea was..."
   "...just give me your number and we'll..."
   "...hi, I'm Trish..."
   "...guys got it in the bag..."
   "...necrophilia song is totally..."
   "...kind of funky guitar is that you're..."

"...hi, I'm David..."

"...awesome band, but what you really need..."

"...but what you really should..."

"...who you have to meet is..."

"...hi, I'm Amy..."

"...hi, I work for..."

"...hi, I'm friends with..."

"...hi, I just want you to know..."

"...I just want..."

"...I just want..."

"...I just want..."

The words come and go, float and dip, sink or swim, bite or sting. The adulation and rush and need and jealousy, it's all one big wash until Püre Venum is over and I didn't hear a note. The judges confab, and then Flog Toggle and Angelo Coxone get back up onstage. They're at the mic. The crowd quiets down. We're all hugging one another, holding shoulders. Flog thanks the bands and the bar and the sponsors and God and his mom, then opens up this oversize envelope just like the Oscars.

He leans into the mic, and in a very low voice announces the winner....

It's the band with the guy wearing Pampers.

There goes Hollyrock.

Much booing from the crowd. Screaming about it being a fix. A chant of *Wise Young Fool! Wise Young Fool! Wise Young Fool!* picks up steam in part of the room and then dies.

The house music comes on, some DJ shit, and then people swamp the bar for fresh cocktails.

I roll cords over my shoulder into figure eights as Flog Toggle comes up behind me.

"You dudes were robbed."

"Yeah," Angelo says. Elliot and Chaos walk over. Lacy is handed a business card by some guy so handsome it makes my teeth hurt.

"You think?"

"I do," Flog says. "On the other hand, if you acted pro and not like a handful of dicks, got offstage at your cue, it might have gone different."

I mime a pen. "By any chance you got something I can write that sage advice down on?"

Flog frowns. And then laughs. "Gotta hand it to you dudes, always staying in character."

Angelo nods. "Yeah, okay, you didn't win, boo hoo. But you want to open up for us next weekend? The original band dropped out, guitar player's got Legionnaires' disease or whatever. So we got an open slot."

"Think of it as a consolation prize," Flog says.

"Screw that!" El Hella roars, a landmass of Proffer-bruises still ripe on his face and not looking too tough at all. "We don't want nothing from ass bandits like—"

Chaos smooths in and shuts Elliot up. He takes Flog and Angelo by the arms and leads them away and tells them we'd love to, how generous they are, cool dudes, how great their band is, don't worry about Elliot Hella, he's just drunk, he loves you dudes, too, no, no, no hard feelings, yes, yes, yes we will open next weekend, no doubt, love to, hey it's cool, it's so cool, let's go out back and have a smoke, right on, glad there's someone with a level head in your band, righteous, you guys were really good, but to be honest, we're better. Ha ha. Ha ha ha ha.

85

I'm in Dr. Benway's office.

"I have good news."

"Okay."

"We're releasing you on schedule."

"That's not funny," I say.

"It's not meant to be. It's true."

"But why? I figured for sure I was a repeater."

"I've filed a number of recommendations concerning your good behavior."

"Huh."

"Also, you've done truly excellent work with your journal."

"I have?"

She holds up the notebook.

"To be honest, I believe you have invested more of yourself in these pages than anyone I've ever worked with."

"That can't possibly be true."

"And yet it is. Further, some of the counselors have suggested it might be wise if you are no longer a member of the population when Mr. Corrigan and Mr. Marcus are released from Preventative Hold."

"Who?"

"Conner and Peanut."

"What, so you believe me now?"

There's a tuna sandwich on her desk. She takes a bite.

"What makes you think there was ever a time when I didn't believe you?"

We're at an after-party. All the bands. All the posses. All the velvet-rope types. A few I recognize, but mostly people I've never seen before. Someone keeps putting beers in my hand. I keep emptying them out in a plant. Chaos is making nine girls laugh. Elliot's standing there in a trance, a huge grin on his face, accepting compliments as is his right and due. Lacy is leaning against the bar, accepting drinks from various slick types, as is her Du and Plais.

One of the Hollyrock dudes tight-pantses it over and stands next to me, playing it cool while he orders a drink. French vodka, top-shelf. He's wearing a shiny leather jacket and tie. He's got one of those Julius Caesar haircuts and rectangular glasses.

"Great set," he says, like he just noticed me.

"Thanks."

"Listen, I think maybe we have something to talk about."

I put down a full beer. Someone hands me a new one.

"Okay."

Hollyrock points at Lacy. "I've seen a lot of bands, believe me, but you guys? You're on fire."

"We are?"

"I think, provided certain items can be agreed upon, that it might be worth flying out to LA to meet the *Real Godz* crew. The casting people in particular."

"Aren't you the casting people?"

Hollyrock laughs. "No, I'm just a regional scout. Talent evaluator. But I'm good enough at my job to think that I might have just evaluated some serious talent."

I look over at El Hella, being mobbed by arty punk chicks. I can't wait to tell him. Can't wait to see him turn red, squat down, and pass a brick.

"But we didn't win. What about the winners?"

"Diaper boy? Um, sorry, no. They lost before they ever got onstage."

Lacy sees us talking and leaves five disappointed guys in her wake.

"Who's this, Ritchie?"

Hollyrock reaches into his pocket, hands us each a business card. It's bone white and soft and expensive, with raised lettering and a logo. It says TREVOR DEMOTIC—ARTISTS AND REPERTOIRE. "I'm the guy who has a proposition for you."

Lacy laughs. "Propose away."

"Well, I was just telling Ritchie here that I think I can get you a meeting with the *Real Godz* producers."

Lacy squeals in a pitch I've only heard once before. "No effing way!"

Trevor holds up his palms. "Don't get excited; it's just a

meeting. No promises. You fly out to LA, get styled, get outfitted. We shoot a little footage, see how you test."

I look down at my black boots, jeans, and AC/DC *Highway to Fred* tour shirt.

"What's wrong with this style?"

He laughs. "Yeah, well, it works for now."

"Are we flying first class?" Lacy asks.

"You buy your own ticket, sister. This isn't the movies. This is barely even TV."

She turns slightly less purple than her Mohawk. "Let me go get Elliot."

"No," Trevor says.

"No?"

"The offer is for you two only."

"But we're a band," Lacy says. "We're—"

"You're a duo. Trust me."

"But—"

Trevor sighs, chewing a mouthful of ice. "Listen, the bongo boy? I like his look, sure. Rich kid slumming it hard. Ghettocrombie. Not very original, but it could work. However, those bongos will not fly. So he's out. And the bass player? Kid's got some chops, but I mean, seriously? He's got a great face for radio. And the legs? We decide to remake *Wizard of Oz*, I'll get him a tryout with the Lollipop Guild. Butch up Munchkinland for sure. Other than that he's a nonstarter. Sorry."

Lacy looks at me. I look at her. "So we just drop the rest of the band? Bang, they're out?"

Trevor signals for another drink, puts it on his corporate Amex. The bartender rolls his eyes and slams the glass down. "I know it's not easy, but it happens all the time. You can't carry deadweight in the biz. You got to think of yourself. Do what's right for you. And the two of you? Believe me, you guys are what's right."

"I guess we don't owe them anything," Lacy says slowly. "We've only been together, what, a month?"

"We don't owe them shit," I agree.

"So what's next?" she asks.

Trevor smiles. "I have some paperwork in the car for you to sign. They don't like you after the screen test? Fine, you come home. They do like you, I'll be your representation."

"Fifteen percent?" I say.

"Exactly."

"I'm ready to sign," Lacy says.

"Me, too. Where's a pen?"

The sound system kicks in. It's so loud Trevor practically has to scream for us to hear. So he screams.

"Okay, but the other thing is, we need a story."

"What kind of story?"

"You two sound good, you look hot, but that's not enough. I need something to pitch you with. No offense, but I'm sure in a shit town like this you don't have a whole lot of drama to dangle, am I right? So we work up character profiles, just to give you a little background."

"Well," Lacy says, putting her arm around me. "Ritchie and I are lovers."

Trevor pulls out a flip pad and starts writing it down. "Good. I like it. Captain and Tennille. John Doe and Exene."

"Better yet," Lacy says, "we *were* lovers, but then we had a huge fight and didn't speak for months. Ritchie's a thief on the side; that's how we finance our band. I told him he has to quit it with the breaking and entering or we're through."

"Love it!" Trevor says, scribbling away.

"Yeah, I pretty much chose crime over her. I need the juice. Gotta have the action. But we both knew we couldn't ever give up on the tunes."

"Nice. What else?"

It's such a good question.

"Well, my mom's a lesbian," I say.

Trevor frowns. "Sorry, don't like it. We have sponsors. Walmart. Miracle Whip. No lesbians."

"Fine. Scratch that. Mom's just divorced. Found religion after my father split for some blonde down in Texas."

"Now you're talking."

"And also, my sister died in a car crash a few years back. Killed by a drunk driver. That's what drove me to music. That's why I'm so committed to becoming a guitar hero but also so detached and enigmatic. It's why it didn't work out with Lacy and me. It's why I'm so edgy and volatile."

Lacy's not smiling anymore. She's looking at me like she can't believe I'm telling him this. I can't believe it, either. But I can't stop myself.

"Wow!" Trevor says. "Where do you come up with this

material? The screen test doesn't fly, maybe I can get you a gig as a writer."

"Yeah," I say. "My sister's death hangs around my neck like an albatross. And the thing is, it's not just because she's gone, it's that there's something I should have done about it. Business I should have taken care of, but never did. Because secretly, like, way deep inside, I'm a coward. I lied to myself that my inaction was all about her, protecting her, but now I realize it's been about me all along."

"Wait," Trevor says, flipping back a few pages in his pad. "You mean the drunk driver? You've vowed to get revenge on him? Great hook."

Lacy's giving me the eyeball, trying to get my attention. "Ritchie—"

"No, the drunk driver's dead," I say. "Worm burned up in the crash."

Trevor frowns, confused. "Listen, if we go the bummer route, it needs to have a really solid payoff. You gotta be real careful with the tragic routine."

"Tell me about it."

"So let's nail what's really motivating your character. What's the one thing he absolutely has to accomplish?"

"That's easy," I say.

"Good. Lay it on me."

"He has to get the fuck out of here. Like, right now."

"I don't get it," Trevor says, chewing a mouthful of ice.

"Me neither," Lacy says.

El Hella finally wanders over with a big shit-eater of an El Smile pasted across his mug. "Who's this guy?"

"Just another fool who is neither wise nor young," I say, ripping Trevor's card into tiny pieces and then sprinkling them all over his vintage Air Jordans. "C'mon, we got to go."

"Now?"

"Now," I say, already starting for the door.

"Why are you driving so fast?"

"Seriously, man."

The trees scream by, the van taking corners hard. Equipment slams from side to side in the hold. Elliot and Chaos grab onto the backs of the seats as best as they can. I see The Paul go flying by in the rearview.

"What the hell, Ritchie?"

"Stop it. You're scaring me."

"Us, dude. You're scaring *us*."

A car comes the other way, hogging the road. I lay on the horn, yank the wheel, miss it by inches.

"Jesus."

"You idiot."

"Slow. The. Fuck. Down."

The roads get narrower, the curves tighter.

Good old Sackville city planning.

I could slow down, but I don't.

I could care, but I don't.

And that's pretty much that.

The gas is floored.

The engine screams in protest.

They all yell at me.

And then we go even faster.

I'm standing on the wet grass and the sky is some weird mixture of orange and black. It's got to be close to dawn. I'm barefoot.

The Perfection Pools van is idling where I left it, which is on top of a huge pile of lumber and Sheetrock.

That was once a porch.

Pretty much exactly what I was aiming for. Bouncing across the lawn, digging up divots, triangulating the front door. The van is like a seesaw, on these granite steps, shrubbery torn and a yard cherub broken in half, the front of the house crushed. There's gonna be a deductible, no doubt. Meanwhile, Elliot and Chaos are yelling at each other at the edge of the property. Chaos thinks we should haul ass. Elliot thinks I need a doctor. Lacy is off somewhere crying. I may have elbowed her when she tried to grab the wheel. My forehead is wet, and I know it's not rain. Blood dries on my scalp, on my lips; it tastes like rust and snot. Kind of good, kind of scary.

I am covered in glass.

I am dizzy with potential.

Looper is, for sure, gonna be pissed.

In the distance, Dice is holding a flashlight. Looking at the hole in his picket fence where I chugged through. It's a van-shaped hole, just like out of a cartoon. You wouldn't figure it would work like that. Then he steps down onto the lawn.

Speaking into his phone. Keeping an eye on me, keeping his distance. Every once in a while I feint, like I'm about to make a run at him, and he flinches.

I dig my toes into the dirt.

"Got anything to say, Dick?"

He's in a bathrobe and slippers. Chest hair pokes from the terry cloth. He doesn't look like a seducer or even a teacher. He looks like just another asshole who bet wrong on too many losing horses, ate too much fried food, and seriously needs a nap.

"No."

"Nothing funny? Nothing charming? No brilliant advice?"

His sad-dude eyes are so fake they look like they were bought at a bodega.

"You're mad, Mr. Sudden. I get it."

"We're not in class, doucheburger. I'm not a mister any more than you are."

He crosses his arms. "Again, I understand you're angry. Perhaps it is, to some small degree, warranted. That may be a conversation we can have at a later date."

"I got an idea. Why don't we say what we've got to say now instead? Huh, Dick?"

He sighs. "Well, for one thing, you're drunk."

"Negative. I don't drink. Guess why not?"

He looks back at his porch. "Well, it's just that...why else would you have driven your..."

"But *you* were drunk the night in question," I say, stepping closer. "Weren't you, Grope City?"

He stares at me. Pale and scared. Or tired and resigned. Or beaten down and defeated. Or fairly accused.

"Yeah, that's right. Beth told me a week before she died how you were at the Pines. Bumped into her near the keg. All talking and laughing and relating to the kids, just like always. Until, you know, you grabbed her shoulder and kissed her."

He clears his throat.

"That did not happen."

"She said it's no big deal, 'cause you were hammered."

"I wasn't."

"She said it's sort of a big deal, though, 'cause she was hammered, too."

"She was."

"She told you to be cool. She pushed you away and asked if you could please just leave her alone."

"That isn't what she said."

"So you were there? Do we at least have that confirmed?"

He looks down at his slippers. It's just him and me, on a wet lawn, the stars and the moon and the crumpled metal. He takes a deep breath, acting out the movie of himself, the one where he's about to give the speech that makes it all okay. That makes me realize how tough it is to be old and getting older. Conflicted. How we're all just human. How temptation is part of our elemental selves, from Eve to the apple to the snake and back.

"I did leave her alone."

"No, you didn't."

Dice claps his hands together. It's like a rifle shot across the lawn. "I've got something that you need to hear, Mr. Sudden. Not for me, but for you. Your sister *liked* drama, okay? And if there was none, she made up her own." He looks back at his house. "Obviously, it runs in the family."

I laugh. "You know what? Beth insisted you groping her wasn't the end of the world. She even had your back. She said people do dumb shit all the time, even teachers, right? So why drag Mr. Isley into anything?"

"Because it never happened."

"I was the one wanted to go to the cops."

"And yet, somehow you never did."

"For what? A bunch of gossip and rumors? I mean, who was going to believe who?"

Dice shakes his head. He expels a bunch of rotten air, trying to regain his Zen.

I step closer. "Maybe you're what freaked her out. Maybe she left that party because of you. Maybe she drove too fast to get away from *you*."

He reties his bathrobe, opens his mouth, about to say something.

"You better not say *I'm sorry*. I swear to gòd, if you do I'm going to—"

Sirens echo off in the distance. We both watch sets of headlights come screaming around the bend.

"I am a good teacher," Dice finally says, and then turns and goes back inside the house.

Through the huge hole where his front door used to be.

Cowardly bitch.

The van's radio still works. It's on softly in the background. Live 105.7 KROK rocking you all night long. And now we got a three-fer from ZZ Top. "Beer Drinkers and Hell Raisers." Makes me want to laugh. Fred Sabbath is no doubt next, laying into a live rendition of "Call Me Paranoid, but I Think I'm Screwed."

The flashing red lights cut across the road and onto the lawn.

It doesn't matter. I've finally let go of my secret talisman, the one dangling around my neck for years, a compressed ball of righteousness I thought was going to protect me.

Nothing can protect anyone.

Elliot yells something about running. He has his arms around Lacy, who is shaking her head.

Chaos is already halfway across the field, arms full of gear, into the woods.

I turn and stare directly into the Perfection headlights. Or headlight, I should say, the one that's not smashed, seeing pink halos and then black dots and then nothing it all, letting it burn my corneas down.

88

It's my last day. They say I don't have to, but I still pull my final shift in the library.

"You drove a *van* into your teacher's house?" B'los laughs, amazed. "That's why your dumb ass is in here?"

"Yeah."

"Oh, shit, homes. You are a bad dude."

"Nah, I'm a pussy."

"No way. You prove yourself. In here and out there. That singing routine? Oh my god. One inch away from crazy, one inch away from genius. Either way, pure stones."

"Maybe. But can I ask a for-real question?"

"Of course."

"Why didn't you help me?"

"Help? You mean like throw a punch?"

"Yeah, I guess."

"And what kind of help is that, but bringing more punches? You rose above. The whole thing. Or you would have been taken under. Either way, nothing I can do. We all make our own life."

"True. I guess."

"When you passed out the chairs? I was the first to sit. That's help. Because you have an idea. And every idea needs one other person to say, yes, this is smart. But fighting? There is no help. It happens and then it's over."

The guy should be writing philosophy textbooks.

B'los laughs. "But wait, you only got ninety days for El Ramo?"

I was lucky. Attempted house murder. Attempted vehicular assault, reckless driving, hauling equipment without a permit, no seat belts in cargo hold, all sorts of possibilities were on the prosecutor's table.

"Dice refused to press charges. The big thing is that I was stone-cold sober, 'cause only a glue-head would have missed that turn. Plus, I pled guilty. People testified about how scared I am to drive. See, we have a history with cars in our family. The lawyer said I lost control. The excitement of the show. Given my past, clean record, blah blah. I told the truth, but the judge didn't listen. He just bought it whole."

"Who is Dice?"

"Guy whose house I ran into."

"What kind of boo-shit name is that?"

"Dick Isley. Calls himself Dice. Like a nickname."

"You can't give yourself a nickname, homes! Everyone knows that. Shit, no wonder you want to run him over."

"And then there was this other thing."

"What other thing?"

"They found some stolen equipment in the van."

"What kinda equipment?"

"Stuff for the band. A compressor. A mixer. Some speakers."

"You jack it?"

"Yeah."

"Nice, dude. You a constant surprise. From who?"

"Dice."

"What, that night?"

"No, like a month before."

B'los howls with laughter. "Oh, shit. Oh my god. You a genius. A mad genius!"

"Yeah, well, he refused to claim the stuff at the trial. Said he didn't recognize it. Said maybe it was mine after all."

"Then what's the cops' problem?"

"Serial numbers were filed off."

B'los nods with appreciation. "So, like, on the house? When you get out, you gotta make...whattayou call it? Reparations? Help him fix the porch?"

"Nah, Dice sold the place. Moved to some other town. Some other school. At least that's what I hear."

"So you won."

"I didn't win. I think it's just sort of over."

"Huh. I guess there is a difference."

"No doubt."

"Man, remember when we were first in here, and you tell me you killed someone?"

"Yeah," I say. "But that was bullshit."

"I think it's still true."

"Whatta you mean?"

"Man, you killed *yourself*. The Ritchie Sudden sitting right here, right now?"

"Yeah?"

"That dude is so not the same dude walked in day one, pissing his pants."

"I wasn't scared."

"Oh, okay, you weren't scared."

"B'los?"

"Yeah?"

"Are you trying to tell me Progressive Progress works?"

He laughs. "Naw, man. It probably would have happened either way. You were just due to evolve."

When it's time for me to leave, B'los and I do the many-gripped handshake. I do it badly. I've never been able to figure that shit out.

"Be cool, man."

"You, too, baby," he says, already checking in the next book.

I get cuffed and processed. Stand in front of the bench. The judge gives me the sentence, ninety days, and the option to start in a week. I say no, let's go right now. I'm put on a bus with a cop who escorts people for a living. In the movies it would be The Rock or some other badass. In real life the guy is so fat and bored I think he might be dead. But he wakes up at the transfer point and shuffles me down the aisle. I get off and stand there for a while, before a van with a counselor and a couple other kids picks me up. The counselor says his name is Yunior, huge dude with a ponytail and gold teeth. The kids all wear scowls. The counselors all wear scowls. The place is a few hours away. We drive through the woods to a big field that looks like an office park. In the center is this mean-looking building, squat and gray. In other words, almost exactly like Killington-Holloway. Except fewer pissing cherubs and way more razor wire. We wheel up and they take us out, cuffed, one at a time. We go through processing, get issued a jumpsuit. They bring me in, sign some forms, look in my ass. A bunch of us are issued soap and blankets, then marched down a long hallway, two to a room. The counselor swings the door closed behind me.

It's crazy how easy it is, the transition.

I was me.

And now I am in a box.

For the next ninety days, I am home.

I get uncuffed and processed. Release forms are triple-signed. It's crazy how easy it is. They issue back my belongings, essentially nothing but clothes, and then sign me out. Meatstick waves good-bye. Yunior waves good-bye. I pop in to see Dr. Benway, but her office is empty. On the desk, like she knew I was coming, is my notebook.

I grab it and slip it into my bag.

"Hey," The Basilisk says.

"The doc said I could have it back."

He can see I don't give a shit either way.

"Fine, whatever."

We walk up to the steel doors. The whole time I'm sure someone's about to yell, "Wait, there's a mistake, don't buzz him through!"

I am buzzed through.

Fence, metal detector, hallway, revolving door.

And then I am free, on the sidewalk, in the sun.

Unless you have stood there, you have never stood there.

I walk down the horseshoe.

Elliot and Looper are in the parking lot.

Leaning against the van.

But it's not a Perfection Pools van.

It's got a new paint job.

LOOPER'S POOL SERVICE.

"I started my own company," she says.

"It's pretty much just like starting a band," Elliot says, muttonchops gone, hair all grown out and slicked back like a Wall Streeter, presumably to piss off the Wall Streeters. "All work and no reward."

"Welcome home, sweetie," Looper says, and hugs me.

I put my face in her shoulder. It feels really, really good.

El Hella gets me in an armlock and flicks my ear.

He smells like sweat. I could swear he smells like Lacy.

It makes me happy.

"Welcome back, brother," he says.

And it's hard not to cry, all lump-throat.

All cell-pale and stupid.

"Where's Mom?"

"Resting," Looper says. "You know how she is about this place."

"Yeah, I know."

I look down at my hands. The calluses on my fingertips are practically gone, weak and soft. It's going to take a while to build them up again. Which is fine, because I owe Rude about ten grand for his van, and it'll take a while to earn that off, too.

"So what now, kingpin?" Elliot asks. "Should we go jam? Get some real chow? Celebrate? Leave you the hell alone?"

Beyond the lot you can see the hills in the distance, nothing but trees.

"Never leave me alone," I say, and they both stare at their feet.

"Okay, you guys do some serious hanging out," Loop says, playing with her feather earring. "I got to get back to work."

Elliot laughs. "Rich fuckers' blocked skimmers won't wait?"

"Don't be..." I say. "Just don't."

Looper kisses me and leaves.

Elliot doesn't kiss me and stays.

"Lacy couldn't make it?"

"Lacy split town."

"Wait, what?"

He nods. "She went to LA after all."

"You are so totally kidding."

"I am so totally not."

"Wow. Sorry, dude."

"Yeah, well. Women."

"So does that mean El Hella is officially stag again?"

"They don't call me Lonesome Dove for nothing."

"And Chaos?"

He shrugs. "Vanished, as far as I can tell. A ghost. It's possible the dude never existed in the first place."

"So we're a duo once more."

"Have been since third grade."

I hug him. This time he really hugs me back.

*   *   *

And there we are.

    In a parking lot.

    A place with no walls.

    I look around and blink and I think

    If I'm just a little bit smarter.

    Just a little bit cooler.

    Just a little less *me* from here on out.

    I won't have to do

    anything on anyone

    else's time

    ever again.

Except maybe Looper's, since I have a feeling she's going to offer me a job.

Assistant douche, minimum wage.

At least to start.

Elliot opens the trunk of the Renault and hands me The Paul.

    It's fucked up, banged up, taped up—duct and Scotch and masking and electrical—yet somehow repaired.

    I toss the strap over my shoulders.

    Plink a few notes

    and it's like

    old home week

    It's

enough to make you want to
laugh
at how right
it is
I finger a G chord
windmill my arm
begin to strut
and I swear, I really don't
even
know how
to explain
how utterly pure
I feel.

LITTLE, BROWN AND COMPANY
BOOKS FOR YOUNG READERS

From the desk of Gloria R. Quill, Editor

And so, sadly, the manuscript ends there. The final page is torn in half, the rest of the notebook empty except for a few crude drawings and what appear to be test essays that were never handed in or perhaps were never intended to be. If you've stayed with Ritchie this far, I'm sure it's as frustrating for you as it was to us not to continue for another hundred pages. Or more. However, over the past year I've come to think that perhaps this ending is for the best. Ritchie is a person not easily wrapped up. And since we do not know who he is, or where he is, or even if he ever really existed, what better way to part than mired in the same brand of confusion (or perhaps enlightenment?) that initially brought us together? We stepped briefly into a few months of his life, and it is no real surprise that he is the one who has decided where we need to step out.

It is typically sudden, if you will allow the pun.

And again, if you have any knowledge of Ritchie or his band, friends, or family, please contact us immediately. I can promise you that your completely confidential information will be forwarded to my desk without delay, and there may, in fact, be some sort of reward. I look forward to hearing from you soon.

Thank you for reading.
Keep rocking!

Gloria R. Quill

Gloria R. Quill
Executive Editor, Quality Division
Little, Brown, Inc.
www.suddenlyfound.com

Sociology II Final Exam
Essay Section
Ritchie Sudden

The 25 Worst Band Names Ever

25. Vampire Weekend

We live in a vampire world. From *True Blood* to *Twilight*, to Tom Cruise slowly draining Katie Holmes, the national vampire obsession is never-ending. Twenty years ago Vampire Weekend would have been fine, even pleasingly nonsensical, but now it's the equivalent of naming your band the Han Solo Experience in 1978, or the Titanics in 1994, or Jeff Probst's Safari Jacket in 2000. It's the worst example of aural product placement since Lionel Richie's last single, "My Toyota Drives So Fine."
Suggested alternatives: Bovine Spongiform Encephalopathy Weekend, Ring Wraith Fortnight, Thank God It's Cannibal Friday, Tom Cruise Blew as Lestat Month.

24. Mötley Crüe, Blue Öyster Cult, Amon Düül, Maxïmo Park, Queensrÿche, Hüsker Dü, Beowülf, The Accüsed, The Crüxshadows, Hüey Lewis and the News

Motörhead gets a pass for being Motörhead. Otherwise, the curse of the umlaut remains an unforgivable stain.

Suggested alternatives: Name your band Umlaut and get an automatic pass from the crucial postmodernist sales niche.

23. Pearl Jam

They can deny it in interviews all they want, but we all know this is hands-down the dumbest allusion for coitus ever used by a band that sold more than six hundred albums. Oddly, all those aging hipster moms wearing Pearl Jam hoodies to Pilates don't seem to have noticed. The Jam should give one half of their royalties to Eric Burdon for his song "Spill the Wine (Take That Pearl)," undoubtedly where they stole the name, like a bunch of sleazy Vedders in the night, in the first place.

Suggested alternatives: Bone Sauce, Hump Wax, Lay Clay, Pork Jelly.

22. Nickelback, Matchbox 20, blink-182, Sum41, Five For Fighting, 24-7 Spyz, 3 Doors Down, Timbuk3, Spacemen 3, Level 42, 30 Odd Foot of Grunts, Sixpence None the Richer, Sham 69, Third Eye Blind, UB40, Maroon 5, Old 97's

Rock and math were born to go together like peanut butter and veiled references to Leviticus. No good band has ever had a number in their name, with the possible exception(s) of Nine Inch Nails and Ten Years After. It's the hip-quotient difference between a skull-plastered Ford Econoline and a turd-yellow Kia, between a thrashed fifties Stratocaster and an endless bassoon solo, between publicly calling your blank-eyed girlfriend "sexual napalm" and playing drums for Napalm Death.

Suggested alternatives: Try something with hyphens, semi-colons, or parentheses.

21. Black Keys, Black Mountain, Black Eyes, Black Rebel Motorcycle Club, Black Nasty, Black Breath, Black Crowes, Blackfoot, Black Star, Big Black, Black Eyed Peas, Ladysmith Black Mambazo, Black Cherry, James White and the Blacks, Black Suede

The only bands that get a pass for having "black" in their name are Black Sabbath, Black Flag, and Black Uhuru. That's it. Well, maybe Joan Jett and the Blackhearts. But that's really it. Everyone else is just plain lazy.

Suggested alternatives: Work out something with the criminally underutilized "azure."

20. Pantz Noyzee

Somehow existing in that rare gray area where The Unfortunate Z and Creatively Dull as Spackle meet Doe-Eyed Men in Leg Warmers.

Suggested alternatives: Pants No More.

19. Counting Crows

A name perfectly encapsulating the desperate, wheedling need that is the band's musical output. Or the ability to translate maudlin lyrics into dates with the cast of *Friends*. And maybe a reach-around from Schwimmer. Apparently a few years ago some kid found one of Adam Duritz's dreadlocks lying in the gutter at the corner of Sunset and La Cienega and sold it on eBay for a dollar.

Suggested alternatives: Counting Crabs, Ignoring Calories, Crutching Crotch, Stuffing Craw, Tallying the Minutes Spent Trying to Erase the Tapeworm of a Melody that Is "Mr. Jones" From Your Brain.

18. Hoobastank

Our generation's least-clever reference to toking up. Puts the listener in mind of floppy Dr. Seuss hats, microwave tamales, scented candles, relationship discussions conducted on two sleeping bags zippered together, and unidentified couch spills. I've never heard any of their songs and am fairly confident I never need to.

Suggested alternatives: A job folding thongs at American Apparel.

17. Live, Bush, Blur, Oasis, Lush, Rush, Low, Train, Muse, Jet, Shins, Vines, Hives, Killers, Korn, Toto

Indistinguishable one-word band names may seem fine individually, like rogue piranhas, but as a group feel like an insidious, soul-killing, Orwellian trend. Essentially the equivalent of when everyone in a café suddenly realizes they're wearing Che Guevara T-shirts but aren't sure whether it's ironically or not. Panic ensues. Fair-trade coffee spills. An abandoned laptop keeps playing *The Jetsons* theme. The day is saved when a barista quickly orders in a gross of Johnny Cash or Nelson Mandela XXL's.

Suggested alternatives: Commodify My Icons. Or maybe just Icon.

16. Prefab Sprout

Evocative of Uggs, incense, seitan, septum rings, cassette bootlegs, and the metric tons of cabbage-y gas scientists eventually had to pump into Biosphere 2 to fertilize the plants and aerate the research teams.

Suggested alternatives: Smell the Tofurkey Glove.

15. Mudhoney, Faster Pussycat, Spiderbaby, Motorpsycho, Vixen

Having one band named after a Russ Meyer movie? Fine, we'll let it slide. But two is unforgivable, and five is a sign of the D-cup Rapture, during which the saved will ascend to heaven while listening to the free-verse poetry of Kitten Natividad.

Suggested alternatives: Roddy Bottum and the Mondo Topless, Beyond the Valley of the Anatomically Accurate Doll Parts, The Immortal Mr. Teas Experience.

14. Asia, Europe, Chicago, Boston, Berlin, Beirut, Kansas, Bay City Rollers, Utah Saints, Manhattan Transfer, The

Bronx, Ankgor Wat, Hanoi Rocks, Alabama, L.A. Guns, Georgia Satellites, Black Oak Arkansas, Of Montreal, Frankie Goes to Hollywood

Taking some sort of subtextual cred from a location seems just plain lazy, the same way that naming your son Brooklyn or your heiress Paris dooms them to an early-twenties paparazzi-and-Vicodin tailspin. Like British Intelligence finally getting their hands on the Enigma Machine, the fact that a high percentage of these bands are keyboard-and-mullet-driven supergroups should begin to crack the code.

Suggested alternatives: Stick with thieving from Greek mythology.

13. Thelonious Monster

Never make fun of, or trade in on, the man who wrote "Crepuscule with Nellie." Monk is musical truth and Monster is a downtown junkie giggle. The totality of the karmic shit-hammer due to descend upon this band is frightening.

Suggested alternatives: Immediately put on an iceberg with Puddle of Mudd and the Blow Monkeys and then shove into the frozen North Atlantic.

12. Collective Soul, Soul Asylum, Soul II Soul, Soul Coughing, De La Soul, Warrior Soul, Liquid Soul

If you have to announce you got it, you don't.

Suggested alternatives: Collective Arrhythmia, Arrhythmia Asylum, Arrhythmia II Arrhythmia, Liquid Arrhythmia.

11. Hawkwind

It's true there are many similar names that qualify at this spot, but there's just something so sadly acid-torched, suede-fringed, and homemade-yogurt-sounding about Hawkwind that it manages to transcend an entire subgenre. The noble hawk. The whisper of a gentle wind. Separately, these ideas epitomize creative honesty and musical rigor. Unified, they represent a commitment to recycling. The Hawkwind concept is the sum of everything wrong with seventies guitar extravagance: Middle Earth lyrics, forty-minute solos, sixty-piece drum sets, leg bandannas, foam Stonehenge, etc.

Suggested alternatives: Emerson Lake and Duritz, Chawking Crowswind, Hawking Lungchunk, Breaking Fatwind.

10. Limp Bizkit

The deep scars from the dawn of rap-metal will never truly heal. A true nadir in American culture—that brief insidious moment in which this band, and the dyed goatee movement in general, was granted a semblance of musical legitimacy. "Pulling a Bizkit" is now street slang for that sense of regret that sets in before your new tattoo of a strip of Velcro is even dry. "No, dude, it's cool. It looks just like...*a strip of Velcro.*"

Suggested alternatives: D'urst, Fred's Limp Speedwagon, Flaccid Bizkit Overdrive.

9. Whitesnake

Ah, David Coverdale. You sort of have to love his willingness to embrace his stature as the walking romance-novel cover of rock. But here he's just gone too far. The beyond-dimwitted sexual allusion is deserving of ridicule enough. Especially considering the neutered brand of hair metal they larded the nineties airwaves with. Throw in Tawny Kitaen air-buffing a Jaguar with her lingeried fanny, plus David's creepy, permed-uncle vibe, and you've got a solid number 9 on any self-respecting list.

Suggested alternatives: My Caucasian Genital Metaphor, Such Crude Caucasian Genital Metaphor As Is Mine Reserves the Right to be Used in Reptile Metaphors As Well, the Queasy Leather-Pants Smell of My Backstage Genital Metaphor, There's a Party in the Groupie Van and Me and My Snake Are Coming.

8. Edie Brickell & New Bohemians

We still haven't recovered from the old self-anointed bohemians, have we? I mean the people who couldn't get into the back room at Max's Kansas City. The people who actually bought Basquiat paintings. The people even GG Allin wouldn't throw his excrement at. Who says we need new ones? The naïveté of Edie's lyrics combined with the band's Industrial Cappuccino sound is a snapshot of a particular strain of nineties dot-com malaise.

Suggested alternatives: Mort Susskind and the Old Napkins, Pathet Lao and the New Communards, Ear Pain and the Delivery Vehicle.

7. T'Pau

When you name your band after a character from the "Amok Time" episode of *Star Trek* you're pretty much screwed from jump. The intersection of arcane *Trek* knowledge and eighties synth pop would seem like a natural, but only if that intersection occurs in the corner of the rec room where the Commodore 64 is stashed. **Suggested alternatives:** Th'pent, D'sposible, A'tLeastNoVocorder.

6. The Goo Goo Dolls

Pretty much saddling a decade with the unwanted mental image of a vinegary baby crap.

Suggested alternatives: Steel Leather Fist, Muscle Wrestle Chainsaw, Golf Golf Beer.

5. Chumbawamba, Scritti Politti, Oingo Boingo, Bananarama, Kajagoogoo, Dishwalla, Milli Vanilli, Linkin Park, Ebn Ozn, Nitzer Ebb, Mr. Mister, Enuff Z'nuff

Alliteration + unnecessary rhyming + neon overalls = a sophomore year of rampant forehead acne.

Suggested alternatives: The By, the At, the On, the Up.

4. Weezer

Quick, you have two choices: 1. You're backstage at *The View*, trapped somewhere between a ravenous Joy Behar and the craft services table, wearing nothing but a falafel Speedo. 2. You're at a party, you've just met someone you're really attracted to, and you have to work Weezer into the conversation three times.

Suggested alternatives: Blather, Chancre, Bleeder, Shafter, Cheeze-It

3. ...And You Will Know Us by the Trail of Dead, Godspeed You! Black Emperor, We Were Promised Jetpacks, Neutral Milk Hotel, My Morning Jacket, They Might Be Giants, Death Cab for Cutie, Everybody Was in the French Resistance... NOW, the Verve Pipe.

There was a while after Raymond Carver's story collection *Will You Please Be Quiet, Please?* came out when almost every other book title tried to emulate his genius sense of off-beat rhythm and unexpected tension. Suddenly arty commas were everywhere, irony abounded, and a cribbed sense of post-modernism ruled the day. It still hasn't completely dissipated. So it should come as no surprise that Ray's stylistic blip has crossed over into music. These are the sort of bands whose name-defenders always say, "But they got it from the first season of *Doctor Who*!" or, "But they got it from *Breakfast at Tiffany's*!" neglecting the fact that no matter how hip the source (yes, that means you, Toad the Wet Sprocket), coolness is not automatically conferred. Hey, Steely Dan is the name of a vibrating personal massager in *Naked Lunch*, but it still manages to work nicely context-free.

Suggested alternatives: They Might Be Turgid and Unlistenable, And You Shall Know Us by Our Trail of Pretension, We Were Promised Relevance, Remainder Bin You Plodding Emperor, Death Stab for the Aggressively Twee, the Corn Cob Pipe.

2. The Darkness

Very, very scary. Like the screen name of a serial killer who also collects Hello Kitty. Like the musical equivalent of failing out of art school. Like soaking in a pentagram-shaped hot tub and then having your bedroom haunted by a pale, Depression-era child only you and Morgan Freeman can see. Dare you listen to this band? Are you willing to risk exposure to solos that may cause you to crawl on the ceiling and suddenly speak fluent Aramaic?

Suggested alternatives: The Comfy Sofa, the Lite Mayonnaise, the Customized Huffy Ten-Speed, the Newly Febrezed Turtleneck.

1. Hootie & the Blowfish

Without question the worst band name ever. It absolutely owns each of the Four Hallmarks of Aural Misery: 1. Unforgivably cutesy.

2. Ultimately meaningless. 3. Unwarranted self-satisfaction. 4. Unmistakable hints of dorm-room horseplay. It evokes the smell of someone else's pizza. It says, "I once broke up with an otherwise terrific girl because she kept whining 'But I love Hootie!' every time I ripped the disc out of the changer and tried to Frisbee it across the quad."

Suggested alternatives: A Merciful Slide into Cultural Oblivion, the same dark, forgotten crease where Poi Dog Pondering nurses the Dandy Warhols at its milkless teat.

BONUS EXTRA CREDIT: The worst band with the best name
I tend to have a soft spot for the universally loathed celebrity. I always think, yeah, sure, but can they really be *that* bad in person? Maybe they just need a quiet place to sit for a while and someone to listen who doesn't want anything from them. For a hypothetically all-male band, Hole is offensive and moronic. For a band fronted by an aggressively nonapologetic woman in a ludicrously macho industry, Hole is a courageous postfeminist statement. It's short, fearless, entendre-laden, and satisfying. It's a big middle finger to a bunch of headbanging gropers who, after fifty years of gleeful misogyny, truly deserve it. Unfortunately, in Courtney Love's case, Hole seems depressingly prescient, if not brutally accurate. And that "you will ache like I ache" song is one of the worst ever written. If they were a bit less abrasive, and Courtney were, say, PJ Harvey instead, Hole might be the single best band name ever.

History of the Americas Final Exam
Essay Section
Ritchie Sudden

The Ten Universal Band Eventualities

1. Band forms, tries to learn some songs, never quite figures out "Cat Scratch Fever," breaks up.
2. Band forms, puts together a set list, plays some bars, no one ever comes, they get paid in drink tickets, breaks up.
3. Band forms, they all chip in for tons of equipment, drummer's girlfriend gets pregnant, breaks up, sells most gear at a brutal loss, trades amp for Pampers.
4. Band forms, is talented, is locally beloved, makes zero money, gets tired of hauling equipment around, breaks up, fifteen years later records go for big $$ on eBay.
5. Band forms, the bass player quits, new bass player joins, he learns the songs and also quits, other band members decide they don't need a bass—the drummer will just play twice as hard—breaks up.
6. Band forms in high school, spends five years practicing together and playing local gigs, they get better, get signed, tour, put out single, it sells less than three hundred copies, breaks up.

7. Band is formed of young boys who dance and lip-synch in sync, is managed by creepy fat dude everyone calls "The Professor," sells millions of copies, is simultaneously loved and reviled, members get old and no longer appeal to teens, breaks up.

8. Band forms, is good, signs with big label, makes great album, label decides album doesn't have much "commercial potential," spends no money promoting it, album sells nothing, breaks up, band members become bitter cranks who work in record stores and make cutting remarks about people's taste in music at the register.

9. Band forms, becomes cult darling and indie icon, never really cares about making it big or making money, so by the inverse laws of physics and justice does make money, is listened to by depressed art majors for decades, and makes just enough off royalties to buy a house somewhere in Maine and raise kids who are into tae kwon do and pottery.

10. Band is Wise Young Fool. Band takes over world.

Official *Wise Young Fool* Discography
A reasonably comprehensive list of ringtones, songs, albums, and bands mentioned (and presumably endorsed by) Ritchie Sudden

Brian Eno. "Burning Airlines Give You So Much More." *Taking Tiger Mountain (By Strategy).* Island, 1974.

Fear. "New York's Alright If You Like Saxophones." *The Record.* Slash, 1982.

The Replacements. "Bastards of Young." *Tim.* Sire, 1985.

Sweet. "Teenage Rampage." *Desolation Boulevard.* RCA, 1974.

The Germs. "What We Do Is Secret." *The Germs.* Slash, 1981.

The Misfits. "TV Casualty." *Legacy of Brutality.* Plan 9, 1989.

Bad Brains. "We Will Not." *Rock for Light.* PVC, 1983.

New York Dolls. "Lonely Planet Boy." *New York Dolls.* Mercury, 1973.

Minor Threat. "In My Eyes." *In My Eyes.* Dischord, 1984.

The Ramones. "Now I Wanna Sniff Some Glue." *Ramones.* Sire, 1976.

Cheap Trick. "She's Tight." *One on One.* Epic, April 1982.

Sly and the Family Stone. "Stand." *Stand!* Epic, 1969.

Stiff Little Fingers. "Suspect Device." *Inflammable Material.* Rough Trade, 1979.

Steely Dan. "My Old School." *Countdown to Ecstasy.* ABC, 1973.

ZZ Top. "Beer Drinkers and Hell Raisers." *Tres Hombres.* London, 1973.

Black Sabbath. "Paranoid." *Paranoid.* Vertigo, 1970.

AC/DC. *Highway to Hell.* Albert Productions (AU)/ Atlantic (outside of AU), August 1979.

Talking Heads. *Fear of Music.* Sire Records, 1979.

Agnostic Front. *Cause for Alarm.* Relativity/Combat Records, 1986.

Bauhaus. *In The Flat Field.* 4AD, 1980.

Carcass. *Reek of Putrefaction.* Earache, 1988.

The Rolling Stones. *Beggar's Banquet.* London (US)/ Decca (UK), 1968.

Siouxsie and the Banshees. *Tinderbox.* Polydor (UK)/ Geffen/Warner Bros. (USA), 1986.

Slayer. *Undisputed Attitude.* American Recordings, 1996.

Johnny Thunders. *So Alone.* Real (UK)/ Sire (US), 1996.

The White Stripes. *De Stijl.* Sympathy for the Record Industry, 2000.

Pavement. *Slanted and Enchanted.* Matador, 1992.

Roxy Music. *For Your Pleasure.* Island, 1973.

Mastodon. *Leviathan.* Relapse, 2004.

Elliott Smith. *Either/Or.* Kill Rock Stars, 1997.

My Bloody Valentine. *Loveless.* Creation, 1991.

Billy Zoom. Guitarist, X. *Los Angeles.* Slash, 1980.

Chuck Berry. *St. Louis to Liverpool.* Chess, 1964.

Joe Walsh. Guitarist, The James Gang. *Thirds.* ABC, 1971.

The Clash. *The Clash.* Columbia, 1977.

ACKNOWLEDGMENTS

The author would like to thank

Henry "Clum" Kyburg, Kristine Serio, Larry Benner, Matt "Sloat" Heller, Steven Malk, Ty King, Daryl Miller Salomons, Mike "Stucco" Nesi, Christian Bauer, Joe Daly, Angelo Gianni, Celestriembryo, Gretna Yardfire, everyone who lived through mid-eighties Hangtown, Greg Olear, Jen Kabat, the entire staff of Dark Coast Press, A Day in Cleveland, Andy Maliskas, Adam Sandone, Gary Skal for his vocals on "My Generation," Eddie Kane's music, Dougie B for knowing that Buffalo Girls go round the outside, Russ at Music Guild, Bleeker Bobs, Bo Diddley, Honeyman Scott's yellow Veeter, Brass City Records, the New Haven line, Yummy Fur, J.T. and his Moog, Michele for introducing me to Nick Drake *and* the Birthday Party, Scene Jenks for taking that crappy bass off my hands, Lennon Studios, the Grove, Segue's own snare-banger Ralph Barsi, Gary and Ricardo and the last gasp of CD-burning, Becks, Madame I'm Adam, Uncle John for laying off all his Traffic and Rick Wakeman albums on me, Bob Mould, Tumast, Dave Renz's cassette of the first Suicide album, Hank Cherry and those early Scrofula practices, Seattle7Writers, Jay and Kymber for pretending to like it all, Jordan "Rock" Schwartz, Alec "Roll" Schwartz, Eric Dolphy, Cap Lewis and the Stellettes, My Bloody Valentine, Alvina "The Hammer" Ling, Bethany Strout, Alissa Parra, Christine Ma, Erin McMahon, Lukas Fauset, Allison Moore, Victoria Stapleton, Zoe Luderitz, Andrew Smith, Megan Tingley, Les Paul, the Gibson custom guitar shop, Mesa amps, the Tube Screamer, Taylor acoustics, a certain lipstick-red Fender Deluxe Reverb, the 1974 Rickenbacker 4001 MapleGlo, Lee Oskar harmonicas, the 1973 Tele Thinline, and everyone over at the Russia House, Hunter's Point's best 24-hour diner and Hollandaise emporium.